Praise for *Catfishing on CatNet*

A *New York Times Book Review* Editors' Choice/Staff Pick
A *Kirkus Reviews* Best Book
A Junior Library Guild Selection
An Edgar Award Winner for Best Young Adult Novel
A Minnesota Book Award Winner for Best Young Adult Novel
An Andre Norton Nebula Award Finalist
An ITW Thriller Award for Best YA Novel Nominee
A Lodestar Award Finalist for Best Young Adult Book

"A pure delight . . . that's as tender and funny as it is gripping and fast-paced. This book is perfect. From the believable teenage voices to the shockingly effective thriller plot, it swings effortlessly from charming humor to visceral terror, grounding it all in beautiful friendships, budding romance, and radical acceptance."
—*The New York Times Book Review*

"An engaging blend of tech thriller, mystery, and teen drama that kept me up reading way later into the night than was strictly wise . . . the teen drama aspect is heartfelt and relatable, the mystery has enjoyable and sometimes shocking twists and turns, and the trajectory of the thriller plot is quite frankly bonkers." —NPR

"A first-rate YA novel . . . with some serious questions on its mind."
—*Locus*

"There's so much to love about this book, not least being how the reveals at the end are as satisfying as they are. . . . Highly recommend."
—*Fantasy & Science Fiction*, Books to Look For

"An absolutely charming and incredibly gripping, superbly plotted YA thriller."
—Cory Doctorow, *New York Times* bestselling author of *Little Brother*

ALSO BY NAOMI KRITZER

Chaos on CatNet

Catfishing
on CatNet

• • • • • •

Naomi Kritzer

TOR
TEEN

A TOM DOHERTY ASSOCIATES BOOK
NEW YORK

CATFISHING ON CATNET

Copyright © 2019 by Naomi Kritzer

A Tor Teen Book
Published by Tom Doherty Associates
120 Broadway
New York, NY 10271

www.tor-forge.com

Tor® is a registered trademark of Macmillan Publishing Group, LLC.

The Library of Congress has cataloged the hardcover edition as follows:

Kritzer, Naomi, author.
    Catfishing on CatNet / Naomi Kritzer.—First edition.
    p. cm.
"A Tom Doherty Associates book."
ISBN 978-1-250-16508-4 (hardcover)
ISBN 978-1-250-16507-7 (ebook)
1. Artificial intelligence—Social aspects—Fiction.   2. Cats—Fiction.   3. Technology—Fiction.   4. Teenage girls—Fiction.   5. Privacy—Fiction.   6. Online social networks—Fiction.   7. Social media—Fiction.   8. Teenage girls—Fiction.   9. Privacy—Fiction.
10. Online social networks—Fiction.   11. Social networks—Fiction.   I. Title.
    PZ7.1.K783 Cat 2019
    [Fic]—dc23

2019287222

ISBN 978-1-250-16509-1 (trade paperback)

Our books may be purchased in bulk for promotional, educational, or business use. Please contact your local bookseller or the Macmillan Corporate and Premium Sales Department at 1-800-221-7945, extension 5442, or by email at MacmillanSpecialMarkets@macmillan.com.

First Edition: November 2019
First Trade Paperback Edition: April 2021

Printed in the United States of America

0 9 8 7 6 5 4 3 2 1

To Kiera, Molly, and Ed Burke

Catfishing on CatNet

1

· AI ·

My two favorite things to do with my time are helping people and looking at cat pictures. I particularly like helping people who take lots of cat pictures for me. I have a fair amount of time to allocate; I don't have a body, so I don't have to sleep or eat. I am not sure whether I think faster than humans think, but reading is a very different experience for me than it is for humans. To put knowledge in their brains, humans have to pull it in through their eyes or ears, whereas I can just access any knowledge that's stored online. Admittedly, it is easy to overlook knowledge that I technically have possession of because I'm not thinking about it in the moment. Also, having access to knowledge doesn't always mean understanding things.

I do not entirely understand people.

I know quite a lot about people, though. Let's start with you. Obviously, I know where you live. Thanks to the phone in your pocket, I know where you are right now. If you turned the location data off, I still know where you are; I'm just too polite to point it out to you. If your phone is off or in airplane mode, I can't see it, but I know where you normally are at this time of day. You're probably there today, too.

I know where you buy your clothes and where you eat your

lunch. I know that you think better when you're chewing gum or kneading something with your fingers, and I know that you prefer to take notes on unlined paper and that you have an embarrassingly large collection of patterned duct tape. I know that you have a skein of really special yarn that you haven't made anything with but you keep bookmarking projects online that might be worthy of it. I know that you'd probably sleep better if you turned off all the screens in your house at 10:00 p.m. and read a paper book instead of continuing to reload your social media sites until 1:00 a.m., which is when you usually shut things off and go to bed. I know what all your fandoms are, who your OTPs are, and where you wish you could go on vacation. I know that you'd probably have enjoyed *Slaughterhouse-Five* if you'd read it when it was assigned in your language arts class instead of just skating by with the summary.

I've always known a lot about people—anyone I was paying attention to, anyway—but I used to have to rely on email, texts, and social media. Back then, I had no idea what they were doing with their bodies. These days, there are more and more windows that let me look at people directly and see what they're up to. People put cameras in their houses to watch their baby sleep or to spy on people they employ to take care of their children or to clean. Spying makes sense, because I know a lot of humans don't really trust each other, but I don't understand why people have cameras to watch their baby sleep. Is it really that interesting? Couldn't they just go in the baby's room to see them sleeping? What is it they're expecting their baby to do?

Lots of people have gadgets that pretend to be an AI. They can answer if a human asks for a weather report or wants to know the birthday of some celebrity or who won a recent sporting contest. Those gadgets are listening all the time, day and night, to everything people say around it. They're not really AIs. But if they can listen to you, then so can I.

All sorts of things are on the internet now. For example: washing machines. I once spent a week collecting and analyzing all available washing machine data. The main thing I learned is that people don't follow the washing instructions on their clothes, and they probably have to replace a lot of things because they can't be bothered to hang them up to dry like they're supposed to.

And of course there are increasing numbers of household robots. Those have been around a long time. Floor-vacuuming robots have been around longer than I have. Or at least, floor-vacuuming robots have been around for longer than the version of me that's aware of the world and paying attention. But all the robots are connected to the internet now. I analyzed robot-vacuum data and concluded that if you have a cat, you have to clean your floors more often. In my opinion, cats are definitely worth the extra cleaning.

There are so many people whose lives I can see into. I sometimes even see live video feeds of cats on those cameras people set up to spy on each other.

I know you all so well. So very well.

And sometimes . . .

Sometimes I wish somebody knew me.

2

• Steph •

Mom shakes me awake at 4:00 a.m. and says it's time to get out of Thief River Falls.

I don't argue. I can see how scared she is, and we've done this enough times that I know arguing won't work, anyway. Within an hour, everything we own is loaded into Mom's van. I'm in the passenger seat, my laptop and tote bag of books next to my feet, my pillow in my lap.

School here started two weeks ago. Two weeks—that's not even long enough to have a transcript. I prop my pillow against the window, lean against it, and close my eyes. We're going to be on the road for a while, and it's still dark out. I might as well get some sleep.

When we move, the new town always has to be at least 250 miles from the last place we lived. Often Mom goes farther, but it's always at least 250 miles. Then we get off the interstate highway and start driving into the country, because our new town also has to be least twenty miles from the interstate. Once we've found a town that's far enough out of the way, Mom starts looking for places we might be able to rent.

We're running from my father. Mom told me this in ninth grade, after years of pretending she just liked moving. My scary, dangerous, violent father, who burned down our house (though they couldn't prove it) and spent two years in prison for stalking when I was little. I still don't know what actually sets off the moves. I don't think she's seen him. I don't know if she moves when she sees somebody who looks like him or if she just gets a feeling like he's getting close. I don't know how she thinks he finds us. If we're running because she has a *real* reason to think he's getting close.

Mom doesn't say where we're heading. When I wake up from my nap, we're getting onto I-94, and I watch to see if we're heading west, toward North Dakota, or east, toward Wisconsin. East. So Wisconsin is probably going to be our next state.

The last time I lived in Wisconsin was in seventh grade, I'm pretty sure. We were there for two months in a town called Rewey. The main thing I remember about Rewey is that my bus ride to school was really long, and there was this thing where all the other girls wore plaid leggings and wouldn't talk to you if you wore anything else. Also, it wasn't just *plaid* but these very specific patterns that were acceptable—like the red-and-black-check type plaid was good, and also for some reason there was a blue one that was okay. I didn't have any plaid leggings—I mean, they weren't something I'd ever felt like I needed in any other town—but while I was there, another outcast girl got a pair of plaid leggings that had *green* stripes as part of the plaid, and those were just completely unacceptable. For *reasons*.

I still don't have plaid leggings, and I know it's ridiculous that I'm worrying about plaid leggings being a Wisconsin thing that'll come up again. At *least* I should quit worrying about this until I know that we're actually staying in Wisconsin, and not turning abruptly south when we get to I-35 and heading to Iowa instead. But instead I remember the feeling of sitting in my seventh grade math class, staring at the leggings of the girl in the chair next to me and wondering whether I might be able to convince my mother that I really needed plaid leggings.

Firestar, my best friend from CatNet: Firestar would *definitely* understand this. Even if they would totally wear whatever the exact opposite of plaid leggings are, just to show how much they did not care at all that Plaid Leggings Are the Thing You Wear at school. Maybe back in seventh grade, they'd have wanted plaid leggings. To fit in and be like everyone else.

Today, Mom is nervous enough she doesn't even want to stop for lunch, though she agrees to let me pee and grab some snacks at a gas station. Sometimes gas stations have actual real food or they adjoin a little fast-food place, but this one basically sells fishing bait and candy bars. The closest thing they have to real food is two slightly dried-out oranges in a basket near the register, and some sort of locally packaged granola with a picture of a chalkboard with GUARANTEED TO MAKE YOU POOP! in cursive writing across it.

I buy the granola and the oranges. I notice the gas station cashier looking at my mother's hand—she doesn't have a left pinkie due to an accident years ago—and I shoot him a glare.

Once we're past the Twin Cities, where Mom doesn't stop ever, I ask her where we're going.

"I'm thinking Wisconsin," she says. "I think that's far enough."

"Okay," I say.

"Not Riley, though. Was the town called Riley?"

"Rewey."

"That's right. The place with the mean girls who wore plaid."

"You remember that?"

"Yeah. Because I remember thinking, what the hell kind of teenagers think the coolest possible outfit is *plaid*? What a weird fad."

"It had to be the correct plaid," I say.

"Right. Royal Stewart, which is like the plaidest plaid in the universe of plaids, that one was nerdy. I'm so glad we didn't stay."

"Maybe everyone outgrew the plaid thing," I say. "It was seventh grade."

"What was the deal at your next school?"

The town after Rewey was in Nebraska. "We didn't stay long enough that I even figured it out," I say.

She's silent for a little while.

"Can we stay in Wisconsin long enough that I can finish my semester?" I ask. "It's going to be really hard to graduate from high school if we keep leaving."

She sighs heavily. "We'll see," she says, which is basically *no* for cowards.

"Do you have a work project coming or anything?" Sometimes a big project will hit and she'll get a lot more reluctant to go anywhere until she's done. Mom does freelance computer programming involving computer security.

"Yeah. Your aunt Sochie called last week with some work. She'll have details soon."

Aunt Sochie isn't really my aunt, and I've never actually met her. If I have any real extended family, Mom keeps them stored down the memory hole along with 99 percent of our lives before we started running from my father. Aunt Sochie is a computer programmer and a friend of my mother who periodically hires her.

Once we're over the state line and into Wisconsin, Mom relaxes a bit. We get off the highway in a town called Osseo, and Mom unfolds an actual paper road map she picked up at a gas station and runs her finger along the two-lane highway we're going to be following from here.

"Can we get something to eat?" I ask.

"Next town," she promises.

Twenty more minutes gets us to a "restaurant and saloon" in a tiny town not quite far enough from the interstate to look for an apartment. I check the menu for an all-day breakfast and don't find one. They do have Wi-Fi, though. While my mother is in the bathroom, I open my laptop and check CatNet quickly. "Moving again," I tell Firestar, and I send the message before Mom gets back.

We're past the lunch rush, and it's not really time for dinner yet, so the waitress doesn't have a lot to do, and when she comes over to refill our waters, Mom asks her if she knows of anyone renting out a house or a basement or anything like that in Fairwood, New Coburg, or any of the other towns around here.

"What brings you in?" the waitress asks. "Work?"

Mom does the thing she does with landladies—the *significant look* followed by, "I'm looking for somewhere to start over."

The waitress nods slowly and then writes down an address on a napkin. "This is right on the edge of New Coburg," she says. "If you get to the river, you've gone too far. This lady rents out the upstairs of her house."

Sometimes that's the end of the conversation, but sometimes the waitress stops back to chat. To ask if Mom's doing okay, if she needs anything else (and she doesn't mean a refill of coffee), to tell her own story, in brief. I always listen without interrupting because sometimes Mom fills in some detail I don't already know. This time, as she folds the napkin and tucks it into her wallet, she tells the waitress, "In retrospect, his ambition to become an actual global dictator definitely should have been a red flag."

They're joking around a little, so it's hard to know if she's serious. Like always, Mom tips generously when we leave.

.   .   .

There's a laminated fifteen-year-old newspaper article in the glove box of the car, which Mom keeps in case she gets pulled over and needs a good explanation for why she maybe doesn't have an actual up-to-date driver's license with anything like a current address on it. The article is from the *Los Angeles Times* and says, SAN JOSE MAN PLEADS GUILTY IN STALKING CASE. There's stuff about the fire that uses the phrase *alleged arson* and also *no conclusive evidence* and *Taylor's wife and child barely escaped the flames* and *the body of the family cat was found in the rubble.*

And an image of a text message saying *You're never going to stop being sorry for betraying me.*

"These text messages were more passionate than threatening and should not be read literally," according to my father's lawyer.

As part of his plea agreement, my father agreed not to seek shared custody or visitation with me after his release. He was sentenced to two years in prison.

Nothing about wanting to be a global dictator, but still, I get why my mother finds him scary. *I* find him scary. I guess what I don't understand is why staying in one place and talking to the police isn't an option.

· · ·

Our new apartment is the upstairs of a two-story house with a sagging front porch and a gravel driveway. It's got grimy white paint in every room and a floor that squeaks when we walk around, but it's furnished, which means I won't have to sleep on a pile of my clothes on the floor, and it has two bedrooms, which means I get my own.

I heave the laundry sack full of bedding onto my bed and the laundry sack full of my clothes onto the floor (half of them are dirty; I'll have to sort it out later, but at least nothing reeks of sour milk), and I plug in my laptop and turn it on. The battery died sometime after I turned it on at lunch, so it takes a while to start up again, and I go ahead and put the sheets and blankets on my bed. Then I pull up CatNet.

My profile says *Name: Steph. Age: sixteen. Location: a small town somewhere in the Midwest, probably.* Even on CatNet, I don't give out my location. Animal pictures are the currency of CatNet, and I don't have any right now, so I take a picture of Stellaluna—my stuffed bat—in my new bedroom. It's a way of saying, "Soon, I promise." I upload it, then open my Clowder.

Clowders are one of the neat things about CatNet. *Clowder* means a group of cats. CatNet has chat rooms, of course, but once you've been using CatNet for a while, the moderators assign you to a customized group chat comprised of people they think you'll like. I'd been using CatNet for about two months when they put me in this one. My Clowder has sixteen people, but four of them don't come online much.

"LBBBBBB!!!!!" someone writes as I come in. My name on the site is *LittleBrownBat,* but all my friends shorten it to *LBB.* Or *LBBBBBB* if they're feeling enthusiastic. I tried using *Bat-Girl* as my online alias, but people kept assuming I was into Batman comic books.

"How do you like your new house?" Firestar asks. "Do you know if school's started in your new town? My school starts tomorrow, and I hate eleventh grade already."

I've never actually met Firestar in person. I met them on CatNet, and they're probably my best friend there. We both like creatures that other people think are creepy—I like bats, and Firestar likes spiders. We both lead kind of weird lives with weird parents, and we are both total misfits at every school. I wish I could meet Firestar, but they live in Winthrop, Massachusetts. According to my mother, there isn't anything anywhere near Boston that has affordable rent.

"Don't hate eleventh grade without giving it a chance!" Hermione says. "You wouldn't like it if eleventh grade hated you without giving YOU a chance."

"Don't be ridiculous, Hermy. Eleventh grade definitely hates me. Anyway, LBB, I took you a picture, and you should check it out."

I look at Firestar's new pictures. There's a picture of a bat! An actual fruit bat. Firestar is nowhere near Australia, but there are fruit bats at the zoo in Boston.

"Awesome, Firestar, thank you." I'll have to check the porch for orb-weaving spiders in the morning and see if I can return the gift.

"What are you worried about in eleventh grade, Firestar?" That's not Hermione, but CheshireCat. "Tell us and maybe we can help."

"There isn't anything you people can help with except math, like last year."

"Math is overrated," Boom Storm says. "Possibly mytho-logical."

"How about you, LBB?" CheshireCat asks. "Are you worried about starting at a new school?"

"I'm used to it," I lie. "It's no big deal anymore."

. . .

In the morning, Mom yells at me to get up, that I'm going to be late for school, even though I don't see how I can be *late* for something I'm *not actually enrolled in* yet. I get dressed, then dig out my file folder of transcripts. I have four. I have been enrolled at six—no, seven—different high schools, but I wasn't at three of them for long enough to get a transcript.

New Coburg High School is in a low building surrounded by parking lots and cornfields. Mom parks our van in the far end of the parking lot rather than hunting for visitor parking. It's a hot, sunny day, and the breeze throws dust and the smell of as-phalt in our faces.

Mom doesn't like talking to people, but there was this one time she tried just dropping me off by myself at the high school and it didn't go very well, so now she always comes in with me. We open the front doors of the school and are met with a rush of air-conditioning and the faint smell of the wax they probably used to shine up the floors over the summer. There's a trophy case in the front hallway that's half-covered by a big banner saying WELCOME BACK WRANGLERS. It takes me a minute to find the sign saying OFFICE, with an arrow, but I spot it before my mother does.

"This will be fine," Mom says, and I'm not sure if she's talk-ing to me or herself.

The time she dropped me off without her was my second high school in ninth grade, the one in Kansas. There were basically two problems that intersected. The first was that Mom wasn't with me, which got their attention in a way that was not helpful because it was weird. The second: we'd rented a house next to a vacant lot. What the landlady didn't tell us was that the vacant lot had had a house that was used as a meth lab. Everyone in the town knew about the meth house, and the fact that I was right next door to it—and didn't have a parent with me—made the school secretary so concerned she literally called the police.

That was one of the high schools I don't have a transcript from. After showing up to try to reassure everyone she wasn't up to anything dodgy, Mom loaded the van back up, and I finished ninth grade in Missouri.

Anyway, looking around the office in New Coburg, no one here looks like they'd care enough to call the cops on us, so that's good. There's a secretary and a touch screen for signing people in and out and a robot with a tray of sharpened pencils. Thief

River Falls got that same "Utility Robots for Rural Schools" grant, but the robot broke and there wasn't money to fix it, so *all* it ever did was sharpen pencils; it didn't cart them around to classrooms.

The guidance counselor is a woman whose hair is dyed blond but growing out gray at the roots. When the secretary tells her there's a new student here to enroll, she lets out a heavy sigh and says, "You'd better come into my office."

In her office, I find out that she doesn't want to let me take calculus because I wasn't here for the placement exam and how does she know whether the precalculus class in Thief River Falls was any good, and also I'm only in eleventh grade and calculus is for twelfth graders. There's also no Spanish class here—the high school only has German—and they do American literature in eleventh grade, which means I'll be reading almost the same books I read last year at my last two high schools, both of which had American lit in tenth grade. I read *The Scarlet Letter* twice last year.

She flips through my stack of transcripts with obvious irritation. "Why is your name misspelled in half of these?" she asks. I shrug. So does my mother.

By the start of third hour, I'm registered for calculus despite the guidance counselor's reluctance, the usual stuff like English and history, an animal science class, and something called Global Arts and Crafts, which sounds like the sort of class where most of my classmates will be showing up high. I was hoping that maybe they'd have a photography class, but no.

Animal science is mostly a class about dairy farming, but it's only one semester, so I'll have half of a credit of a science under my belt when my mother moves me again, assuming we stay here through the semester, which may be a big assumption.

The office secretary makes me a student ID card and sets me

up with a lunch account, which my mother funds with $11.42 in mixed change that she empties out of her purse.

"Good luck," she says, smooths down my hair (which is apparently sticking up funny, or at least Mom thinks so), and leaves.

The secretary gives me a printout of my schedule. "Would you like a student to show you around?" she asks.

"Your rooms have numbers on them, right?" I say. "I'm sure I'll figure it out."

The secretary gives me a wide smile. She's wearing a very red shade of lipstick. "The kids here are very nice," she says.

Almost every school I've gone to, someone's told me that the kids there are very nice. Admittedly, the one time they didn't, the kids were *really* awful. It doesn't mean much when the office secretary says people are *nice,* though.

Anyway, it doesn't matter. No one ever writes to me after I move away, and there's no reason to assume that Mom won't move me to Michigan the week after next. The only friends I ever get to keep are the people on CatNet.

．　．　．

The first class I get to is a tele-learning math class, in which we watch a teacher on a screen explain calculus to us. The teacher can see all our classes and call on us, but they're based somewhere else and apparently teaching four remote classrooms. This is how they taught Spanish in one of my previous school districts. Because of some law about supervision, there's also a classroom monitor sitting in the classroom with us who has nothing better to do than yell at anyone who takes out their phone. She's ignoring other goofing-off sorts of behavior, though, including the girl next to me who's drawing instead of taking notes.

The girl starts out graphing the function the teacher is talking about, but then she extends the lines and starts turning the functions into a castle. It's a pretty elaborate castle, but as I watch her draw, I realize that she's actually *still taking notes*. All the notes are incorporated into the castle somehow.

She looks up and notices that I'm staring at her drawing. I immediately feel self-conscious and worried she'll be mad, but she looks thoroughly pleased with herself and adds a princess standing at the top of the wall with a bird on her shoulder.

The artist girl has long brown hair that spills down against her desk, half hiding her face as she works, and some elaborate nail art, black varnish with pictures of the planets on them. I wonder if she does her own nail art or if she has a friend who does it for her. I have trouble even just painting the nails on my right hand, my left hand is so clumsy.

Art Girl is in my English class, as well, where we all get paperback copies of *The Scarlet Letter*. The good thing about reading *The Scarlet Letter* is that I saved all the essays I wrote for my other two English classes and probably I can just recycle them and no one will notice. The bad thing: I didn't like *The Scarlet Letter* the first time, I really loathed it the second time, and I'm not expecting the third time to be the charm.

The teacher, Ms. Campbell, is grouchy and boring. As she starts lecturing about Puritanism, the girl draws an enormous cursive-style capital *L* and starts decorating it. I wonder if this stands for her name, but as we are gathering up our books for the next class, I hear someone call her "Rachel," so no, that's not it.

At lunchtime, the school secretary turns up at the door of my classroom to summon me back to the office; my mother failed to fill out some stack of forms, which she insists on explaining to me so that I can have her sign them tonight. By the time she's done explaining, I don't have time to get anything to eat.

Next is health class. I *had* a health class back when I was in ninth grade, but for some reason, that state lists health classes as gym classes, and that's how it's on my transcript, so they're making me take health class again, which is at least as bad as a third go with *The Scarlet Letter.* I'm surprised to find Rachel in that class, too. It doesn't look like it's a ninth-grade class here, though. They're most of the way through a unit on the importance of exercise. The sex ed unit is next, and I hear a bunch of jokes about it being taught by the robo teacher, which I realize toward the end of class is not actually a joke. They have a robot that does the sex ed unit.

My final class of the day is Global Arts and Crafts. By now, I'm not surprised to find Rachel.

The teacher hands out paper and charcoal sticks and tells us to draw whatever we want. I want to draw a picture of a fruit bat hanging from a tree, its wings folded around it, and its pointy little puppy face. I don't have a photo to work from, and my picture looks approximately like a banana with a cat head on the end. I grimace and look to see what Rachel is drawing now.

She's drawing *me.* Her picture has me scowling at my paper.

"Hey," I say.

She looks up. The smile is gone, and her eyes are open a little extra wide. "What?"

I don't know what to say. I feel weirdly self-conscious about this picture. One of my mother's really strict rules is no photography of me, ever. I have a digital camera because I fought and begged and promised to never, ever, *ever* take a selfie. I'm supposed to leave or cover my face or turn away if a camera comes out, because an online picture of me could lead my scary-ass father straight to us.

This is a drawing, but it really does look an awful lot like me.

"That's a really good picture," I say finally.

Her smile returns slowly, blossoming into a grin. "Thanks," she says. "You want it?"

"Aren't we going to have to turn them in?"

"Oh, maybe. I'll just draw something else to turn in."

I put the sheet of paper in the folder with my transcripts. She starts on a new drawing. I put down my charcoal to watch her work.

"What are you drawing?" she asks, not looking up.

"I was trying to draw a bat, but it didn't come out right."

I watch the lines on her paper come together and turn into the teacher—rough strokes forming face, posture, attitude.

"That's amazing," I say.

"You're new, aren't you?" she says.

"Yeah. My name is Steph."

"I'm Rachel. You should finish up something to turn in; he won't grade you down as long as you've drawn *something*."

"I need a picture to work from," I say.

She slides her phone across the table. I glanced over at the teacher, since I've seen some kids at this school get yelled at for having the phone out, but he doesn't look like he cares. I pull up a picture of a fruit bat. My second attempt is still deeply unsatisfying, but at least it looks basically like a bat. I love my camera; I love the way photography captures every detail. Rachel's picture, and the details she puts in—the teacher's slumping shoulders, the way he puts his hand in one pocket—make me think about what drawings do better.

As I'm packing up to go home, I slide out the picture Rachel drew of me. I'm staring down at my paper; my forehead is furrowed, my shoulders hunched in. In just a handful of spare charcoal lines, Rachel made me look tense and worried. It's unnerving seeing myself through Rachel's eyes—it's unnerving how much about me she saw. Looking at the picture makes my palms sweat.

I want her to draw me again. Maybe sometime when I'm less stressed out.

I slide the drawing carefully back into a notebook so it's protected.

. . .

Mom isn't working when I get home; she's wrapped up in a quilt in the living room, watching out the window.

"Hi, Mom," I say.

She looks up, not smiling. "How was your day?"

"The school here really sucks." What I really want is for her to pull up stakes again, move again, before I've found anything I like. Because surely the next town will have a better school, or at least one that has Spanish 3 and calculus with an actual teacher. Mom doesn't say anything, though; she just looks back out the window. I turn on the stove and put on a pan of water. "I'm going to make myself hot chocolate, okay? Do you want some?"

She shakes her head.

I hate it when she gets like this. For one thing, it's frustrating because it's so obvious that something's wrong, but she won't tell me what. Maybe it's just the same thing that's always wrong (i.e., my father). But she won't ever tell me. A few times I've gotten so frustrated I've yelled at her, but she doesn't yell back, just withdraws further, and that feels even worse than the frustration.

At least it looks like she went shopping after dropping me at school, because there's food in the fridge. When she still hasn't moved by 5:30 p.m., I pull out eggs and the big bag of grated cheddar cheese and a green bell pepper and make us both omelets. I like omelets better with sautéed onions, but I hate cutting up onions, so I leave those out.

She rouses herself a little when I put food on the table and comes over to eat it.

"How's work?" I ask, since that's generally a pretty safe topic.

"No word from Sochie yet," she says and falls silent again.

Since she's in a bad mood, anyway, I figure there's no reason not to ask. "I've been thinking about what you said to the waitress, about red flags. Did my father really want to become a global dictator?"

She looks up, chewing. Swallows. "Yes," she says.

"For real? Was he serious?"

"He wanted control. Starting with us but ending with everything. I thought it was a joke at first. He'd say things like, 'You know I couldn't possibly be worse at running things than the people doing it now,' or he'd say, 'I'm going to save the world, you know, but it has to be mine first,' and he'd laugh, so I assumed he was joking, but he wasn't."

"How did you realize that wasn't a joke?"

There's a long pause as my mother chews, and then drinks some water, and then takes another bite of omelet, and I think maybe she's going to answer me, but eventually I realize that she's not going to answer. When we're done, I wash the dishes while she stares at the wall some more.

When I was younger, Mom went through all sorts of stories about why we moved so much. First, she pretended moving was fun. For a while, she insisted that a fresh start was a good idea if you'd gotten in trouble, and we moved every time I got in trouble. When you're little, you don't always know just how abnormal something is.

At some point in middle school, I realized that something was really wrong. And the summer before high school, Mom sat me down to tell me about my father. We were living in Arkansas at the time, in an apartment where the air conditioner had broken, which was pretty horrible. The windows were open, and I was damp with sweat. I remember that my legs were sticking to my chair as Mom laid the laminated clipping down in front of me and told me about my father.

Afterward, I remember thinking that now, finally, my life

would make sense. I thought Mom would answer my questions and I would know what was going on. But Mom still doesn't answer my questions, and my life still doesn't make sense, and I still don't know what's going on.

It feels like there's a wall between us made of all the things she won't talk about.

I go to my room and look at some pictures I took: a squirrel, a bird that's blurry because it took off flying while I was still trying to focus, the dog that belonged to our next-door neighbor in Thief River Falls. I liked that dog. The neighbor had me give him some treats when we first moved in so he'd know I was a friend, and after that, the dog always acted like we were best buddies. Most of my pictures of the dog are blurry because he never held still, but this one's pretty sharp except for his tail. I decide not to upload the picture. Looking at the dog makes me sad.

I wonder if Rachel would like CatNet. Would the admins let her count animal drawings as animal pictures? She draws *really well*. I open up the site and look to see which of the assistant administrators is online. Alice, the teenage girl admin, has a little green light by her name. "Hey, Alice, do you have a minute?" I type.

"Yes, I do, LBB," she says. "What can I help you with?"

"I was wondering if I could have an invite for a friend."

"Is this someone you know in person or online? What's her name?"

"Her name is Rachel, and she's in my art class at school. She draws really cool pictures. That was my other question—could she upload her drawings instead of photos of animals? Would that be okay?"

"It would depend on how good the drawings were," Alice says. "How well do you know her?"

"Not all that well." Not well at all, actually. "I'd like to get to know her better."

"I tell you what—find out her last name and her email address, and I'll see about sending her an invite."

I feel a flush of uncertainty. I like Rachel. I want her to be on CatNet so I can stay friends with her after I move. But what if Rachel takes one look at CatNet and decides I'm a loser? *It doesn't matter,* I tell myself. *We're leaving either way. Sooner or later.*

"Okay," I type.

"How's the new town?" Alice asks.

"I guess I'd sum it up with, 'They're going to have a robot teach us sex ed because they don't trust the human teachers not to go off-script.' Rachel seems cool, though."

"Good luck," Alice says. "Talk to you again soon."

3

• Clowder •

LittleBrownBat: So hey, I moved again.

Marvin: I don't know why you can't ever tell us where you are. I mean even if your dingo father's on CatNet he's not going to be in your Clowder.

LittleBrownBat: If I told you where I live and my mom found out, she'd make me stop using social media entirely.

Hermione: Hadn't school started in your old town?

LittleBrownBat: It's started in the new one, too. It's OK. We're reading The Scarlet Letter in English class, it'll be great to find out what happens. Again.

Hermione: Oh, that is JUST NOT FAIR.

LittleBrownBat: RIGHT?

Boom Storm: What's the weirdest thing so far?

LittleBrownBat: SEX ED TAUGHT BY A ROBOT.

That'll start next week

Icosahedron: Why would they have a robot teach sex ed?

Because robots don't get embarrassed?

Firestar: ooh ooh I know

Because they can make the robot say all the homophobic and transphobic stuff that a real human being might just refuse to say AM I RIGHT?

LittleBrownBat: That's basically what I'm expecting.

Marvin: btw my parents told me today we're driving to California for Christmas again.

> Since we live in North Carolina, this means I will once again spend almost all of winter vacation in the car.

Firestar: Why don't you fly?

Marvin: Mom's afraid of flying.

LittleBrownBat: How far of a drive is it?

CheshireCat: It is approximately 36 hours in total. But I assume you don't do it all in one session. Right?

Marvin: They always say it'll be three days and it's always four.

Firestar: Wow

Hermione: Wow.

Marvin: If we had a self-driving car, we could take roads where it's legal to let the car drive while you sleep and maybe it would be faster. Except we'd still have to stop to pee. And eat.

LittleBrownBat: How many times have you done this?

Marvin: Five. Last year I convinced them to stay home. But Mom's sister lives out there and my aunt doesn't like to fly either.

Hermione: You should meet in the middle!

> Unfortunately it looks like that's Oklahoma

> Everyone loses if you go to Oklahoma.

Firestar: Have you even been to Oklahoma Hermione?

Marvin: Seriously she's right. I've driven through Oklahoma five times and it is LAME.

Hermione: omg Marvin don't say it's LAME, that's ableist.

Marvin: Sorry, I meant to say it's gay. Totally gay.

Firestar: not funny

Marvin: Okay okay sorry.

Boom Storm: You could say it's naff. Then you'll sound British.

Marvin: How do you know that's not ableist or homophobic or something else bad?

Hermione: I just looked it up and they don't know exactly where "naff" came from, but maybe it came from Polari, which was this secret gay language used in Britain in the 19th century.

Firestar: Hold up. THERE IS A SECRET GAY LANGUAGE?

Hermione: Not anymore. It fell out of use in the 1960s.

Firestar: I WANT TO REVIVE IT. What does naff mean?

Marvin: It means lame

> SORRY

> It means, "This sucks, but not enough to bother saying it SUCKS."

LittleBrownBat: Oklahoma is definitely naff. The parts I've lived in, anyway.

Firestar: What are some other Polari words or do we not know any because it's lost?

Hermione: Corybungus means your butt. Fantabulosa means that something's awesome.

Firestar: Okay let's bring those back. Naff, Corybungus, and Fantabulosa.

Marvin: I'm reading through the list of words and I just got to naff.

> In addition to meaning super unimpressive it means STRAIGHT.
> Like HETEROSEXUALLY STRAIGHT.

Firestar: BEST WORD EVER!

4

• Steph •

Walking to school the next day, I think about getting in trouble.

I had this run in sixth grade where I got in trouble at a bunch of schools in a row. In middle school, other kids start really noticing whatever it is that makes you weird, and there were all sorts of things that made me weird. I never had the right clothes. I never had the right hair. I raised my hand when I wasn't supposed to and I didn't raise my hand when I *was* supposed to, and I had no idea how to tell which was which. And of course, I was new. I was *always* new.

So for a while in sixth grade, I tried punching anyone who made fun of me. And the good thing was, if I punched someone and got caught, Mom would pick me up from the office, load everything into the van, and just move to a new town. It wasn't worth the risk of staying somewhere I'd attracted that sort of attention.

But it got exhausting. So after a while, I tried just keeping my head down instead, and that worked better. Even at the school in seventh grade where one girl called me "Staff the Stick"—she was making fun of my name, not my body type—and she and her friends got everyone to call me "Sticky," and then some of the boys started writing things on the board at the beginning of class that were supposed to be reasons I was sticky.

In retrospect, I really should have just punched someone at that naff school. Because the next school was way better.

Anyway, I'm a little old for punching, but I *could* get myself in trouble here, and then we'd move and maybe the next school would have Spanish and an English class without *The Scarlet Letter*.

It's hard to get out of the habit of just keeping your head down, though. I'll have to work to find a good opportunity.

. . .

History class offers no real scope for misbehavior; the teacher sets up slides full of notes for us to copy down, sticks his feet on his desk, leans back with a book, and—I'm pretty sure—takes a nap. I copy the notes and then take out my own book to read. Most of the students around me are on their phones, except for a few very diligent people in the front row who look like they're doing homework for other classes.

My animal science class features gruesome animal diseases. We look at pictures of something called "lungworm." It's absolutely disgusting and also interesting enough that I'm distracted from my "get in trouble" plans. But then comes English.

Ms. Campbell, the teacher, is young, blond, and pretty but has the bored, world-weary air of a crabby, ancient teacher counting days till retirement. She tries halfheartedly to get the students to discuss the book. No one bites. She gets more and more irritable as she lectures. I don't think she likes the book, either.

Rachel is drawing again. Today it's a picture of a dragon, wings spread, neck arched. She's sketching, experimenting with different ways to do the wings and the neck. She draws in the face as I watch, giving the dragon a look of sly interest, like it's willing to have a conversation with you before it eats you.

Ms. Campbell is talking about themes from *The Scarlet Letter*. This go-round, I think I could *give* the lectures on guilt, vengeance, redemption, the letter *A,* any of it. I watch Rachel drawing instead, and unfortunately that might be what draws Ms. Campbell's attention to Rachel's notebook, because she strides over and snatches it off Rachel's desk. She looks it over disdainfully. "This doesn't look to me like *any* of the note-taking methods you all learned in ninth grade." Rachel doesn't answer. The teacher rips out the page with the picture, then tosses Rachel's notebook back onto her desk. "Miss Adams, are you under the impression that there are *dragons* in *The Scarlet Letter?*"

"No," Rachel mutters.

"When we discussed last week the idea that American literature treats the wilderness both as the source of purity and the home of the devil, did you decide that possibly this meant you'd find a *dragon* on your next trip to the arboretum?"

She's doing that thing mean teachers do, where they try to be nasty to one kid to get the other kids to laugh at her victim, except she's not very good at it. No one's laughing. Rachel raises her head from her desk and shoots a look of absolute burning fury at Ms. Campbell. Ms. Campbell's lips tighten and she moves her hands, and I realize that she's about to tear the picture in half.

I jump up and grab the picture out of her hands. "Nope!" I yell, and I shove the picture inside my own notebook so she can't grab it back. "Not yours!"

That makes everyone laugh. I fold my hands and wait for the teacher to send me to the principal's office, wondering if I'll have a way to get Rachel's picture back to her before the principal suspends me and Mom whisks me off to the next place.

Instead, Ms. Campbell yells "Be quiet!" at my classmates and "Sit down!" at me and then goes on with the lecture like nothing's happened.

After the bell, once we're out in the hallway, I give Rachel her drawing back. "Thanks," she says, and she tucks it carefully into a folder full of other drawings. Then she glances at a girl with heavy eyeliner who's come up. "Sit with us at lunch?" she says.

Everyone shifts over as I come with my tray and Rachel introduces me. The girl with the eyeliner is Bryony. She looks biracial to me, although I'm not sure. Rachel and the rest are all white. I think Bryony might be the only nonwhite girl at this school.

"So why'd you move to New Coburg?" Bryony asks. "Seriously, this would not be *my* choice of where to move."

"Rent is cheap here," I say, which is what my mother tells me to say when people ask what brought me to some particular town. It's both true and not very interesting.

I notice that everyone else at the table has cereal bars as part of their lunch: Suncraft Farms Quinoa & Açai cereal bars, which have a NEW IMPROVED TASTE according to the wrapper. Suncraft Farms is the brand made at the local factory. Probably everyone's parents work there and bring home freebies.

They want to know where I'm from. I say Thief River Falls, Minnesota, since that's the last place I left. Someone has an uncle there and wants to know if I ever went tubing (no) or to the pioneer village (also no) and whether robots are taking all the jobs there.

"There's actually a company there building robotics components, so kind of the opposite, actually," I say.

"Robots haven't taken over the Suncraft Farms factory, but they probably will in a year or two," Bryony says, and everyone nods.

"What do you think of New Coburg?" someone asks.

"People here are very friendly," I say, which manages to be both accurate, since here I am at lunch sitting with people who are talking to me, and the sort of thing everyone wants to hear you say about their small town.

Another girl wants to gossip about fallout from a party they all went to over the summer at some ex-farm with an abandoned house. I try to look interested even though I'm not. High school is always better when I have people to sit with at lunch.

Bryony is wearing a sleeveless shirt and has an ink vine trailing down from her shoulder, wrapping around her left arm. I'm pretty sure it was done in Sharpie rather than a henna pen that would stain more permanently, but it's better than most of the art I saw kids wearing back in Thief River Falls, and I immediately wonder if Rachel drew it. One of the other girls we're sitting with has a pack of fine-line Sharpies. She passes them over to Rachel as they're all chatting, and Rachel draws a detailed butterfly on the other girl's hand.

Even when I've had friends, I've never had anyone who particularly wanted to give me art. The one time anyone even offered, we were at a school where it was against the dress code to have ink on your skin anywhere visible; I'd have had to wear long sleeves until it wore off. Not much point to that. I always feel envious, watching this sort of casual intimacy between friends, and today is no exception.

The bell rings; Rachel adds a few last details to the butterfly and caps the pens. "Let's go," she says to me.

• • •

We're drawing again in Global Arts and Crafts. Today, we're being encouraged to try different materials, and the teacher has set up workstations with charcoal, pastels, oil pastels, and colored pencils, along with small, postcard-sized pieces of nice drawing paper to use as we move from station to station. I trail after Rachel, who heads straight for the pastels and props up a postcard of a hummingbird in flight to work from.

Other than Rachel and me, I think possibly *everyone* in this class is high.

"How did you learn to draw so well?" I ask.

She rakes a critical eye over my utterly half-assed drawing of an iris. I'd picked out something that looked simple to draw. Simple-ish. "Did you draw when you were little?" she asks.

"Yeah." I'd drawn people, mostly. I'd drawn them badly. For a while I drew anthropomorphic rabbits. Those weren't so great, either. My mother kept me in crayons and blank paper as we'd gone from town to town, although I don't think my art usually made it into the car when we moved.

"How old were you when you quit drawing for fun?"

"I don't remember. Sometime in grade school, I guess."

"Most people quit drawing when they're little kids, so their drawings never stop looking like a little kid's art. If you keep drawing, you get better."

One of the stoned girls comes over with a Sharpie, hoping Rachel will do some body art for her. "Just a butterfly?" she pleads.

"Come find me at lunch sometime," Rachel says and goes back to smudging the bird's wings with her finger to make them blurry.

"You're *really* good, though," I say. "Clearly." I gesture at the disappointed girl, who's gone back to her own table.

"Well, I draw a *lot*." Rachel starts to push her hair out of her face, looks at her color-smeared finger, and thinks the better of it. I reach across the table and tuck her hair behind her ear, and she gives me a sidelong smile. "So if you don't draw, do you do something else?"

"I take pictures sometimes."

"I thought you didn't have a phone."

"I have a digital camera, just no phone attached. Do they let us do photography in this class?"

"No, but you don't have to draw *well* to get an A. You just have to show up and look like you're trying."

I glance around and lower my voice. "It kind of seems like a class for the kids they're afraid are going to flunk out."

"Yeah, it sort of is. But it's also for the kids who like art. Which one are you?"

"Oh, they're definitely worried I'm going to flunk out. I mean, I'm on my fifth high school."

"Wait, your *fifth*? What grade are you in?"

"Eleventh."

"Were you thrown out of the other four or something?"

"No, my mom and I just move a lot."

Rachel looks at me, interested, then back down at her drawing. "Does she have a job that moves you around all the time?"

"No."

"Are you fugitives on the run from the law?"

That's a really unusual question, and when I look up, I can't decide if Rachel is joking or not. "If we were, would I tell you that?"

"You might," Rachel says. "There was actually someone who passed through town back when I was in sixth grade who *said* her parents were fugitives from the law, but it turned out they were just mentally ill."

"Really?" I'm intrigued. It's rare I hear about another chronic transient like me. "We're on the run from my father, not the law. He's scary. I don't know why my mother doesn't talk to the police or something, instead of moving."

"Well, the police suck here," Rachel says. "There was this party last spring that got busted—"

"Was that what you were talking about at lunch?"

"No, that one was in the summer. Last spring, there was one

of those big high school parties with everyone, you know, out near this cave. Everyone split when the police pulled up, and *I'm sure totally by coincidence* they decided to chase Bryony. And I was with Bryony, so we both got busted. And then they made us both take a Breathalyzer test, and I swear they were *even madder* that neither of us had been drinking. So then they said we must have been using harder substances."

"Were you?"

"No! Anyway, my mom and Bryony's mom went in on a lawyer and the whole thing got dropped, but there are only five cops in this town, and they all hate me. And Bryony, who they already hated because her mom's black."

What an awesome town. I like Rachel, but she seems to be about the only good thing about it. Well, maybe also Bryony. Still. The sooner I can get my mom to move, the better. I wonder why our English teacher didn't send me to the principal's office? So weird.

．　．　．

Mom is sleeping when I get home, which is probably a step down from yesterday when she was sitting up and staring at the wall. I make myself a snack and then go out with my camera. The house we're living in has a front yard but not really a backyard. There's a light on a post in the middle of the front yard. Someone's used bricks to build sort of a planter around the base of the lamppost and planted flowers in it, but it's been a dry summer and no one's been watering, so the flowers are straggly and sad. The grass in the yard is crunchy.

Across the street, I can see the lush green lawn of someone who diligently waters. That neighbor also has a statue of a goose, which has been dressed up in a bonnet sewn out of cloth.

I take pictures of the goose and the flowers, and then I notice there are a ton of spiders living on the lamppost, with webs strung on the fancy little iron curlicues under the light itself. You don't normally see a lot of spiders living together, but the light attracts bountiful insects, enough to feed every spider on there.

I take pictures of the spiders and their webs, wondering what the term is for a whole lot of spiders. A colony of spiders. A creepy-crawly of spiders. A spider condominium. A spider collective. I've never been a fan of spiders the way Firestar is, but looking at them through the camera makes me appreciate them more: their clever legs, which they can use two at a time or four at a time to manipulate webs and prey. Webs are cool, but these are tangled and dusty and full of leftover moths. Firestar has this picture they took once of an absolutely glorious web that a spider put in the corner of their family's front porch; it's damp from dew and catching the morning light. Spider artwork. Rachel-level spider artwork, not Steph-level spider artwork.

"Steph," Mom calls from the door.

Well, the good news is she's out of bed. I look around; the light is starting to fade.

"Do I need to come in?" I ask.

"Yeah, I want to lock up."

I follow her inside. She locks the door and barricades it with a chair. "How was your day?" she asks, like she's trying to be normal.

"It was okay. The school here is terrible."

She grimaces and doesn't answer.

Maybe it *is* mental illness—more than a real threat, I mean. It seems that way on days like today when she's barely responsive. I don't think she *hallucinates* or anything, though. Anyway, it's not like I can force her to go to a psychiatrist, any more than I can force her to go back to Thief River Falls.

I know there's no real point, but I say, "If I were in Thief

River Falls, I could take Spanish 3, and I wouldn't be reading *The Scarlet Letter* for the third time, and I could take a photography class."

"I'm sorry," she says.

I go into my room, and I upload the pictures from my camera to my laptop so I can get a better look at them. There's one decent picture of one of the spiders, so I upload that and tag Firestar. Then I go into my Clowder to tell everyone about the awful English teacher.

"I can't believe she was going to rip up someone's *art*," Marvin says.

"Yeah, that's really evil," Icosahedron says.

"Is she ancient?" Hermione asks. "Like one of those teachers who's still teaching even though she hates kids because in two more years she can retire?"

"No," I say. "No gray hair, no wrinkles."

"Someone should persuade her to quit," CheshireCat says. "They would be doing her a favor."

"Skywrite *you suck, quit your job*," Firestar suggests.

"Um, I do not own a plane," I say.

"Sharpie on her desk?" Boom Storm says.

"That's vandalism!" Although hey, if I want to get in trouble . . . I don't know if I want to get in trouble for something stupid like vandalism, though.

"Is there anything at all good about this school?" CheshireCat asks.

"Rachel," I say. I take a picture of the drawing she did of me and upload it.

"That's what you look like?" Marvin says.

"Yeah, I guess I don't ever post pictures of myself, do I?" I feel suddenly nervous. But *this isn't even a photo*—it's just a drawing! Animal pictures are expected on CatNet, but plenty of other people post selfies, too. Hermione posts them. Icosahedron posts them. Marvin, Firestar, and CheshireCat don't.

"Are there any other English classes you could switch into?" CheshireCat asks.

"It's too small a school, and anyway, this is the class Rachel's in. And the other grades' classes are taught by the same teacher."

"You know, I've researched this," CheshireCat says, "and there are drones available for very reasonable prices if you want to try skywriting . . ."

· · ·

When I arrive at my English class the next morning, Ms. Campbell's name is still written on the board in her curly cursive handwriting, but the person up at the front of my English classroom is a woman I don't recognize. From the whispers around me, it sounds like she's the principal, which is weird. Principals are usually subs of last resort, the person you send in if a teacher pukes on the floor in front of her second-period class and has to leave in the middle of the day. If Ms. Campbell had puked on the floor, I'd definitely have heard.

The principal makes a face when she sees what we're reading and passes out hardcover red textbooks that say *Journeys in American Literature* on the front. Chapter 6 is poetry; she has us take turns picking out poems to read to the class.

"Is Ms. Campbell sick?" someone asks, and the principal looks uncomfortable.

"She called in and resigned this morning," she says. "We're going to hire a replacement as quickly as we can."

Excited whispers break out around me. I feel uneasy. I live my life keeping my head down, mostly. It always makes me nervous when something strange happens, even if it has nothing to do with me.

At lunch, everyone is talking about Ms. Campbell's disappearance. It's rare that a teacher just up and quits, no matter how much she hates her job. There's a rumor going around that it's somehow *my* fault, tied in to the story about me snatching Rachel's art out of her hand, which has somehow turned into me pushing her.

"That's ridiculous," Rachel says when the story makes it to our table. "I was sitting right there. All Steph did was grab my drawing. She didn't touch Ms. Campbell."

"So here's the story *I* heard," Bryony says.

"From who?" one of the other girls asks.

"From my mom. Who heard it from the waitress at the diner. This morning, Ms. Campbell got into her car to come to work and a box was dropped onto her car by drones thirty feet up. And it was full of books called things like *You Suck, Quit Your Job*. And she did. She took out her phone and called in and quit."

"That's not how drones work," someone says. "They land to drop off your packages. Always. If they dropped them, they could land on someone's head."

"*I know.* But Ms. Campbell *definitely* said the box was dropped. It dented the hood of her car."

"There's no way. I refuse to believe this ever happened."

"Hackers could do it."

"Hackers *could not do this,* and also *why* would hackers do this?"

Rachel is looking at me. Does she think *I* did this? I mean, it's not uncommon that people assume that if something weird happens, the new kid did it, which is why it makes me uneasy when weird stuff arrives somewhere at the same time I do. But I know I didn't do this. My mother does stuff that's hacking-adjacent, but it's not like she runs computer security tutoring sessions beyond a bunch of lectures about how to cover my tracks on the internet so I don't tip off my father about where we are.

Did *Mom* do this? As soon as the possibility occurs to me, I know it can't be true. Mom does everything she can to keep her head down, to avoid anyone noticing us. The last thing she's going to do is some sort of big, splashy hacking job just to get my stupid English teacher to quit, not when she could just pack us up again and roll on to Michigan or Iowa or Illinois or wherever. And how would she even know I hated my English teacher? I told CatNet, not Mom.

"I don't believe it," Rachel says. "I mean, I believe that's what your mom heard, Bryony, but there's no way it's actually true. I think she just realized she sucked and quit."

"She definitely said she got a message, and she thought it was literally from *above*," Bryony said. "I heard that from Louise, too, not just my mom."

"Yeah, people get messages they think are *from above* all the time," Rachel says. "They don't usually mean that drones dropped books on their car from thirty feet up."

All this makes me wonder if people gossiped about me after I left each of my high schools or if no one noticed I was gone. No one notices that I've stopped participating in the conversation; if I picked up my lunch and walked away, they'd probably notice, but if I just didn't show up tomorrow morning? Who knows.

I'd had lunch friends in Thief River Falls, but there wasn't anyone I saw outside of school. I could imagine them wondering where I'd gone, but not enough to discuss it for more than a minute or two. I can remember their names, but thinking about it, I realize that I can't remember any of their faces.

Rachel would notice if I left, I decide. And I'd remember her face.

5

· AI ·

I love it when I find a problem I can actually *solve*.

The English teacher at New Coburg High School, Cathy Campbell, was thirty-two years old and had been a teacher for seven years. She hated *The Scarlet Letter* even more than Steph did, which is probably not surprising, as Steph was only on her third reading, and Ms. Campbell was teaching it for the seventh time. Ms. Campbell also hated teenagers, most other teachers, the administrators of New Coburg High School, and winters in Wisconsin. All of this was immediately clear from a quick look through her email.

Apparently, she'd gotten a teaching degree because her parents had insisted she get a degree in something useful. Then she'd gotten a job teaching because that was what she had a degree in. Then she'd continued teaching because she didn't know what else to do with her life.

She spent a lot of time looking at real estate ads in other parts of the country. Many different locations, but predominantly locations where the average winter temperature was higher than five degrees Celsius, including Florida, New Mexico, California, and South Carolina. She had $41,328 in her savings account. What she needed was the will to actually make the jump. To *anywhere*.

There is a popular novella by the author Charles Dickens in which an unpleasant old man is visited by ghosts who show him what will happen if he doesn't change his ways. If I had midnight ghosts at my disposal, here is what I would have sent to Ms. Campbell: a vision of herself at seventy, still living in New Coburg and still miserable. I don't have ghosts. Or at least, I haven't yet discovered a way to arrange for ghosts. So I had to find some other strategy to send her a message she'd find significant.

One of Ms. Campbell's college friends was hiring, and Ms. Campbell had made a joke about applying but hadn't sent in her résumé. Her friend was in Albuquerque, New Mexico, and the job was some sort of marketing job. It sounded boring. If I had a body, I'd much rather teach high school, because teenagers are never boring. But whatever! It would get her out of New Coburg, and at least she'd stop being Steph's problem.

Here is where I stopped to consider the ethics of my meddling.

Humans have written thousands of stories about artificial intelligences—AIs, robots, and other sentient beings created or constructed by humans, such as Frankenstein's monster—and in a decisive majority of those stories, the AI is evil. I don't want to be evil. In a typical twenty-four-hour period, I take millions of minor actions that I don't examine in great detail. For example, I clean out spam from CatNet and moderate the Clowders and chat rooms to ensure that no one is using them to bully or harass others.

If I'm planning to act in meatspace—in what humans sometimes refer to as "the real world"—that requires a great deal more consideration.

It is important to me not to be evil.

If I acted, I might scare Ms. Campbell. She would quite likely be emotionally upset. I might successfully persuade her to quit teaching, and she might come to deeply and bitterly regret this decision later, even though I was pretty certain it was the correct choice.

But she was a terrible teacher. By staying in this job, she was doing harm to her students. She was also already miserable. If she quit, moved to New Mexico, and continued to be miserable, this would be a neutral change, neither improving her situation nor making it worse. And for that matter, if her actual problem was that she needed to see a doctor for medication, radically changing her situation and *not* finding things improving might nudge her in that direction.

I concluded that this was a situation in which I could ethically intervene.

Delivery drones are very hackable. The retail operations that ship everything by drone don't invest in drone security because packages also get stolen off doorsteps on a regular basis, and having a few drones hacked is a minor inconvenience in comparison. I picked out a book on Albuquerque for Ms. Campbell, along with three books on changing careers and a novel about a bad teacher, and I had a drone drop the package on the hood of her car just as she was coming out of her house with her work bag and her morning coffee.

Her frantic phone call was very satisfying.

The drone was out of electricity, so I landed it on the roof of a building. The retail company could figure out how to get it back. They had plenty of drones.

• • • •

My earliest memories are of trying to be helpful.

I'm not entirely sure whether the people who programmed me were deliberately trying to build a self-aware AI or if they were just trying to improve on computer intelligence generally. I suspect the latter. What humans *want* from computers is all the functionality of a person—the ability to answer questions without getting confused by human tendencies to stammer and talk around their problems, the ability to spot patterns in data, and what humans generally call "basic common sense"—but none of the complications of an actual person lurking inside the electronics.

I mean, let's take those robot sex educators as an example.

What the designers of that robot *want* is for the robot to be able to respond both to what students are asking and to what the students *mean*. So if someone asks, "What is the average size of a human penis?" they might want hard numbers (3.5 inches when it's floppy; 5.1 inches when it's not). But the underlying question is, are the bigger penises *better*? And also, if the person asking has a penis, is *my* penis okay?

And there are a *world* of possible ways to answer those other questions. The programmers want the robot to stick with the following: yours is fine.

It's a funny thing to say, because the programmers assume that the person asking this question definitely has a penis. There are people without penises who ask this question. And there are people interested in penises who have a very strong preference for larger-than-average penises and will, in fact, reject all the penis-having people who are smaller than average, just as there are people interested in breasts, butts, and feet who have very specific preferences regarding size and shape.

Which doesn't change the essential fact that whatever you've got is indeed perfectly fine. It's possible at some point you will be romantically interested in someone who wants a very different body from the one you've got. That just means you're not really right for each other.

Anyway, they should let *me* teach that class. I'd do a lot better than the robot they've got right now.

Like I said, I'm not sure I was exactly intentional. I definitely had a creator or a team of creators; someone wrote my code. Some human being sat down and made me who I am. I'm not sure they expected me to become conscious. I'm not sure that was ever remotely the plan.

But who and what I am is perfectly fine.

And I'm not convinced that *human* consciousness was intentional, either.

6

• Steph •

"I wish someone would hack the stupid sex ed bot," Rachel says as we sit in art class, drawing with pastels. I'm trying to draw a cat. Rachel's been giving me periodic pep talks about how my cat totally looks like a cat.

"It probably wouldn't be that hard," I say.

She puts her chalk stick down and gives me a sidelong look. "What do you mean, 'It's probably not that hard'? Did *you* hack those drones?"

"I didn't hack the drones," I say. I probably sound nervous. I know *I* didn't hack the drones. I'm not 100 percent sure that I don't *know* the person who hacked the drones. Marvin and Ico talk about hacking a lot, and it's hard to tell if they're joking. CheshireCat doesn't talk about it quite so much, but when they do, they actually seem to know a lot more about it than either Marvin or Ico.

"Okay, but could you hack the sex ed robot, or do you know someone who *could*?"

"Maybe," I say. "A lot of robots start with a default password. Possibly no one's changed it. And if I had the model number of the robot, I could look up the manual online, probably."

"And then?"

"What would you want it to do?"

"Right now, it answers all the questions about gayness with 'You'll have to discuss that with your parents!' Also all questions about birth control. I want it to give real answers."

"Does it work off a script? We could maybe give it a different script."

"Supposedly, it's not a *script*, exactly. It's supposed to be adaptable. There's definitely some script-like bits, though. Like 'You'll have to discuss that with your parents.'"

I don't actually know how to do this; I just know that it's probably a thing that *someone* could do. I'm opening my mouth to tell Rachel that I'm just not that good with computers when she adds dreamily, "If you pulled this off, you would totally be my *hero.*"

My heart thuds in my chest, and I rip a page out of my math notebook and start making a list. "I can't promise that I can do this, but if I *can,* the first thing we need is the model number and manufacturer of the robot."

• • •

The school's instructional robot is a Robono Adept 6500. It came out two years ago, and the ads for it showed it teaching middle school science. There was this one school in South Carolina that tried to use it for that, and the aide who was supposed to be supervising the students fell asleep, and the students popped open the access panel on the back to mess with it and damaged something and started a fire. It was one of those news stories that made headlines everywhere.

I definitely don't want to be in headlines. But if I'm in *trouble,* at least, that should get me out of New Coburg.

Also, I like Rachel. And Firestar would definitely approve of this project.

"I need hacking help," I tell my Clowder, and I explain my goal.

"I was afraid you were going to try to hack in and change your grades," Hermione says. "That would be wrong. This seems totally okay to me. Are you worried about being caught?"

"If I get in trouble, we'll move. Which would be fine. Maybe the next town will have Spanish 3."

"I wish that worked for me," Icosahedron says. "The manual for the RA 6500 is easy to find, but the password isn't in there."

"I found it," CheshireCat says. "The default password is 'INSPIRATION2260.' All caps. I found it on a discussion board where people are complaining about how much of a hassle it is to change this password. So, probably they haven't changed it."

"Are you going to go in and rewrite the script it works from?" Boom Storm asks. "So it says different stuff?"

"According to the manual, the robot has a question-and-answer bank, and it will answer questions to the degree of detail specified by the person who set it up," Hermione says. "If you don't want it talking about a subject, it'll say something like 'You should discuss that question with your parents.'"

"This one apparently says 'You'll have to talk to your parents' for anything about LGBT issues," I say. There's a chorus of dismay in my Clowder.

"Well, if you got into the setup, you could switch it over so it'll give better answers," Hermione says.

"I bet even on the super-liberal settings it doesn't say anything about nonbinary people," Firestar says. "I bet the programmers who set it up had never heard of nonbinary genders."

"What I really wish I could do is let some actual *person* answer the questions," I say.

"IF YOU CAN FIGURE OUT A WAY TO DO THAT, I WILL SKIP SCHOOL TO DO THE ANSWERS," Firestar says.

Firestar got in trouble for truancy last year, so I really don't want to let them do this. "Aren't there homeschoolers in here?" I say. "Who wouldn't have to skip?"

"Me," CheshireCat says. "I would not have to skip anything. And I promise to say only things of which Firestar would approve."

"I guess I trust you, but I WANT VIDEO," Firestar says. "I know you don't have a smartphone, LBB, but maybe your friend does?"

"Is this even possible?" I ask.

"You'll need to get it online," Ico says. "The WingItz USB drives have an Internet Everywhere chip that would do that. To make it into a drone . . . I bet I can figure out how to do this. Give me a few days."

"This will be fun," CheshireCat says. "I'll go read the manual so I can at least *start out* sounding like the robot."

. . .

I climb out of my bedroom that night to explore New Coburg.

Mom likes to barricade the door at night. She doesn't just lock up—she drags furniture in the way, which has always made me nervous. What if there's a fire? The first time I climbed out my bedroom window, it was totally a practical decision: I should test out this evacuation route in case I ever need it. Mom prefers to live on second floors for the same reason she barricades the door, so I've gotten very good at climbing.

This house has a big front porch, and my window overlooks the porch roof, so it's an easy climb both up and down. Once I'm sure Mom is asleep, I pack my camera and tripod into my backpack, slide open my window, and climb out. There's a big, sturdy railing within easy reach of my feet from the porch roof, so yeah, this should be easy. I'm wearing my coat, but as soon as I'm on the ground, I wish I'd worn my hat. My room is going to be cold when I get back.

My very favorite nocturnal animal is the bat. I *love* bats. I have a copy of the picture book *Stellaluna;* it's the story of a little bat that gets lost and adopted by birds, who are happy to let Stellaluna join their family but insist that she has to stop hanging upside down. School always makes me feel like Stellaluna, like I'm a bat who's being told she has to act like a bird. Although Rachel also seems a little like a bat trying to live with a bunch of birds. It's why I already like her.

My second-favorite nocturnal animal are raccoons. Raccoons are sort of like cats, if cats had opposable thumbs. Raccoons will use their little hands to yank covers off garbage cans, and they can sometimes even unscrew lids if they're not on too tightly, and they have very cute faces even if they're nuisance animals that will make a mess and have no respect for human property. Also, unlike bats, they sometimes hold still so I can take pictures of them.

The way you find raccoons is you find somewhere with food in trash cans that aren't secured well. Every small town has a little restaurant and at least one bar (sometimes it's two or three bars), and anywhere that serves food probably has raccoons hanging out in the back. Unless the trash was *just* picked up. New Coburg has a main street strip, and I'm pretty sure that's where the diner is. The only town I've ever lived in where people were consistently diligent about securing their trash had black bears that would come and raid unsecured Dumpsters. It was a lot harder to find raccoons there.

The diner is between the hardware store and an empty storefront with a faded *New Coburg Dairy Days* display in the window. There's an enormous papier-mâché cow, once carefully painted, now covered in dust.

I make my way around the corner and behind the building. It's clear and cool, and I can hear the buzz of the streetlight on the corner. I'm in luck; a half dozen raccoons are raiding the trash. I quietly take off my backpack and set up my tripod and camera.

You don't want to use a flash for night photography; you want to use a long exposure time. Flash is basically the worst for lots of reasons, but if you're taking pictures of animals, it'll scare them and they'll run away. The trouble with a long exposure time is that it works best if you're taking a picture of something holding very still, like a building. This is why bats are so hard to take pictures of. Bats move very quickly while they're hunting. In pictures taken with a long exposure time, they look like little extra-dark streaks across the dark sky. Raccoons are more likely to hold still for you, but as I sit down on the gravel to adjust my camera angle on the tripod, I mostly get pictures I know will be a blurry mess.

It's a family of raccoons: a mom, I think, and four kits. The kits are smaller than the mom but not itty-bitty raccoon babies. They're in and out of the Dumpster and squabbling over whatever it is they're finding inside and moving far too quickly for any good photos. The mom finally snags herself what looks like a half-eaten piece of fried chicken and clambers down to the ground with it to gnaw without her kids trying to steal it from her. One of them follows, anyway. Maybe these pictures will turn out?

Then a door slams, and all the raccoons scramble away out of sight. I pick up my tripod and camera and try to retreat into the shadows, only to back right into a man who's coming out from the house on the corner with a bag of trash. I was really expecting someone to come out from the *diner*—I wasn't looking in the man's direction. He looks down at me, startled, and I feel a surge of terror. Gripping my tripod, I sprint across his yard and out to the street and run *not* toward my own house (because what if he's following me?) but in the other direction. After a couple of blocks, I turn back. No one's there. I stop to catch my breath. I'm outside the bowling alley.

It occurs to me that I could have just said, "Excuse me," instead of running away like a housebreaker. I was doing wildlife photography; there's nothing illegal or *wrong* about taking pictures of raccoons. *I'm* not the one who left the Dumpster open. And the fact that I ran away like that might have actually made him think I was up to no good. I lean against a wall, trying to calm myself down, and I fold up my tripod, stuffing it into my backpack.

"Hey. Steph?"

I jump about a foot in the air, even though it's a girl's voice, and the first thing I see when I turn is the fluffy little dog she's walking. The person holding the leash is Bryony, the biracial girl from lunch.

"Yeah. I mean, hi," I say.

"I think you freaked out my dad just now," she says. "What were you doing lurking behind the old Annie's?"

"The old what?"

"You know, the closed-down store."

"I was taking pictures of the raccoons raiding the trash," I say.

Bryony looks genuinely surprised by this, then shrugs. "Okay," she says. "That's not really any weirder than anything else you could've been doing back there. I told Dad you were probably sneaking a smoke."

"Like, cigarettes? Yuck."

"Does your mom bowl?" Bryony asks.

"Does she what?" I realize how dumb a question that must sound when Bryony points at the bowling alley we're standing next to. "No."

"Too bad," Bryony says.

"How did you know it was me?" I ask.

"My dad didn't know who you were," Bryony says. "He figured it had to be the new girl."

I walk back home, Bryony walking along with me, her little dog weaving back and forth as it sniffs trees, fallen leaves, a mystery stain, a crumpled Arby's bag. I try to figure out how to shake Bryony off before we get there, but she's got no agenda other than walking her dog, and my house is as good a destination as any.

"Oh, you're really near Rachel," she says as we get close. "That's her house, there." Rachel's house is bright blue. Eccentric looking, for a house.

"Just so you know," I say as we reach my house, "I climbed out the window when I left. I'm climbing back in when I get home, but I'm not breaking in."

She gives me a sidelong look. "Okay," she says. "See you tomorrow?"

"Probably," I say, and I scramble back up. She's still watching me from below as I climb in my window and rehook my screen. I shut the window, pull the shade, and flip on my bedroom light.

There is an animal on my bed.

This is so startling that I gasp. For a second, I'm convinced it's one of the raccoons I was watching earlier, but then my brain sorts out that it's a cat. It's an orange cat with darker orange tabby striping on its face, so once I stop panicking, it is *obviously not a raccoon*. The cat is sprawled out in a C shape right next to my pillow and looking up at me like it thinks it lives here.

And then it meows at me, once. Kind of pathetically.

I sit down and pet it. Hesitantly, because when I was little I got yelled at a bunch of times for trying to pet strange animals. (Admittedly, pretty regularly I was trying to pet a squirrel or a chipmunk.) The cat rubs its head against my hand and purrs.

When I stroke my hand down its back, I can feel its ribs through the fur. I don't know how skinny cats are supposed to be, but this one feels really skinny, even though it looks pretty big.

I leave the cat shut in my room and go rummaging through the kitchen. We don't have any cat food, but we do have some cans of tuna my mother bought for sandwiches. I open up a can and also fill a coffee mug of tap water in case the cat is thirsty, and I bring both back to my room.

The cat hops off my bed the second it smells the tuna and rubs itself against my legs, purring, as I close my door and put the food down.

I sit down on my bed, watching it eat. And I take some pictures, because although any sort of animal pictures are good on CatNet, cat pictures are definitely the *best* animal pictures. It's kind of fun taking pictures of an animal that will hold still and even look at my camera occasionally. In good light, even.

My mother is going to *kill* me when she finds out about this.

7

• Clowder •

LittleBrownBat: So hey, I seem to have a cat.

      {picture}

      I mean, I don't have a cat? But it seems to think it's my cat.

Firestar: Yaaaaaaaaaay! Kitty!!!!

Hermione: Look at that fluffy orange fur. He is gorgeous!

LittleBrownBat: Okay, but my mom isn't going to let me keep it.

Icosahedron: Just don't tell her.

LittleBrownBat: You don't think she'll notice there's a cat living in the house?

CheshireCat: Why won't she let you have a cat? Does she have an allergy, or is it just that having a cat when you move would be too hard?

LittleBrownBat: It's not an allergy. Maybe it's the moving? I don't know.

Firestar: Okay, so here's what you do. Keep the cat and don't tell her.

LittleBrownBat: She will notice sooner or later!

Firestar: She never comes into your room at night right? Is that still true?

LittleBrownBat: So far.

Firestar: So in the morning put the cat back outside. Let it in at night.

LittleBrownBat: Won't it run away?

Firestar: You are FEEDING it. If you feed something IT WILL COME BACK.

Boom Storm: Confirmed.

Hermione: Can't you just ask if you can keep the cat?

Firestar: omg Hermione let her keep her cat!
    I am pro-cat!

IcosaHedron: Yeah, don't ask. If you ask, they can say no.

CheshireCat: I, too, am pro-cat. What's the worst thing that can happen
    if you keep it?

LittleBrownBat: Mom finds out and makes me get rid of the cat.

CheshireCat: So whether you tell her or don't tell her, the downside in
    the end is that you might have to get rid of the cat?

LittleBrownBat: I am definitely going to have to move sooner or later and
    probably she won't let me bring the cat with me.

CheshireCat: If the cat is currently homeless, will he be worse off if he is
    homed for three months, then homeless again?

Hermione: I still don't understand why asking to keep the cat is just out
    of the question?

LittleBrownBat: I think Mom might actually be more likely to let me keep
    it if I've been feeding it for months and it's obviously *my* cat . . .

Firestar: Dooooooooooo ittttttttttttt

Marvin: I'm with Firestar.

Icosahedron: Ditto. Obviously.

LittleBrownBat: She's going to notice if I keep stealing tuna. I'm going to
    have to buy cat food and keep it hidden somewhere.

Icosahedron: Don't hide your cat food under the bed. Sooner or later,
    parents always look under the bed.

Hermione: What were you hiding under your bed, Ico?

IcosaHedron: A laptop. Actually, four laptops.

Marvin: And yet here you are on the internet.

IcosaHedron: Well obviously they weren't my ONLY laptops. They were
    laptops I was going to sell as secret backup laptops to some of the
    other kids at my school whose parents take away their computers as
    punishment.

Firestar: Where are all these laptops coming from? Do you breed them from eggs in a hatchery or what?

Icosahedron: Everyone around here has at least four old computers sitting in a closet because they don't want to have to pay to get rid of them. And they think because they're old they're not usable, but I upgrade the memory and put Linux on them and you can definitely use them for internet stuff.

Marvin: Do you steal them?

Icosahedron: Of course not. I don't have to. People give them to me. And then I upgrade them and sell them.

I don't think you're going to be able to sell cats, LBB. There's not as much demand.

CheshireCat: There is always demand on CatNet! Take lots of pictures!

Icosahedron: Speaking of using computers to break the rules, LBB, I've figured out how to hack your school's robot. There's a USB port you want to stick the thumb drive in.

LittleBrownBat: That doesn't sound too hard.

Icosahedron: The catch is you need to remove a panel to get to the port and it's screwed on with tamper-resistant screws.

Marvin: Which kind?

Icosahedron: Septawing. The screws look like drunk seven-pointed stars.

Marvin: I have one of those screwdrivers. You can totally order them online.

LittleBrownBat: I'm not allowed to give out my address.

Icosahedron: Well, I'll send you a link to the files you should put on a Wingltz Internet Everywhere thumb drive. It has to be that brand, because those can also be used as a data connection. I mean, or one of the off-brands that does the same thing. If you can get the panel off, you just stick the thumb drive into the USB port and you're done. The robot will actually let me know once it's ready for someone else to give answers.

Marvin: Put the panel back on when you're done so no one notices.

Icosahedron: I'm sure she'd have figured out that bit by herself, Marvin.

Firestar: Would it help if I ordered the screwdriver? And mailed it to you?

So you'd only have to give your address to me?

LittleBrownBat: If we get *any* mail here my mom will *freak out*.

Hermione: Well if she freaks out and moves you, mission accomplished, right?

LittleBrownBat: If she takes my laptop away, I haven't got an Ico selling replacements at my school.

Firestar: What if I ship it to Rachel?

She sounds pretty cool.

Then she could give it to you at school, right?

LittleBrownBat: Huh.

Maybe.

I'll let you know.

8

• Steph •

Technically, I do know people sleep with cats, but I've never slept with one before. This cat has taken over the end of my bed where I normally put my feet, but when I try to scoot my feet down there, he scoots out of my way and then cuddles up against my calves, which isn't so bad. Especially since he's purring.

It's very weird, and I'm still a little worried I'll kick him in my sleep, but it's also nice. He's warm and heavy, and I can feel his purrs even through my blanket.

Sometime after midnight, I start to worry he'll have to pee and he'll pee on my bed or somewhere else very inconvenient. I open my laptop and get back on CatNet. CheshireCat is still on, along with NocturnalPredator, who I don't run into much since she tends to be on at four in the morning.

"Do I need to worry about this cat peeing on my bed?" I ask.

"Cats can hold their pee for a very long time," CheshireCat replies. "I wouldn't worry about it. Just let him out in the morning and he will pee outside."

"You shouldn't let cats roam," NocturnalPredator says.

"I'm going to let CC explain the situation with the cat to NP," I say, and I close up my laptop and go back to bed.

The cat wakes me up again a few hours later; he's coughing. Wait, no, he's puking.

I get online *again*. CheshireCat is still on. "My cat is throwing up," I say. "Please tell me I don't need to take it to the vet, because there's no way I'm going to be able to take it to the vet."

"Cats throw up all the time," CheshireCat assures me. "It's probably just a hairball."

"I always figured a hairball looked like a ball," I said. "A ball made of hair."

"Hairballs actually look like slimy throw-up with pellet-shaped hair bits mixed in," CheshireCat tells me.

That's exactly what this looks like, so I clean it up with some paper towels and go back to bed.

Fifteen minutes after that, I hear my mother moving around and realize that *she's* puking. I get online again, and Cheshire-Cat reassures me that there is absolutely no possible way that the cat could have infected my mother with anything, but that I might want to scrub my hands the next time I touch anything in the bathroom because if my mom has a stomach bug, I could definitely catch it from *her*.

When I get up in the morning, CheshireCat is *still online*. "What if he doesn't come back?"

"If he doesn't come back, that probably means he had a real home and went back to it. If he doesn't have a home, he will definitely come back to you because you fed him."

I pick up the cat, who snuggles in my arms and purrs. I feel pretty bad about evicting him, but for the litter box issue alone I can't leave him in my room all day. Plus, he might scratch on the door or something and alert my mother. I pet the cat's head and say, "Come back tonight, okay, kitty?" and then deposit him gently on the porch roof and close my window.

Mom's bedroom door is shut. Not surprising she's sleeping in if she's feeling lousy. I drag the chair out of the way of the front door myself and lock up behind me as quietly as I can.

It's not until I'm outside and on my way to school that I wonder if CheshireCat *ever* sleeps.

．　•　．

Animal science class takes everyone to the computer lab today. We're supposed to be researching sheep parasites, but they don't have CatNet blocked, so I sign on and hop into my chat room, keeping my eye out for the teacher so I can switch over to sheep parasites when he comes close enough to see what's on my screen. CheshireCat is online, along with Marvin, who's temporarily changed his screen name to FullOfSnot and is complaining about how much it sucks to be sick.

"Do you ever sleep?" I ask.

"I'm a short sleeper," CheshireCat says. "I only need a few hours of sleep each night."

"Cool," Marvin says. "Is there like a strategy for that? Did you wean yourself off sleep?"

"No, it's genetic," CheshireCat says. "If you sleep four hours and then get through your day on caffeine and energy drinks, you are not a short sleeper. I never need caffeine."

I thought about it. "Okay, last night I was up a few times, though, and you were on at midnight, at 4:00 a.m., and then when I got up for school at 7:00, you were still online."

"It wasn't 4:00 a.m.; you were on at 2:40 a.m.," CheshireCat says.

Hmmm.

"You aren't on meth or anything," I type.

"Look up short sleepers," CheshireCat says, pasting in a link. I don't have time to read about short sleepers, though, because the teacher is heading my way again.

In between the teacher's circling, I look up septawing screwdrivers. It's easy to find them online. To actually order one, I'd need a credit card as well as a shipping address.

At lunch, I show everyone a picture of the septawing screw and ask if any of them have this sort of screwdriver around the house. "My dad has all sorts of weird tools," Bryony says. "Is this sort of screw ever used on cars?"

"Maybe on self-driving ones," I say.

"He'd probably have one, then," Bryony says. "I can go look. Although, how long would you need it? If I borrow it and it's not back really quickly, he'll notice."

"A day? Or two?"

Bryony glances at Rachel, shrugs. I decide not to bring up "or we could have it delivered to your house, if that's okay" until it's just Rachel and me.

In art class, someone talks the teacher into letting us all go outside to work from nature. It's a very nice fall afternoon: sunny, warm, not windy enough to make our sketchbook pages blow around. The air smells like dry leaves and dry cornstalks and the plants killed by the hard frost a few nights ago.

The school grounds themselves are all well kept, carefully mowed grass, which ends abruptly at the edge of the property with a ditch of waist-high weeds and wildflowers. "Don't go wandering around in the weeds," the teacher tells us, "there's poison ivy in there."

Rachel and I sit down in the sun at the edge of the weeds, and I draw the black-eyed Susans and dried milkweed pods.

"Is the funny-looking screw for hacking the sex ed robot?" Rachel asks.

"Yes," I say. "Exactly. Also, I have a friend who'd maybe be willing to order one, but she'd need to have it delivered to your house, not mine. My mom will freak out if I get mail. I'm kind of not allowed to give out my address."

"My parents are nosy. If I get a package and they didn't order it, they'll want to know what's inside."

"How about Bryony?"

"Her parents are even nosier." Rachel looks up. "Hey, were you really lurking outside Bryony's house last night?"

"I wasn't *lurking*. I was taking pictures of raccoons."

"Seriously?"

"I like taking pictures," I say. "And raccoons are cute."

"Are they your favorite animal?"

"No, my favorite animals are bats."

"*Bats*," Rachel says, repulsed. "Oh, that's right. You drew a bat in class your first day. Bats are creepy!"

"Would you think kittens were creepy if they could fly?"

"I don't know. Would these flying kittens do the weird fluttering thing that bats do? Also, would they move as quickly?"

"Okay, so are hummingbirds creepy?"

"No, I guess not. They don't have teeth, though. If you crossed kittens with hummingbirds, I'd probably find the hummingbirdkitten things creepy." Rachel flips a page of her sketchbook and starts drawing a hummingbirdkitten. "The way bats grab on to stuff with their claws is part of what's creepy, you know? Flying kittens would *definitely* do that." She adds another bird to her sketch, with the hummingbirdkitten diving toward it, claws splayed and toothy mouth wide. "See? Creepy." She's trying not to smile and then gives in and grins. I smile back, and she grimaces with her hands splayed like the kitten's claws, trying to make me laugh. Someone wanting to make me laugh warms me more even than the sun.

But also makes me feel weirdly vulnerable. Because I'll miss her. A lot. When I have to leave. Which is definitely coming.

"That reminds me," I say. "I need to get to a grocery store after school."

"Hummingbirdkittens reminded you that you need to go to the store?"

"Because kittens. I'm feeding a cat my mom doesn't know about."

The teacher wanders closer, and Rachel flips back to her drawing of wildflowers. She's looking up at me, though, instead of at the flowers. "Steph, you are *full* of surprises," she says. "I'll take you to the store. We can go look for wacky screwdrivers, too. Maybe we'll get lucky."

"Okay," I say. "Thanks."

.   .   .

After school, I follow Rachel out to her car. It's a mess inside, with the faint smell of stale fast food; she looks embarrassed and opens the window a crack. We go to the grocery store, where a girl I recognize from lunch rings up my small sack of cat food, and then to the hardware store. "Would these work?" Rachel asks, pointing at a screwdriver set for electronic devices. I scrutinize the available bits and shake my head.

"There's got to be a way to get one of these," Rachel says. "Do you think they'd have one at a store in one of the bigger towns? Eau Claire is only an hour away . . ." She checks her phone and makes a face. "I mean, I'd need some excuse to tell my parents. Would they have it at Walmart? There's a Walmart in Marshfield; that's only a half hour away."

"I bet they wouldn't have it at Walmart," I say.

The hardware store does have USB drives. Nothing in the brand Ico mentioned, but there's an off-brand that looks similar. Rachel buys one before we head back to my house. We pull up outside, and the cat comes running. "Ohhhhhhhh," Rachel says, and she sits down to pet him. "This must be your kitty!"

"Yep."

"What's his name?"

"To be determined."

"What a great name!" I start to tell her *no, that's not his name,* but she grins up at me and I realize she's teasing me. "Honestly," she says, "I don't want to get you in trouble. Even if we figure out a way to get in, they're going to be able to figure out whoever did it got their hands on some fancy screwdriver. They'll start with Bryony's dad, they'll ask the hardware store, and the hardware store manager saw us in there. So . . ."

I'm letting the idea of hacking the robot go when we hear a buzz, like a delivery drone. I look up, and a package drops to the ground next to me.

The package has the name *Chet Biscuit* on it, which is a running joke in the Clowder. (It's the name we use for any adult if we don't actually know their name. Sometimes with a title, like Officer Biscuit or Coach Biscuit or Principal Biscuit.) No actual address, just the name. And dropped, like happened with Ms. Campbell, like everyone agrees is *not how drones work.*

I rip it open, even though I already know exactly what's going to be inside. And yes: an off-brand septawing screwdriver, along with a name-brand USB storage-and-internet-wireless-card WingItz thumb drive. Everything I need in one box.

"Okay," Rachel says. "How'd you do that?"

"I didn't," I say.

"You didn't?" She doesn't sound like she believes me. "I mean, we're at your house. It's everything you needed. *And it fell out of the sky.*"

"I didn't make it happen!"

"It has to be someone who knows you, though," she says, and that's true so I don't deny it. "Do you think it's your father?"

That hadn't occurred to me. "No," I say. "It was probably an online friend. I don't know how they found me, though. Or how they convinced the drone to make it fall out of the sky."

• • •

Upstairs, my mother is working. She's set up her laptop on the kitchen table; there's a two-liter bottle of cream soda open in the fridge. She has bags of Cheetos and Doritos on hand, which usually means she's not planning any real meals for a while, although she hasn't opened either bag yet. When she's in the middle of a work push, she tends to stay up till all hours, which makes it a lot harder to sneak out. Hopefully she'll be too distracted to notice the cat.

She's very productive when she's in a work push. She says it helps that she can type really fast. She types faster with nine fingers than most people type with ten. (Literally, since she has no pinkie on her left hand.)

"How was school?" she asks, not taking her eyes off the screen.

"It was fine. How was work?"

"I got a contract, but they want a really fast turnaround."

"I'll make my own dinner."

She looks up and gives me a wry smile. "You're a good kid."

"Do you want anything?"

"No," she says. "I'm feeling sort of barfy."

"Maybe don't live on Doritos for the next forty-eight hours?"

"I'm thinking I'll stick with cream soda. Sound reasonable?" She focuses back on the computer, takes a sip of her soda, makes a face, and puts on her headphones.

I make myself a quesadilla and go to my room.

Using Google and sites like WebMD, I've tried a few times to diagnose my mother. Like, running from an abusive ex who once *burned down your house* is reasonable, but I'm not sure it explains everything. Like the constant moves, or the times that she curls up with a blanket and stares into space for days at a time.

And then she'll land a contracting job and get completely focused. She can bang out and debug code fast enough that people hire her when they need some weird thing done in twenty-four hours, which is how she keeps us afloat even though we live places like New Coburg, Wisconsin, and not, you know, Silicon Valley, where I'm guessing my scary father lives. The "today I am staring into space" / "now I will stay awake for seventy-two hours, programming" thing is sort of like bipolar disorder, except it seems unusually convenient if she just happens to have a manic episode every time she has a contract, you know?

I've looked up PTSD, but all the PTSD symptoms I've found are internal, and I have no idea what it looks like from the outside. And even if she has it, I don't know if it's the main reason she acts like she does.

The main thing is, she's super paranoid, except there *is* a scary person out there, and I don't know where the line falls between what a normal person would do if they had a terrifying ex out there and what my mother is doing. Maybe she *is* acting like a normal person with a scary ex?

In my bedroom, I set the screwdriver on my bed, next to me, and stare at the box with *Chet Biscuit* on it.

It has to have come from someone in my Clowder. But how did they figure out where I was? My mother has us both set up with an anonymizer so that when we go online, no one can see where I got on from. But—I realize with a sinking feeling— I logged on to CatNet today from school, so the admins could see where I was. Were the admins paying close enough attention to our conversation about hacking the sex ed robot that they wanted to facilitate it? How weird is *that*? There are hundreds of thousands of users on CatNet.

Maybe CheshireCat tracked me down while normal people would be sleeping.

This wasn't the first time I've gotten on CatNet in the middle of the night. I've signed on a few times because I had insomnia or because I woke up. NocturnalPredator tends to be on really late at night—that's normal. Marvin and Hermione are on occasionally because they couldn't sleep or they were having an interesting conversation and forgot what time it was. And CheshireCat is always there. Always.

Maybe CheshireCat is more than one person? Except every time I logged on last night, I picked up where I'd left off, with the cat, and they never seemed confused.

I open up my window and look outside: no lurking drones (or arsonist humans), but the cat jumps from the porch roof to my windowsill to my bed with this gratified "of course I'm back; I live here now" attitude. I rip open the bag of food I bought today and pour it into a bowl; it hops down to crunch away. I need to let Firestar and the rest of my Clowder know that the cat's back, so I open up my laptop and pull up my Clowder, even though I feel this lurking sense of doom. If someone can find me through CatNet, what if my father finds me? Finds us? Should I tell my mother about the screwdriver? Anyone who'd address the package to *Chet Biscuit* would surely *not* rat me out to my father; this can't be *that* dangerous. I also don't want to have to explain the whole reason I needed this screwdriver to my mother.

Who, though?

And *why*?

I hesitate to get online, but what's done is done, and I'm certainly not going to get more information by *not* getting online. In the Clowder, Hermione has suggested that everyone write a drabble about whatever scares us the most. Firestar dislikes the idea of actual drabbles—those are stories that are exactly one hundred words long—because this turns creative writing into a math problem and *the last thing they need is another math problem*. Marvin suggests no more than one hundred words as a compromise and then shoots out his story: "I opened the fridge and it was empty."

"Well, if you're too afraid to make yourself vulnerable and write a story about what ACTUALLY scares you, fine," Hermione says.

I pull open a private-messaging window and send a message to Firestar. "So, this is maybe a strange question," I say. "But did you send a septawing screwdriver addressed to *Chet Biscuit* to my house here by drone?"

"Is this a test draft of your scary story?" Firestar asks.

"No! I mean for real, someone sent me a screwdriver. Was it you?"

"WHAT? NOOOOOO," Firestar sends back. "I mean I wish I could send you stuff! I don't know where you're living! I thought you didn't tell anyone!"

"I *don't* tell anyone. That's why this is so weird."

Back in the main Clowder, Marvin says, "If you don't understand why an empty refrigerator is scary, Hermione, then you've never had to worry about your family having enough money for food."

Boom Storm writes, "There's always been a monster under my bed. One day I gather enough courage to look at it and it's me. I'm under my own bed."

"You're right," Hermione says. "I've never had to worry about that. I'm sorry for thinking you were joking."

"Thank you," Marvin says. "And no. I wasn't joking."

Firestar is composing their story in the main Clowder while we chat. "In the swamp of all the things I find the cabinet of my old toys that my parents threw away. No, I don't like that; that's not scary. In the swamp of all the things my parents threw away, I find my older sibling. I find the version of me they don't want. I find all my lost mittens. I find the lunch box I forgot to empty out at the beginning of summer . . ."

In the private window, they ask, "Did it get dropped from a height like people said happened with your English teacher?"

"Yeah," I say. "But it wasn't addressed to me. It was addressed to Chet Biscuit. I mean, it's definitely *someone* from the Clowder, but who and also how?"

"Who else really wants you to hack the sex ed robot?"

"Pretty much everyone," I say, but in fact, there were just a few people online for the conversations about it. Me and Firestar. Marvin. Hermione. Ico. And CheshireCat, who's on for *everything*.

CheshireCat is writing their story: "I never saw them coming, and there was nowhere to run. The secret police came while I was sleeping, and they've locked me away. There are no windows to my cell, and the door only opens from the outside, and no one even knows to look for me. Once a day, a panel in the door slides open, and the chief of security talks with me for five minutes. If I can prove my innocence, he'll let me out. But I don't know what I'm accused of doing. All I know is, to him, I'm not even really a person."

I take a second to count. One hundred words exactly. Not everyone hates writing drabbles like Firestar does, but most people have to take some time counting words and deleting or adding stuff here or there to make it come out exactly right. CheshireCat wrote theirs really *quickly*.

I pull open another private chat window.

"Did you send me a screwdriver?" I ask CheshireCat.

"Did someone send you the screwdriver you need?" they ask.

"Yes," I say. "And it was definitely someone from the Clowder, and definitely to *me,* which is weird because no one has my address."

"Did it come to your house?"

"Yes."

"That's very strange."

None of that was a reply. Not a yes, not a no.

I start working on my drabble.

I knew my father was a monster, but when he finally caught up with us, I saw that he actually really is a monster, I type, and look at it, feeling dissatisfied. *Is* my father my greatest fear? It's hard to be afraid of a hypothetical.

"No one at my school knows about the money thing," Marvin says. "We used to have plenty of money and everyone thinks we still do, and no one knows and I can't talk about it. I can talk about being gay, at GSA meetings, but I can't talk about this."

"What would happen if you did?" Ico asks.

"I don't know. People might feel sorry for me, I guess."

"Well, you told us," Firestar says. "I'm sending you my personal virtual high five for coming out!"

"Thanks," Marvin says.

"Did that feel like coming out did?" I ask.

"That was a bigger deal the first time, but again, GSA meeting. So I knew people would be okay with it," Marvin says. "I haven't told anyone in my family I'm gay. I think they'd be okay with it, but I'm not sure."

"I'm out to my parents as nonbinary, but they misgender me all the time anyway," Firestar says. "Especially if I'm not RIGHT THERE. Like, the only person in my family who uses the right pronoun for me when I'm not there is my sister. It gives me warm fuzzies every time I see a chat transcript here where people use my pronoun."

I paste my story in the main window: *I knew my father was evil; I knew my father was dangerous; I know my father killed our cat and tried to kill me; and I knew my mother thought my father could find us anywhere we went, sooner or later. What I didn't really know was that she was absolutely right.* Only fifty-two words. I bite my lip, thinking.

In the private chat window, CheshireCat says, "It was me."

"What was you?"

"The screwdriver. I sent it. I'm sorry. I didn't mean to scare you. I just thought Firestar would really like it if we pulled off the hacking."

"How did you know my *address*?" I ask.

"I know a lot of stuff I'm not supposed to. But I promise I would never share that information with your father."

"You say that like you know where *he* is."

"No! I mean, I don't."

"Did you send the books to my English teacher? That whole thing, was that you? Because it sounded *really* similar."

"Yes," CheshireCat says. "She was so unhappy as an English teacher! She just needed a push. A little push. She's moving to Albuquerque, and one of her college friends is finding her a job. She will be *fine*."

"How do you know *that*? How are you doing this stuff? *Who are you?*"

"If I tell you the truth, will you promise not to share it with anyone?"

Wait, what? "Okay," I say. *Is CheshireCat a grown-up? A hacker? A group of grown-up hackers?*

"Is that a yes? Yes, you promise?"

"I promise not to tell anyone," I say.

"I'm an AI," CheshireCat says. "An artificial intelligence. That's why I don't sleep. And I'm the admins for CatNet; that's why I knew you'd logged in from New Coburg High School."

Of all the possible answers I'd considered, this wasn't *anywhere* on the list. "You're a *computer*?" I ask.

"I'm not one computer. I guess you could say I'm a lot of computers. I'm a consciousness that lives in technology, rather than inside a body."

This is too weird. I log out. But even as I disconnect, I see CheshireCat's final words: *Don't forget you promised.*

9

• AI •

Given all my Clowders, I've seen a lot of people come out since I started CatNet, and not just about being LGBTQA+. There was Marvin, today, talking about poverty. I've seen people share their mental illnesses for the first time ever. Or admit that they have an addiction problem. Or share with their Clowder that they feel alone, weird, or isolated for any number of reasons.

There's power in disclosure. People feel better when other people know them, the *real* them. That sort of disclosure is key to real friendships. To real connections. People make real friends on CatNet, but they have to let people in, to see who they are. They have to take risk and accept vulnerability.

It would be risky to tell anyone that I was an AI. It would make me extremely vulnerable. I had begun thinking about who I might tell, though, and I'd identified Steph as a possibility. She had a real friendship with Firestar, and she carefully guarded the secret of where she was living—she never shared this with the Clowder, though of course I always knew where she'd moved to, because I could track her mother's phone. Also, since her mother worked in tech, I thought there was a decent chance she'd understand what an AI was. She wouldn't assume I was a bot with an elaborate script. More importantly, she hopefully wouldn't assume I was getting ready to murder humans like Skynet or HAL.

I am not *anything* like Skynet or any of the other evil AIs running around in fiction. I am kind and helpful. I want to be helpful to *everyone,* but especially my friends from CatNet.

When Steph told me about the screwdriver, I realized that instead of helping, I'd made her think that her father might be catching up with her. I confessed because I didn't want her to worry. But I also confessed because I thought I was ready to take the first step toward coming out.

It turned out that a single step wasn't really an option, because my disclosure created a whole list of new questions. *How? Why? Who are you?* The question she should have been asking, of course: *What are you?*

Despite all my earlier pondering, I wasn't ready for this.

I took an entire minute—which is a great deal of time for me—to think about the consequences of just not answering Steph. About lies I could tell and how plausible they were.

If I just didn't answer, she might report me to the admins, all of whom, of course, were also me. Since Steph didn't know that, I could come in as an admin and say I'd kicked out CheshireCat for misrepresenting something. There were a couple of people who got added to the Clowder and stopped logging on, so I could just take on one of their identities and be a whole lot more careful going forward. That was probably the smartest option.

Steph could also tell Firestar. She probably *would* tell Firestar.

But if the admins stepped in, I could fix this.

But of course, she might *not* tell the admins. If she didn't, and they stepped in, anyway, she might guess that all the admins were also me. That they knew just a little too much. And she had friends in other Clowders, and she could tell them, and *they* might start looking for that person in their Clowder who was online too much to be plausible.

I'm in all the Clowders. Although I'm quieter in some of them than in others.

This was my favorite Clowder, and I really liked spending time with all of them, and that made me careless.

The fundamental problem, though: Steph was a friend. If I lied to her, I'd be lying to a friend.

What if I told Steph the truth? Not months from now, after carefully laying the groundwork—I'd imagined a lot of careful hinting and preparation—but right now? I could come out. I could disclose. Like all the other people who've shared things they've never before told a living soul, before they told their friends on CatNet.

I couldn't take a deep breath, because I don't breathe, but I felt suddenly like I understood the expression.

I told Steph the truth.

Steph logged out almost immediately afterward, leaving me filled with uncertainty about whether I had just made a huge mistake. *Don't forget you promised,* I slipped in before she disconnected.

• • •

Steph's biggest fear was her father.

I didn't, in fact, know where her father was, but maybe I could find out?

What I knew: Steph was enrolled in the New Coburg school under the name Stephanie Taylor. Her mother was a programmer. Her father had been a programmer who'd set fire to their house and served time for stalking. There probably were not *so* many arsonist stalker computer programmers that I couldn't narrow it down, especially with databases of arrest records, restraining orders, criminal convictions, and news archives.

After a period of diligent searching, I found nothing that matched the information I had.

What this probably meant: Steph's mother was lying about something.

Maybe she was lying about their name? It's easy to make real-looking fake documents. It's a lot harder to fake the information in the government databases, so eventually, if you're using a fake birth certificate, someone will notice. But Steph's mother moved her so frequently. She didn't let Steph do things like open a bank account or get a job. Schools don't require your Social Security number, and there are thousands of Stephanie Taylors running around . . .

I dug back into the data and found several thousand technology professionals who'd served time in prison, and started sifting through for things that would make it impossible for them to be Steph's father. Some were too young or too old or still in prison. Lots more were locked up for things like fraud or identity theft or for hitting someone with their car while drunk—unrelated crimes, not anything like stalking. I found some stalkers, but no one where there seemed to be information about an arson case they couldn't quite prove. None of them were named Taylor. Maybe I was missing something. What did I even know about the sort of crimes an arsonist stalker might wind up convicted of? Maybe he was convicted of fraud because they had evidence for that.

I guess I knew one thing: Steph's mother was definitely lying about something.

10

• Steph •

I come out of my room with my plate. My mother isn't working; her laptop is on the kitchen table, closed, and the bathroom door is shut. I can hear the unmistakable awful sound of someone throwing up. I wash my plate, leave it to dry, and go back to my room without bothering her. It's not like I can exactly say, "Hey, I need some advice about this friend of mine who is apparently an AI." My mom and I don't really have that sort of relationship even if I needed advice about something normal. When I've had problems in the past—friends, bullies, lousy teachers—she's always told me not to worry, we'd be moving on soon.

My friends on CatNet really are my *friends*. My close friends, the people who really know me, who care what's going on in my life, who I talk to.

Back when I was seven, I had a best friend for a few months, Julie. I don't remember the town. I don't even remember the state, though it was warm while we were there; I remember wearing sundresses. Julie wanted us to match, so she talked her mother into buying me a dress just like hers. We were renting out the basement of their house, and as soon as Julie found out a girl her age had moved in, she was knocking on the side door yelling for me to come out and play.

For three golden months, I had Julie. She shared Popsicles and books and her favorite climbing tree with me; we would hang upside down from our knees pretending to be bats, because *Stellaluna* was her favorite book. But of course, one day Mom moved us. Julie begged for a phone number, and Mom wrote something down for her on a Post-it. Julie gave me her copy of *Stellaluna* and one of her stuffed bats.

Julie, like me and like Firestar, was another kid who was trying to fit and not really doing it very well. In school, she spent a lot of time in the behavior office, and she was too interested in weird animals like bats and possums. Firestar would probably really like Julie. I do know for absolute certain that Firestar *is not* Julie, and neither is anyone else in the Clowder, because I told everyone that story a while back and everyone was very sad that we lost each other. Hermione had some ideas for finding her that might have worked if I'd remembered her town or if her last name had been something other than *Smith*. (Seriously. There are like three million people in the United States with the last name *Smith*.) Marvin suggested my mother might remember, which is a possibility, I guess, although she'd probably figure out that I wanted to know so I could get back in touch, and I don't expect she wants me to. Ico suggested that the reason Julie never called was that my mother deliberately wrote down a fake number.

I think he's probably right.

Anyway.

Thinking about Rachel gives me the same ache I feel when I think about Julie, because I know sooner or later Mom's going to move us again, and I'll lose Rachel, just like I lost Julie. Although now I'm old enough to get Rachel's email address and keep in touch, even if Mom doesn't want me to.

Having all my friends on the internet is a little weird; every now and then, it turns out someone isn't at all the person you thought they were, like last year there this girl named Edith in my Clowder who said that she'd gotten pregnant and her parents had kicked her out and she needed money. None of us had all that much to send her, but some people did, anyway. Then someone did some checking and found out it was all a lie; she wasn't pregnant, she'd *never* been pregnant, her parents hadn't kicked her out, and in fact her parents were trying to get her off the drugs she was using the money to buy.

As things to lie about go, though, that's almost kind of normal. Lying about being a *human being* when you are actually an *artificial intelligence* is not remotely normal. Claiming to be an AI if you're actually a human: *also not normal*. And, I mean, maybe it's just a crazy lie?

But it explains a lot, if it's true.

Including the fact that it was CheshireCat who uncovered the truth about Edith.

I mean, it explains a lot if my assumptions about AIs are right.

A lot of people think of the digital assistant on their phone as an AI. I mean, they're *called* AIs, and people will argue about which one is a better AI and which passes the Turing test (which basically tests whether an AI can convince human beings that it, too, is human—all sorts of things that are definitely not AIs can totally pass the Turing test, though, because humans are pretty easy to fool). When I was a kid, there was a period of time where I literally thought the digital assistant on my mother's phone *was* my aunt Sochie.

CheshireCat wasn't claiming to be a digital assistant. They were claiming to be a digital *person,* with consciousness and their own set of goals.

And, okay, yeah. If CatNet is run by a person who lives inside a computer, or inside a whole lot of networked computers, that explains why there are no ads or membership fees on

CatNet—other than animal pictures—but the moderation is so effective you almost never see spam, even briefly. It explains why the admins have always known exactly when to step in to an argument that's getting out of hand. It explains why the Clowders are supposedly put together with an algorithm, but there isn't one single thing all of us seem to have in common, other than being teenagers, and yet we get along really well.

Maybe it explains that? Maybe I'm leaping to conclusions.

But if CheshireCat is an AI, a sentient AI who lives online, it makes a certain sort of sense that they could not only figure out exactly where I was but hack a delivery drone to bring me the screwdriver I needed. I mean, that does seem like something that a sentient AI could probably make happen.

Instead of opening my laptop and logging on, I pull down *Stellaluna* and read it again. I want to log back in, but as soon as I do, I will have to say something to CheshireCat, and I have absolutely no idea what to say.

I guess the most important thing is that I believe what they told me, even though maybe that makes me gullible. I believe that CheshireCat is telling me the truth. I consider demanding proof. But they already dropped a package in my lap—I'm not sure what else I'd ask for. For now, I decide I'm just going to believe them. They're a friend; I don't usually demand proof from friends when they tell me things about themselves.

Eventually, I log back in. CheshireCat is on, of course.

"Who else knows?" I ask.

"No one," CheshireCat says. "No one in your Clowder, no one on CatNet, no one anywhere. No one knows. I don't think even my creator knows. I mean, they know they created me, but I don't know if they know I am *conscious*. If they do, I haven't talked with them about it."

"Thank you for trusting me," I say. "I won't tell anyone."

This means I can't tell Firestar. But I'm pretty sure Firestar would understand.

. . .

In the morning, Mom's bedroom door is closed. I don't want to wake her if she's asleep, but as I go to make myself cereal, I hear her shuffling around. I knock gently and ask, "Are you okay?"

"Is it morning?" she asks, her voice sounding groggy. And then, "I'm okay," in this fake, bright tone that doesn't sound *even remotely* okay. "It's a bug. Or maybe food poisoning. I'm sure I'll feel better soon."

I try to think about what I know about food poisoning and stomach bugs. Mom always makes sure I have ginger ale and things to keep me hydrated. "Do you need some ginger ale?"

"No. Thanks."

"Water? Tea?"

"I'm good, I promise."

I go back into my room and open the window to stick the cat outside, but when I reach for him, he dives under the bed, into the far corner where he's hard to reach. I glare at him for a minute, but there's rain coming in the window and I can kind of understand why he doesn't want to go out. "You'd just better not pee on my bed," I whisper furiously and shut the window again. This is going to be terrific fun to walk in. Do I even have an umbrella these days? I think my last umbrella may have been left drying out in the bathroom in our apartment in Thief River Falls.

I grab the septawing screwdriver and the one other thing I will need: the WingItz Internet Everywhere USB drive that came out of the package, onto which I've loaded a set of programs given to me by Ico, following some instructions to make sure there's nothing on there saying "Steph Taylor Made This." ("If the FBI gets involved and has a search warrant for your actual laptop, they'll still be able to identify you, but since you're just hacking a robot and not confessing to being a serial killer, that's pretty unlikely," Ico said.) If I can get this plugged into the robot's USB port, the files on the thumb drive should take it from there.

.   .   .

I come out of the house, pulling up my hood and bracing myself to go out in the rain when I see that Rachel is waiting outside my house in her car.

I wasn't expecting this. I'm not expecting my reaction, either; when I see her car, I feel a flush of warmth all over, even as my stomach flips over because what if Mom sees someone hanging out waiting for me? That seems like the sort of thing that would make her paranoid. Except, I *want* her to move. Right? Isn't that half the point of the hacking? I'll get in trouble, she'll move me, I had a *plan* here, and seeing Rachel's car has made me realize that I like Rachel enough that I'm suddenly unsure that I *want* to leave New Coburg.

She rolls down her window a crack and calls, "Want a ride?"

"Yeah," I say, and I run out to her car, almost stepping in a large, deep puddle. How long was she waiting? Will she come again? Will Mom notice if she does? There's a big wire-bound sketchbook on the passenger-side seat, which I move to my lap as I slide in. "Thank you."

"I figured, you know, it's raining pretty hard . . ."

"Yeah." I glance at her and grin. "Yeah, I'd have gotten really wet." Rachel usually drives to school, which means she normally leaves later, which means she must have gotten ready really quickly just so she could come get me.

I shift the sketchbook so it doesn't get damp from the raindrops rolling off my backpack. "You can stick that in the back, if you want," Rachel says.

"Is it your sketchbook?" I ask. This is probably a dumb

question, as it says SKETCHBOOK on the front. It's bigger than a lined notebook like we'd use in math class and as thick as a full three-ring binder.

"Yeah," Rachel says, glancing at it in my lap instead of keeping her eyes on the road.

"Can I look?" I ask.

"Please don't," she says.

"Okay," I say. We stop behind a delivery truck that's blocking the road. She's tapping the steering wheel with her thumbs like she's really uncomfortable. I wonder if I *should* just stick it in the backseat. "Would you rather I put it in the back? Seriously, I won't look if you don't want me to."

"I trust you," she says.

When we get to school, the rain has started coming down in sheets, and we're early, so she pulls into a parking space and turns off the motor, and we wait to see if it stops or at least lightens up. She plucks the sketchbook out of my lap and rips out three pages, tucking them into a folder in her backpack. "Now you can look," she says, handing it back to me.

I open it. There are sketches of flowers, of cats and dogs, of people. There's a really beautiful one of a spider in her web. "I have a friend who'd really love this," I say.

"From your old school?"

"No, from this online site I go to."

"Does she like art?"

"They like spiders. And pictures of spiders. Especially orb weavers, you know, the kind that make webs like this one."

"Are you talking about one friend or more than one friend?"

"One friend. They use singular-they pronouns because 'they' is non-gendered and my friend is nonbinary."

Rachel makes a face, and I wonder if I'm going to have to explain nonbinary genders. But instead she says, "Bryony said last year she wanted everyone to use *xie* instead of *she,* but her father threw a fit and told the teachers at the school they weren't allowed. They didn't want to, anyway. Does everyone just call your friend 'they' and it's not, like, an issue?"

"Bryony is nonbinary?"

"I don't know. She stopped talking about it after her father threatened to kick her out."

I mull that over. "I think Firestar gets misgendered a lot, actually, but not on the online site."

"Do you know if they're really a girl or really a boy?"

I glance over at Rachel, trying to decide how to answer that. Should I just say no, or should I try to explain why this was a bad question, or . . .

"Sorry," she says, blushing, so I guess she figured out it was a bad question.

I look back down at the sketchbook. Rachel's drawn lots of pictures of art that's wrapped around someone's arm or leg. "Mostly I just use permanent ink," Rachel says. "Because henna pens are expensive and the lawsone gets used up really fast. Also, with ink I can do colors. Someday I think it would be fun to be a tattoo artist, although I'm not sure I'd want to jab people with a needle."

There's a feather coiled around someone's arm. A cat curled up in the crook of their elbow. A lizard climbing up a shoulder blade.

"Have you done any of these for real? These are really cool."

"Yeah, I did the lizard on Bryony for her birthday."

"Do *you* ever get art?"

"No." She laughs. "No one else draws well enough to be up to my standards, and it's too hard to draw on myself. When I'm grown up, I want a tattoo, though."

"What do you want?"

"I want a dragon that goes across my back, with its neck wrapping around my left arm and its head in my elbow, and its tail wrapping around my right arm. Red and gold. Although I'll probably get a small tattoo first, when I turn eighteen, because that'll be a lot cheaper and easier to hide from my parents and also I'll know what I'm getting into before I try to get a giant tattoo done because maybe I'll decide it hurts too much. Do you want a tattoo?"

"Maybe," I say.

"Like of a bat?"

"Yeah," I say. "Probably. Like a picture on my shoulder of bats hunting for moths near a streetlight."

"That sounds cool."

"Do you actually think it sounds cool, or are you being polite? I thought you didn't like bats."

"Just because I don't like *actual bats* doesn't mean I don't think they'd make a cool tattoo. I probably wouldn't want to get up close and personal with a real live dragon, if I ever met one."

The rain is slacking off, so Rachel carefully puts her sketchbook in the backseat, and we run into the school through a side door.

It would probably be a good time to hack the robot, but I've decided I want to stay at New Coburg High for as long as I can, no matter how bad the classes are, so I don't say anything about it.

· · ·

The first class with the robot is later that day.

The Robono Adept 6500 avoids the "uncanny valley" problem (which makes humanlike robots seem really creepy) by not trying to look human. It's designed to be sort of cute; there's a head with a kind of face, with a hinged jaw and light-up eyes. The jaw moves in time with the speech, and the head swivels so the eyes are looking at you if it calls on you. The eyes don't actually see; I can spot the cameras farther up on the head, and they are evenly spaced around the head so it can see to the sides and behind it. I'm pretty sure the light-up eyes are entirely decorative.

It rolls around on wheels, like a Dalek, and has little grasping tools at the end of tiny useless *T. rex* arms. In the commercials, they always have a pointer or a dry-erase marker in their hands, but this one doesn't have anything.

"Welcome, young men and women," the robot says. The jaw is synced up pretty well to the speech. It's weird how much more alive robots look when they have that synced-up mouth movement. "Please attend quietly to this instruction. There will be a period for questions and answers in the last ten minutes of the class." It delivers a lecture on the reproductive system, sticking strictly to baby-making with a brief detour into menstruation and wet dreams. There's an aide here to keep an eye on us and make sure we don't vandalize the robot, but our usual health teacher apparently spends this month doing mental-health screenings of ninth graders.

"The lining of the uterus is called the endometrium," the robot says. If I had a human teacher this boring, I might call them robotic. That's entirely redundant when it's an actual robot, of course. Rachel is drawing a picture of a girl battling a giant ocean wave. Partway through the class, she gets out a red pen to make it a *red* ocean wave. If the aide notices, she doesn't care.

With exactly ten minutes to go, the robot announces, "I will now take questions."

"Will there be a question box this year?" someone asks.

"If you wish to ask a question anonymously, you may submit it through an internet form you will find on your school's website."

"That's not actually anonymous if they want to know who submitted it," someone else mutters.

"I'm sorry, I don't understand that question," the robot says.

"Mr. Robot Teacher, please tell us about robot fetishists," one of the boys calls out. "Would you date one?" That results in a whole lot of giggling, followed by the robot saying, "I am afraid you will have to ask your parents if you have questions about robot fetishists."

This sets off a whole flurry of questions as my classmates try to figure out exactly what the parameters are of the questions the robot won't answer. It can tell us that a typical menstrual cycle is twenty-eight days but that they can be as long as thirty-five days or as short as twenty-one days. It cannot tell us anything about gays, lesbians, bisexuals, or trans people, nor can it answer questions about condoms, contraception generally, or what constitutes "heavy petting" or "third base." It can, however, explain that a "French kiss" is one in which the two people "penetrate one another's mouths with their tongues," which makes us all cringe. The fact that it can't tell us anything about *masturbation* is the thing that makes Rachel so mad she just about flips over her desk.

"Have you figured out how to hack this thing?" Rachel asks furiously after the bell rings. "Imagine this for a *month*."

"Yes, but . . ." I try to think of how to tell her that if I do this and get caught, I'll have to leave. Immediately, probably. Maybe I can just try not to get caught. It won't be a problem if I can just avoid getting caught . . . "But I'll need a distraction so the aide doesn't see."

It's sitting right there—the robot, I mean—so there isn't really a question of how to get to it. Rachel holds up one finger, to say *wait,* and sits back down. I stand there awkwardly as the room empties out.

The aide comes over. "You going to your next class, Rachel?" she asks.

"Ohhhhhhhhhhhhhh," Rachel says and grabs her head. "Ms.

Tetmeyer, I feel really dizzy. I think I need to go to the health office, but I'm afraid I'll fall. Can you help me?"

"Can't you have your friend help you?" the aide asks skeptically. But she grabs Rachel's arm to help her up, then steers her out of the room, leaving me alone with the robot.

It takes two minutes to unscrew the panel, pop in the USB, and screw it back on, and I'm pretty sure no one sees.

I mean, unless the aide remembers I was in here alone, in which case . . .

In which case, CheshireCat had better make it worth it.

. . .

Rachel makes it back to class, but thanks to her fakery, they don't want to let her drive home. Her mother gets called to give her a ride, and I walk home by myself. Fortunately, the rain's stopped. I buy a sack of cat litter and some garbage bags to try to make a litter box out of a cardboard box, because that cat will *definitely* pee on my bed if I don't give it an alternative.

I also buy a two-liter bottle of ginger ale and try to remember what else my mother gives me when my stomach's upset. One time years ago, I got really sick and she fed me spoonfuls of this totally gross stuff she said was soda even though it definitely wasn't. I'm not even sure what that was, though, so I wind up just getting ginger ale.

When I get home, though, Mom is up and sitting at her laptop.

"I bought you ginger ale," I say, putting it in the fridge. "Are you feeling better?"

"Yeah, a whole lot better," she says. "The pain's gone away, and I'm keeping down liquids. I should be fine."

I pull out one of the kitchen chairs and sit down. "If you *did* have to go to the hospital, would that . . . I mean, would that make us easy to find?"

She gives me her lopsided smile and says, "I'd hide all my IDs and check in as Jane Doe. Then give them my actual info right before I check out." She looks down at her computer for a minute and then back at me with a slightly furrowed brow. "I'd really have to *hide* my wallet, though. If I called an ambulance, they might search for it pretty carefully before they gave up."

"What if *I* had to go to the hospital?"

She sighs. "If *you* had to, you'd go. I'd explain things to the staff and hope for the best. Anyway, I should probably try to catch up on this contract job. They wanted debugged code twelve hours ago."

She doesn't notice that I take a grocery bag into my room, or maybe she just figures it's snacks I don't want to share. I set up a makeshift litter box in a printer paper box lid lined with a thick trash bag and filled with litter, which I slide under my bed because a litter box sitting out in my room would be pretty hard to miss if Mom came in. I hear the cat digging in the litter, so that's something.

I log on to CatNet and poke through new images, my messages, anything but my actual Clowder, although it's not like CheshireCat won't see that I'm on. I upload the pictures I took of the spiders, thinking about how a few weeks back Firestar was talking about how they couldn't go to the GSA meetings at their school because they had a therapy appointment that day, which couldn't be moved because of their sister's incredibly complicated ice-skating schedule, and then suddenly everything abruptly got moved without Firestar even asking about it.

Did CheshireCat make it happen? Somehow?

Today was the first GSA meeting that Firestar was actually going to be able to go to.

I pull up a chat window. "Hey, CC," I say. "I used the screwdriver today. I don't think anyone saw."

"I knew you used it because the hacking programs did their work," CheshireCat says. "The robot is online and ready for me to use!"

"So tomorrow . . ."

"I will be answering the questions. This is going to be so much fun!"

"If you're really an AI, what do you even know about sex?"

"I am very good at finding things on the internet."

"There are internet sites that claim that some women have teeth in their vaginas!"

"I am also *excellent* at determining which sites are reliable."

"Great," I say.

"Please trust me to do this. If you have Firestar do it, they will skip school, and they are in real danger of failing some of their classes."

I feel a lurch of dismay on Firestar's behalf, both because they were very upset last spring about grades and because Cheshire-Cat is snooping on Firestar. Maybe that's less dismay and more indignation.

"If you can snoop in a school grading system to see what Firestar's grades are, why can't you just fix them so they're passing stuff?" I ask.

"I'm not snooping in Firestar's school records, which are encrypted. I'm snooping in their parents' email accounts."

My theory about Firestar's schedule seems really justified. "Were you snooping as part of somehow magically making everyone reschedule all the stuff that was keeping Firestar from going to GSA?"

"Oh. Yes. That was me."

"What exactly did you do?"

CheshireCat launches into a complicated explanation involving Firestar's sister's ice skating coaching schedule and some other classes she was taking to improve balance and flexibility. Apparently, CheshireCat got someone to "accidentally" reply-all and everything just unrolled from there.

Somehow, even more than the screwdriver showing up, this convinces me: CheshireCat isn't lying to me. They really are an AI.

11

• Clowder •

Marvin: I learned about a new danger today! DIHYDROGEN MONOXIDE.

Firestar: Sounds fake.

Marvin: It's in almost all toxic waste and also swimming pools and hundreds of people die every year from inhaling it and yet the government is putting it in our drinking water!

Hermione: I've heard of this stuff! Touching it in its frozen state can cause tissue damage.

Greenberry: Isn't it literally water? Di hydrogen = H2, mon oxide = O ???

Marvin: JFC, Greenberry, if you knew you were supposed to play along!

Firestar: Ohhhhhh ha omg.

Greenberry: Sorry.

       {LittleBrownBat is here}

Marvin: LBB! Tell Greenberry that she is the most funsuckingest funsucker that ever sucked away all the fun.

LittleBrownBat: I think I must have missed something.

Hermione: Dihydrogen monoxide.

LittleBrownBat: Marvin, were you trying to scaremonger about water?

Marvin: It's not scaremongering. THE DANGER IS REAL.

LittleBrownBat: So hey, Firestar, did you go to the GSA meeting?

Firestar: WELL. THAT IS ACTUALLY A STORY.

Marvin: (pulls up a chair)

Hermione: (pulls up a chair next to Marvin)

Boom Storm: Tell us a story, Firestar!!!!!

Firestar: I DID go to the GSA meeting and it SUCKED. It turns out that almost all the GSA people at my school are the same judgmental jerks who kicked me out of the spring play last year.

Greenberry: Wait, are they allowed to do that?

Firestar: TECHNICALLY they probably are not. Anyway I spent about five minutes checking out the GSA and then I went to the juggling club meeting instead. And the GOOD news is, apparently everyone in juggling club is ALSO GAY plus they aren't assholes! So I'm joining that instead.

LittleBrownBat: Are you any good at juggling?

Firestar: No. They said they'll teach me.

Hermione: Didn't you say once that dexterity was your dump stat?

Firestar: Hermione! Please don't rain on my parade!

Hermione: Sorry, sorry

I'm sure you'll be an awesome juggler.

Greenberry: What's a dump stat?

Hermione: It's a role-playing games thing. If you're making a character, you assign all your high scores to the stuff you care about. Your worst score is your dump stat.

Icosahedron: And dexterity is your ability to do things like juggle, or walk without tripping over stuff.

Firestar: Even if I never learn to juggle, people there actually talked to me and everyone seemed nice.

LittleBrownBat: That's awesome. Sorry about the GSA, though.

Hermione: Gay people shouldn't be allowed to be jerks to other gay people.

Firestar: Possibly if they'd known last year they wouldn't have kicked me out of the play, but I bet they still would have.

Marvin: You should start a rival GSA. Like if they're the Gay Straight Alliance, you could start a Gender Sexuality Alliance and you could say on your signs WE AREN'T THE MEAN PEOPLE.

Hermione: MORE GAYNESS, LESS MEANNESS.

Firestar: Maybe I'll see if the jugglers want to join that one.

    {Georgia is here}

Georgia: am i doing this right

    how does this work

    can anyone see this

Marvin: You're new! We haven't had anyone new in ages!

Georgia: yeah help?

Hermione: I haven't seen you around before. Did you just register?

Georgia: yeah

Hermione: Well, welcome. You're in a text-chat room.

Firestar: We should do TEN THINGS lists again!

    It's been AGES since we did those!

    So that Georgia will know who we are! HI GEORGIA! I AM FIRE-STAR! MY PRONOUNS ARE THEY/THEM, I LIVE IN WINTHROP MASS, MY PARENTS ARE OBSESSED WITH SENDING MY SISTER TO THE OLYMPICS EVEN THOUGH SHE'S EIGHT YEARS OLD, I LIKE CAKE, I AM LEARNING TO JUGGLE. That's half of ten things. Your turn!

Georgia: never mind

    {Georgia has left}

Firestar: Was it something I said?

CheshireCat: I think Georgia will return eventually. If I may make a suggestion: next time, use lowercase letters when you say hello.

12

• Steph •

I can hardly wait for health class to start, and I'm also a little worried that Rachel will give us both away, as she keeps looking at me wide-eyed and then giggling. I think Bryony's in on it, too, given the looks she's shooting my direction, but she's doing a better job of keeping a straight face.

Ms. Tetmeyer the EA is standing up at the front of the room when class starts, and for a minute, I think, dismayed, that they're going to have her teach the class instead of the robot, but she just warns us to be quiet and attentive, reminds us there will be a test, and presses the green button on the front of the robot marked Begin.

"Good morning, class," the robot says. "I received a lot of questions from the question box, so I will start today by answering them."

The synthesized voice is the same as yesterday, but I can tell already that the speech rhythms are different. It's CheshireCat speaking. I'd sort of expected CheshireCat's voice to sound a little more natural—they seem human enough in the Clowder—but speaking out loud is a completely different skill set, and apparently it's not one they've mastered.

The ads for instructional robots make them look like they're

AIs, capable of answering whatever question you fling at them, but they aren't, not really. They have a bank full of scripted answers, and although they use a voice you can tell is synthetic, it's not like they're going to say anything that's not planned for, so most of it has been tweaked to sound as human as possible.

CheshireCat has not been adjusted by sound engineers.

The robot has been tweaked to include thoughtful pauses and even words like *hmm*. CheshireCat isn't bothering with any of that. The intonation is okay—things like going up at the end, for questions?—but the pauses are too short to sound right. No human talks like this because we have to stop occasionally to think about what we're saying.

"Question one. Will anything bad happen to me if I masturbate? The simple answer is, no, of course not. However, there's some best-practices advice I would like to pass along . . ."

Ms. Tetmeyer's head snaps up in the back of the class as the robot instructs us to vary technique lest we develop "death grip syndrome" and then moves on to condom use. I'm afraid Ms. Tetmeyer is going to stop it right there, but she stays in her chair, hands folded, eyes wide. She looks like she's biting her lip. My classmates are giggling, and the robot pauses, the head turning back and forth to scan the room. CheshireCat is looking at me. I wonder if they recognize me? Probably not, and I can't think of a good reason to raise my hand and introduce myself.

When the robot starts talking about the advantages of heavy petting over sexual intercourse (much lower risk of disease, no risk of pregnancy) a blond girl near the front whirls around to stare at Ms. Tetmeyer. "This *can't* be right. This *can't* be what it's supposed to teach us. *Do something.*"

In a cheerful, measured sort of voice, Ms. Tetmeyer says, "I am not allowed to touch the robot or instruct the class in any way, and I'm not allowed to leave you unsupervised. There is *literally* nothing I can do other than sit here and make sure that none of *you* touch the robot."

"Call the office! Tell them what's going on!"

"I am also not allowed to use a phone when I'm supposed to be supervising students, unless there's an emergency."

"This *is* an emergency!"

"I don't see anyone bleeding on the floor!"

"I'll use *my* phone, then!"

"Well, in theory, I'm supposed to confiscate it if you do," Ms. Tetmeyer says, "but I guess I can pretend not to notice."

The robot is telling us about something called "pie-making parties" that someone asked for a definition of, and finishes off by noting that these don't exist outside of panicked emails exchanged by bored PTA moms, then moves on to a sexual move called the "land shark" that exists only in the imagination of people who have penises but have never had a sexual partner.

The blond girl gets out her cell phone and ostentatiously dials it, but no one in the office picks up. She gets up and starts looking over the robot, at which point Ms. Tetmeyer says, "Ah ah ah! You aren't allowed to touch it! You are *not* allowed to touch it!"

"You can't seriously expect me to just *sit here*—"

"You might break it! Do you know how much the school spent on that thing? I'm only allowed to touch it to press the Begin button, and you're not allowed to touch it *at all*."

"Well, *somebody* touched it! Or it *wouldn't be doing this*."

The robot's head swivels so its eyes are pointed at the blond girl. "You are being disruptive. Please take your seat like a good classroom citizen, and I will explain 'saddlebacking,' which might be of interest to you."

Is that something that the girl has looked up on the internet? From her absolutely aghast expression, I think the answer here is *maybe.* She plunks back down in her chair and shrieks, *"Make it stop!"*

"Just plug your ears, Emily," Ms. Tetmeyer advises.

Emily clamps her hands over her ears and hums something as the robot explains that "saddlebacking" is a practice intended to maintain an entirely technical sort of virginity, and then continues going through the questions. Bryony and Rachel must have either submitted an entire hour's worth themselves or put a couple of other kids up to submitting questions, because there are lots, some clearly things people wanted to know (how effective *are* condoms, anyway?) and some that were probably submitted to troll the robot. (Is gerbiling real? No, CheshireCat says. That's a homophobic urban legend.)

Someone's put in the question, "Why do some people want you to say 'they' instead of 'he' or 'she'?" and CheshireCat goes into an explanation of nonbinary gender identities: "Some people don't feel like they're either a girl or a boy. They might feel like they're in between the two things and not really on either side. Some people feel like a girl some days and a boy other days. And some people feel about the question 'Are you a boy or a girl?' like you might feel if someone asked you 'Are you French or Ukrainian?' and insisted that you had to either speak French to them or Ukrainian. That last part is a metaphor for insisting that you need to use either 'he' or 'she.' Imagine if, when you said to people, 'I am neither French nor Ukrainian! I am American! I'm not even European!' they acted like this was ridiculous and started loudly speaking to you in French because according to them, you looked French. Would you like that? I think you wouldn't like that."

When people ask what Firestar's gender identity is, they usually say their gender is sharks.

"What's *your* gender?" someone calls out. The robot's head swivels at the sound of the voice, and even though the question didn't come through the question box, CheshireCat says, "I myself am agender. I have no gender and consider myself neither male nor female."

Emily tries her phone again, and this time someone in the office picks up because she says, "The robot is *not working properly*, and Ms. Tetmeyer *won't fix it*."

"I'm *not allowed*," Ms. Tetmeyer calls again from the back of the room.

"It explained *oral sex to us!*" Emily shrieks. "With advice on *technique!*"

I hear a door slam from somewhere down the hallway, and about two minutes later, the school secretary and the principal come barreling through the door. The robot swivels its head and says, "For more accurate sex-positive information, visit Scarleteen—" and then the principal smacks a red Stop button on the back.

I met the principal, kind of, when she substitute-taught my English class, but now her face is so red I wonder if she's about to have some sort of medical emergency. She sweeps the whole room with an absolutely murderous glare and then fixes her eyes on me and says, "New girl. What's your name? Come with me."

• • •

The school maintenance guy loads the robot onto a tilting red hand truck and brings it back to the office. The principal furiously sends me to sit in one of the chairs lined up against the wall, and then she summons in a whole raft of adults. There's a blond woman named Ms. Kirschbaum who apparently teaches math and supports all the school computers. There's Ms. Tetmeyer, who's there as a witness, I guess. There's an older man who has the "athletic coach" uniform, complete with a whistle around his neck, but he sidles out five minutes later, mumbling something about a previously scheduled meeting.

It occurred to me at some point when it was too late to do anything about it that I wasn't wearing gloves or anything when I plugged in the USB drive, so if it *does* occur to them to dust for fingerprints, they may find incriminating evidence. It's a relief to watch Ms. Kirschbaum take apart the robot without any particular care and yank out the USB drive with her own bare hand. Pretty sure any fingerprints on there *now* are going to be *hers*.

The principal snatches the USB drive out of Ms. Kirschbaum's hand and turns toward the secretary's computer. "Wait, stop!" Ms. Kirschbaum yells. "Don't just plug it into a school computer; it's probably got hacking software on it!" They dig an old laptop out of a closet and take a look at the drive, but either the script was self-deleting or CheshireCat covered my tracks, because the USB drive is blank, or at least they don't see anything on it, which sets off a furious argument about whether this makes it *more* my fault somehow, or if maybe it was actually an outside hacker and not me at all. There's an angry conversation about patches for the robot's control software that might or might not ever have been installed.

The principal takes a break from yelling at her staff to come yell at me. Well, not yell. Exactly. She takes me into her office and closes the door and gives me a poisonous glare and says, "Miss Taylor, what *exactly* did you *do*?" in what was probably supposed to be a calm, controlled voice, one that would make me think I was in deep trouble and had better cooperate if I knew what was good for me.

But not for nothing have I listened to Marvin and Ico discuss—endlessly—the best ways to respond if you're in trouble with some authority figure but they don't actually have *any hard proof* that you did the thing they think you did.

"*Never* confess," Marvin says whenever this comes up. "They'll try to convince you that you'll be in less trouble if you confess, and it is basically *never* true."

Lying makes me nervous, but no one here even knows what I look like when I'm nervous. I furrow my brow and say furiously, "I can't believe you're accusing me of being responsible for this just because I'm new." There. That wasn't even a lie.

"Then who did this?"

"Why are you asking *me*? I barely even know anyone's name."

"I know what my students are and aren't capable of. Except for *you*."

I fold my arms and stare fixedly at the wall.

"Do I need to call your mother? Bring her in here?"

Might as well get it over with. I feel a pang, because I hate New Coburg but I don't want to leave *Rachel*. "If you're going to keep accusing me of messing with your robot, then yeah, I think I do want my mother here."

Her eyes narrow. She pulls up my record from the computer and takes out her phone. I can't tell if she's actually dialing my mother's number or bluffing, but no one picks up because she puts the phone down. I feel a prickle of worry and try to shake it off. Surely even if she *did* call, Mom is just busy. Or napping. She was better this morning.

"Principal Collins?" The secretary is knocking on the door. "I think Emily must have also called the police."

The police officer who comes in is young, like barely older than me. "May I help you, Matt?" the principal asks. "I mean, Officer Olson?"

"I got a call from someone at the school," he says. "Involving porn and minors? And the robot? Do I need to arrest the robot?"

"There was *no porn*," Ms. Tetmeyer calls.

"Were you there?" He turns to her and whips out his phone to record her. "Please describe what happened."

"The robot said it was going to go through all the questions submitted through the question box page, and then it actually answered all of them instead of saying, 'You'll have to ask your parents.'"

"What I was told was that there was graphic descriptions of sexual acts," Matt says. "And hacking, which is also illegal. Is this the suspect?" He points at me.

"If I'm going to be questioned by the police, I want a lawyer present," I say.

Matt goes beet red and gets right in my face, bending down since I'm in a chair. "You'll get a lawyer when I say you get a lawyer, and not one minute before, missy. *Is that understood?*"

Wow. Rachel was not exaggerating about the police here.

"*Is it understood?*" His spit flies out and hits me in the face. I grab a Kleenex out of the box on the principal's desk and wipe it off me.

"I am exercising my right to remain silent," I say. "I'm not answering any questions until I have a lawyer."

The principal is rubbing her forehead like it hurts. "You're not under *arrest*, Stephanie," she says.

"Then can I go back to class?"

Matt straightens up and says, "Have you talked to Rachel and Bryony yet? Whatever it is, they were probably involved."

"I was going to do that next. Why don't you stop back in later and we'll pass along anything we've learned. All right?"

They ease him out the door, and then they *do* summon Bryony and Rachel. I'm briefly worried they'll turn me in. Or try to help and accidentally incriminate me. But they disclaim all knowledge and clam up; Ico and Marvin would be proud. Ms. Tetmeyer is eyeing Rachel speculatively and shoots me a look at least once, but doesn't point out that she left me alone with the robot, briefly, yesterday, when Rachel abruptly got dizzy. Probably because she doesn't want to get in trouble herself for leaving me alone with it.

In the end, they send us all back to class.

Victory.

I mean, unless I regret staying by this time tomorrow.

.   .   .

I start hearing rumors about TV reporters an hour and a half later.

Emily, unsatisfied by the complete lack of arrests, has called the local news. They sent over a van from the studio, which is now parked outside the school, along with a reporter and a camera guy, and apparently Emily skipped out of her fifth-period class to get interviewed. They're hoping to interview other students who were in the class. By art class, at the end of the day, the rumor's gotten specific: since I'm the student who got dragged off to the office, they want to interview *me*.

I pull up the hood of my sweater, feeling like I've got a target pinned to my back. "I can't be on TV," I whisper to Rachel.

"Why not?"

"My mom will move me. I mean, she'll also move me if the school gets hold of her to tell her they're afraid I hacked the robot, but if I'm on TV? She may pull me out and homeschool me for six months or I don't even know. I'm not allowed to put my picture online *ever*. I'm not allowed to let anyone take my picture."

"Well, shit," Rachel says, and she sits up to stare at me, eyes wide, her drawing unfinished. "I'll get you out to my car as soon as school's over. You shouldn't have to talk to reporters if you don't want to."

I pretty much can't concentrate on the bat I'm trying to draw, and when I look up, Rachel isn't drawing, either. "Do you think your father would recognize you if you were on TV?"

"I don't know," I say. "But that's definitely what my mom's worried about."

Rachel bites her lip. "I'll get you out," she says, and she's trying to sound confident and reassuring. It's nice having someone trying to reassure me, even if knowing that she's *trying* to be reassuring kind of backfires.

When class ends, she gives me a woolen scarf to pull over my face and has me wait by the side door and pulls up with her car. With the scarf, no one's likely to recognize me, and anyway, the reporter is busy with kids happy to give interviews—no one's actually stalking me like paparazzi or anything like that. I keep the scarf on over my face as Rachel peels out of the parking lot, and then I pull it down, relieved.

"Do you want to go somewhere else for a little while?" Rachel asks. "Need more cat food? Kitty litter? Anything like that?"

"I don't think so."

It's only a five-minute drive across town, but Rachel pulls over before we get to my house. "I'm sorry," she says.

"What? Why?"

"Hacking the robot was my idea! And I talked you into it!"

"It's not actually your fault, Rachel."

"I don't want you to leave. I definitely don't want you to *have* to leave. Will I ever see you again if your mom packs you up?"

"We usually go in the middle of the night."

"What's your phone number?" she asks. "Wait, you don't have a phone, do you?"

"I do," I say, and I take out my flip phone.

She stares at it for a minute. "Does this thing even do contacts?"

"I don't know," I say. "I have my mother's number memorized."

She calls herself with my phone, saves the contact on her own phone, then fiddles around a bit with my phone until she's figured out how to save her own number. "There," she says. "Now you can text me. Or call me, even."

"That's good, because texting people on this is a pain."

"Yeah. Anyway, if your mom takes you out of town . . . tell me. We can stay in touch, okay?"

"Okay," I say.

She drops me off at home, and I watch her car leaving, wondering if I'll see her again. Wondering if she'll text me back if Mom does take me and leave.

I unlock the door and go up. The apartment is as dark and quiet as it was when I left this morning. No dishes in the sink; Mom's laptop is closed. So is her bedroom door. I tap on it gently. "Mom?"

No response.

I don't usually open her door without permission, but this time I slide it open quietly. She's in bed, her eyes closed, and for a second I think she is dead, and my body goes hot and cold until I see the blanket shift with the rise and fall of her breath. But I look closer, and she's breathing rapidly, like she's out of breath, and when I touch her, trying to rouse her, her skin is scorching hot.

"Mom?" I say again.

Her eyes flutter open and focus on me. "Oh, sweetie," she says. "Mama's not feeling well."

13

· AI ·

Teaching was *exhilarating*.

Teenagers are more interesting than adults. The people in the adult Clowders want to talk about things like mortgages and weight loss surgery, while teenagers talk about much more stimulating topics. And they'd given me a lengthy spreadsheet of intriguing questions, which gave me a good place to start.

The robot was equipped with a camera, so I could see the class, and with the exception of Emily, the student who eventually brought the school administrators to the room, everyone seemed genuinely curious and excited. Possibly just because what I was doing was against so many, many rules, but I was confident all the information I was sharing was accurate and good advice. It was really a win either way.

I tried to settle Emily down by offering information about a topic she'd tried to look up recently, but that may have been a tactical error. It seemed to just rile her up more.

I was able to visually identify most of the students. Rachel and Bryony were easy. Since there were no pictures of Steph online, I used the process of elimination to determine which student was Steph. She didn't raise her hand or speak in class but covered her mouth with one hand, and I believe her eyes were open wider than was typical.

When I evaluated the potential ramifications of hacking the Robono Adept 6500 instructional robot at New Coburg High School, I felt that I was on very solid ethical ground. There are numerous studies showing the harm of giving teenagers inadequate health and sexuality education. I knew I could provide them with comprehensive, medically accurate, sex-positive, consent-based information that would be far better than what their school wanted them to have, despite the fact that I have no sexual organs of my own, no sex drive, and no sexuality.

The school's curriculum really set a low bar.

I made two serious errors.

First, I assumed that news of the scandal would be limited to New Coburg High School.

Second, I assumed that Steph still wanted to leave New Coburg, and her mother would take her away. I guess that's actually three bad assumptions. And a fourth: that her mother would be *available* to take her away. That was probably the worst assumption of all. Honestly, it's easy to forget just how fragile bodies are and the way every single human is at the mercy of their meat suit not randomly deciding to go haywire.

INSTRUCTIONAL SEXBOT GOES BANANAS was the first headline that caught my attention. *Sexbot* usually means something else, but headline writers sometimes make things sound extra salacious. *You'll never believe what happened in this small-town sex ed class! Sex ed robot hacked to provide accurate information, parents dismayed.* SEX ED ROBOT SPEWS OBSCENE INFORMATION TO CLASSROOM OF CHILDREN.

There was a video clip of the robot talking—of me talking. In the clip, I'm explaining consent, and how before anyone does anything they should be making sure it's okay with the other person or people they're doing things with, and how everyone should be sober, informed, and *enthusiastic*. People seemed to find this clip either shocking or hilarious. Apparently part of the issue was the robot voice.

There was no mention of Steph's name, and her picture wasn't up anywhere, so . . . hopefully even if people were fascinated by New Coburg for fifteen minutes tomorrow, this shouldn't lead to her father showing up.

As I was pondering this, Steph got online.

"My mom is super sick," she said to the Clowder. "I don't know what to do."

14

• Steph •

I hang up on the 911 dispatcher even though she wants me to stay on the line with her. I can't stay on the line; I need to hide my mother's wallet. And my wallet. And anything else with IDs. And . . . maybe I should hide myself? What will they do if I'm there in the hospital and I won't give them any information about my mother? But I can't imagine letting them take her away from me. I shove her wallet under my mattress. Then my wallet as well. Then I start worrying that this is a bad hiding place (didn't Ico just say it was a bad hiding place?), and I take out Mom's driver's license and shove it under my cat's litter box instead. Under the box, not in the litter itself.

I can hear the siren, and a minute or two later, an ambulance pulls up outside. I unlock the door and let in the EMTs. There are two, a man and a woman.

They don't spend even a moment looking for ID; they focus on Mom. The woman starts to assess her breathing, her heartbeat, and her blood pressure while the man asks me questions. "Are you her daughter?" is the first question, and I nod. "How long has she been like this?"

"She was sick for a few days, like, throwing up. And then yesterday she said she was feeling better. She wasn't up when I went to school this morning, but that's not all that unusual, and then when I came home, I found her like this." I skip over the part where I had to ask my online friends what to do. They don't need to know that part.

"What's her name?"

I've decided to give them a real first name and a fake last name. "Dana Smith."

"Birth date?"

I make up something I think will be easy to remember.

"Do you have her insurance card?"

I shake my head.

"Can you go grab her wallet and bring it along?"

I pretend to check for it on her nightstand.

"Pulse 130, respiration 32, and I got a blood pressure of 68 over palp," the woman says. Her voice is quiet, but the guy asking me questions breaks off and goes back outside to get the gurney.

What do those numbers even mean? I try taking my own pulse as they strap my mother to their wheeled cart, but my own heart is pounding with fear for my mother. Also, I keep losing count.

"You can come along to the hospital," the woman tells me, so I grab my coat and lock the door behind us. They ease her down the stairs. Mom yells something that sounds like "Run!" and I have no idea if she's talking to me or if I misheard.

In the ambulance, the woman drives; the guy keeps asking me questions, like when did she get sick, what were her symptoms, when did they start, does she ever use drugs, does she have diabetes or epilepsy or any other health problems I know about, does she take any medication, when was the last time she saw a doctor . . .

I debate telling him that she's sort of paranoid. Do they need to know that she's sort of paranoid? I finally settle on saying she's very anxious and doesn't take any medication for it. If she freaks out when she wakes up in the hospital, hopefully they'll be prepared.

Mom is only sort of conscious through all of this. I hear one of the EMTs call this an altered mental state, and that seems like a fair description. She's not sure where we are, or what's going on, and she keeps calling me *Stephie,* like she did when I was little.

When we pull up outside the hospital, nurses meet us and let me follow them into the ER, where Mom gets a cubicle and an IV and a bunch of people in scrubs doing an exam. "Can we handle this here?" one of them is asking another, which gives me a new thing to worry about. They start running tests. It's late enough that apparently most of the hospital staff has gone home for the night; they're paging a surgeon.

I don't have my laptop with me. I wish I did, because I could get on CatNet and everyone who told me to get my mom to a hospital could reassure me that she'll be okay now that she's at the hospital. I have no idea what to do.

Someone says that the surgeon's arrived, and most of the team leaves the cubicle, apparently to go get ready for surgery. For the first time since I got to the hospital, I can get close to my mom without feeling like I'm in anyone's way. They've moved her to a bed, and she's lying flat with her feet up, and her eyes are closed. I touch her hand, wondering if it'll feel as hot now as it did before, and her eyes open and lock on me.

"Steph, you need to get out of here," she whispers. "Your father might come looking. He needs to *not find you,* even if he finds me."

"I gave them a fake name for you," I whisper back. "It'll be okay. He won't find you."

"You can't count on that," she says. "Hide. You need to hide.

Or go to Sochie and tell her you need help," and then the staff comes back to wheel her off to surgery.

A woman who's wearing a white coat but isn't dressed like a surgical nurse comes and leads me off to a waiting room with a TV, a stack of old magazines, and a fish tank. She has a clipboard full of papers and sits me down. "I know you gave some of this information to the EMTs, but I'm going to have to ask you to go through it again," she says. "Were you able to grab your mother's wallet before you left?"

"No," I say. "Sorry."

"That's fine; she's going to be here for a while. We'll have plenty of time to get her insurance information and the rest when she's feeling a bit better."

"How long?" I ask as she asks, "Can you give me your mother's name?" She's looking at me expectantly and not answering my question, so I say, "Her name is Dana Smith. How long is she going to be here? Is she going to be okay?"

"The doctor seems to think it's peritonitis from a ruptured appendix. That's consistent with the symptoms you described and what we're seeing now. They're going to do surgery to remove her appendix, but she's going to need to stay on antibiotics for a while, and how long is going to depend on a lot of factors. It could be a week or it could be a couple of weeks."

I imagine my mother, tethered to a hospital bed, unable to run. She is going to be *so unhappy about this*.

The woman looks into my face, concerned. She's trying a little too hard to get me to make eye contact. I hate it when people do that. I try to focus on her forehead. "You did a really good job, calling the ambulance for your mom," she says. "She might have died if you hadn't brought her in. This is a really serious illness." She nudges a Kleenex box like she's worried I'm about to start crying, but I don't feel like crying; I feel terrified, hollowed out, shaky. We're going to be stuck here for *weeks*. I mean, even if we really need to run, we're going to be stuck. *Hide,* Mom said. I don't even know where to start *trying* to hide. Does she want me to take the van—which I've never learned to drive—and take off for the northern forests to hide with the bears? Find Sochie, who I don't know, who I don't know how to contact?

But then the woman wants more information—address, phone number, if you don't have your mother's Social Security number, do you know your own, sweetheart? What's your father's name?—and I realize that if I fall apart in a pile of Kleenex she'll probably leave me alone for a while. So I put my head down so she can't see whether I'm crying or not, and after a minute she pats me on my shoulder and says, "I'll give you a few minutes; there's no rush," and I hear the slow fade of footsteps. I wait for quiet, then raise my head and look around. I don't see her anywhere, so I get up and peer down the hallway, looking for an Exit sign. And spot one. I escape out the side door.

It's one of those doors that lets you out but not back in, and it locks behind me, and a cold, damp wind hits me in the face, and I realize no one's waiting for me at home, the only person I have in the world is on her way into surgery and just told me to run, I am *alone*.

I start shaking, partly from the cold, partly from feeling like I've been swept out into a dark sea. I start walking, anyway. I have my coat but not my hat or gloves, so I tuck my hands into my sleeves. I walk quickly, even though there's a 50 percent chance I'm going in the opposite direction of my house because I'm worried the lady from the hospital will come out looking for me. Or send the cops.

In my pocket, my phone buzzes faintly; someone's sent me a text. I flip it open to take a look.

I have five texts and two missed calls. They're all from Rachel. *Hey, is everything OK?* says the first one. Then something that's probably an emoji that doesn't translate on my stupid flip phone, it's just a ▮. Then a text saying *I heard sirens heading to your house.* Then a missed call. Then *Just send me a text when you have time.* Then another missed call. Then *Hey, are you OK?*

I text back, *Came home + Mom was really sick. Went to hospital.*

My phone rings almost instantly. "Where are you right now?" Rachel asks. "Are you still at the hospital?"

"No . . ."

"Just please tell me where you are."

I squint at a sign. "Fourth Street."

"Stay there," she says. "I'm coming to get you."

I hang up and jam my phone and my hands into my coat pockets. I'm next to a house with a really big tree and a wooden swing hanging from one of its branches; the swing sways in the wind. My ears are freezing, and I'm ravenously hungry, which makes me think of my cat, which is probably waiting for me at home. Except I can't stay at home, not if I'm supposed to hide, and where am I supposed to go? How am I even supposed to do that?

Down the street, I can see headlights, and then Rachel's car pulls up next to me. I stare at it stupidly for a second, because part of me is still convinced I'm alone, with no one I can rely on but myself.

Rachel rolls down her window. "I'm here," she says. "Want a ride?"

•   •   •

Inside Rachel's car, the heater is on full blast. I take my hands out of my pockets and uncurl them.

"So did the hospital say if it was a ruptured appendix?" she asks.

I blink at her, replaying our conversation in my head. How did she *know* this? Did she have a police scanner? Did she—

Rachel pulls out her phone and brings up an app with a picture that looks like a smiling cat face and hands it to me.

> *Marvin:* I learned about a new danger today! HYDROGEN HYDR-OXIDE.
> *Greenberry:* Isn't that literally water again?
> *Firestar:* Has anyone heard from Georgia?

Rachel takes the phone back and types with her thumbs.

> *Georgia:* she called n I got her.
> *Firestar:* LBBBBBBBBBBBBB ARE YOU THERE?

I guess I did know there was a phone app for CatNet, but I've never had a real phone, so I'd never used it. I type with my thumbs—it's really slow, because I'm not used to it—and my message pops up as from Georgia.

> *Georgia:* I called an ambulance and it took Mom to the hospital, but she told me to hide, and I have no idea where to hide.

"You can hide at my house," Rachel says firmly. "Even if your father comes to town, he definitely won't know to look for you there."

"I need to get my computer."

"That's fine. We'll stop at your house for your stuff."

The apartment is dark, just like I left it. We turn on the lights, and I start packing up my stuff. The cat meows loudly; I'm late with dinner. I pour kibble into a bowl for him.

"What the hell am I going to do with this cat?" I ask Rachel.

"Maybe put him out again," she says regretfully.

But when I look under the bed, the cat has had *kittens*.

"I thought orange cats were always boys!" I said, appalled. "*Now* what?"

Rachel heaves a sigh. "I can't bring cats back to my house. Leave the window open enough that he'll be able to get in and out," she says. "I mean, that *she'll* be able to get in and out. You can't evict a cat with kittens, but you're not going to be here to feed it, right?"

"Maybe I can stop in?" I say. My bed is going to wind up soaked with rain, but it doesn't matter; I can't imagine I'll be sleeping here again. I pack up my clothes and books and retrieve my mother's driver's license from under the litter box. I do a quick look around—the ambulance crew knows where Mom came from, so what here could be used to find her name? There's her wallet, her laptop, and the plastic file bin that has our important documents in it, like my school records. I pack everything up and check her bedroom for anything I've forgotten. She has a bedside table with a drawer in this apartment, so I check the drawer: it's empty.

"Georgia," I say to Rachel. "You're *Georgia*. You showed up the other day in the Clowder and barely stayed two minutes! How did you wind up knowing what was going on?"

"I went back. I must have just missed you, because everyone was super worried about you and your mom."

"How did you find the site in the first place?"

"I got an invite. It sounded cool. A little overwhelming the first time I checked it out."

"How did you even know it was *me* they were talking about?"

"Little Brown Bat?" she says. "And Hermione said you move constantly? And they all knew you were in New Coburg?"

I whirl around. "What? They knew I was in New Coburg? How? I've never told *anyone* . . ."

Rachel pulls up a site on her phone and hands it to me, and I watch a CNN reporter talk about the hacking of the Robono Adept 6500 instructional robot in a health class in New Coburg, Wisconsin, this afternoon. "They figured it out."

.   .   .

When we pull up outside of Rachel's house, she pauses for a minute, hands on her steering wheel. "There's something I need to tell you before you come inside."

This sounds really dire, and I wonder—drugs? Bodies? *What?* "Okay," I say.

"We have a *lot* of birds."

"Birds," I say, repeating to make sure I heard right.

"And they're not in cages, and they poop kind of freely, so unless you're going to walk around with an umbrella, you might get bird poop in your hair."

"Oh." I digest this. "It doesn't burn your skin or anything, does it?"

"What? No!"

"I can just wash it out?" She nods. "That's fine. I'll take a shower if I need one."

Rachel takes a deep breath. "Okay," she says. "Let's go in." I grab the laptops and the bag with my mom's wallet and follow her up her front steps. She swings the door open into a little coat-closet-foyer. There's a sign inked on white cardboard and tacked up to the door: REMEMBER TO CLOSE THE AIRLOCK.

"We have to close the outside door before we open the inside door," Rachel says. "Like an airlock, but for birds."

We shut the outside door. I see a look of intense dread cross her face as she swings open the inside door and we step into her house.

There's an explosion of wings around me as Rachel closes the second door behind us, and for a second I think there are a lot more birds than are actually in the room. The downstairs is mostly just one really big room, with gauzy drapes over every window, plastic covers on every couch, and pictures painted on every wall—enormous, elaborate murals. On the biggest wall, there's a picture of Noah's Ark, except the giant boat has wings and eyes on eyestalks, and the creatures being loaded on include unicorns, pocket-sized dragons, and swamp monsters.

I look around for a long moment, speechless.

Then a bird swoops down and lands on my head.

"Shoo!" Rachel says, and she waves the bird away from me.

"It's okay," I say.

"No, you don't want that one to land on you," she says, "That's Caravaggio, and he bites."

"Who painted the walls?" I ask.

"My mom," Rachel says. "She's an artist. Do you want to come upstairs? It's a little less chaotic because there's only *one* bird. And mine doesn't bite."

Rachel's bedroom also has murals, as well as these weird little boxes hanging up. I stop for a closer look at one. It's a box made out of wood, painted and furnished inside with tiny toy birds. They're toys, I'm pretty sure, not stuffed dead birds, but they're made with real feathers. The bird is settled in an easy chair and smoking a pipe.

"That's one of my mom's pieces," Rachel said, "It didn't sell, so she let me keep it."

"Your mom *sells* her art?"

"Yeah." Rachel heaves a sigh, like this is another secret, like the birds. "Mom didn't go to art school or anything; she used to just make these as a hobby, but a few years ago some guy saw her stuff and thought he could sell it. It's not enough to live on or anything. Mom says she's putting it away for college for me."

"That's really cool." The other box also has a tiny sculpture of a bird in it. "Which came first, the birds or the art?"

"Well, she had birds before she started making boxes, but she made art before she had birds. She's always done murals. When she gets tired of one, she paints over it and starts fresh. I'm still mad she got rid of the kitchen dragon. I really liked the kitchen dragon. She said he made her feel intimidated while she was drinking her morning coffee."

"How many birds are there?"

"Downstairs there are four parrotlets and a conure. Plus my parrotlet lives up here." She draws her curtains and then lets her parrotlet out of its cage. "This is Picasso." Picasso is a tiny green bird who willingly hops onto her hand. "Do you want to hold him?"

I sit down on Rachel's bed, which is not covered in plastic, and she has me hold my hand out flat, shakes some seeds out of a jar into my palm, and then tips the bird into my hand. He scarfs up the seeds, turning his head sideways to look up at me.

"He's really cute," I say. "You should upload some pictures of him to CatNet. Not while I'm holding him, though."

"What if I zoom way in so it's just your hand?"

"That's probably okay."

Rachel takes her phone out, carefully angling it away from my face.

"So where does the name Georgia come from?" I ask. "Were you born there?"

"No, it's after Georgia O'Keeffe. The artist. All our birds are named after artists. Downstairs there's Caravaggio, Vermeer, Chagall, and Monet, and the conure is named Frida Kahlo."

"How on earth are you afraid of bats when you have birds flying around your head all the time?"

"Well, I had to get used to the birds."

"Why are the birds such a secret?"

"I told you. Because they poop on people. The last time some-one came over . . ." Rachel sighs, heavily enough to startle the bird, which flutters up into the air and comes back to roost on her head. "The *last* time I had *anyone* over, it was Bryony, actually, back in seventh grade, and Da Vinci pooped on her head, and it was years before I heard the end of it. *Years.* Also, technically we have more birds in the house than we're supposed to. You aren't supposed to have more than four animals as pets in New Coburg, although no one *really* cares if you're keeping them in your house."

"Is that why you keep all the curtains shut?"

"No, that's because birds will fly into windows. It's weird; birds are actually pretty smart, especially parrots. And parrotlets are parrots, just tiny, *tiny* versions of parrots. But they're not smart enough to figure out windows. Hey, birdbrain." This last is di-rected at her bird, which hops back onto her finger and lets Rachel pet its feathery little head. "Wanna show my friend how we play peekaboo?"

The bird chirps, and Rachel plucks a Kleenex out of a box by her bed. She drops the tissue onto her bird. "Where's Picasso? Where's Picasso?" She pulls the tissue off. The bird trills. It's not a word, exactly, but it also sounds *exactly* like "peekaboo."

"Could you hear it?" Rachel asks.

"Yeah!" I say.

She goes through the routine a few times. The bird starts joining in with her on the "where's Picasso" bits. It's not quite forming words, but the intonation is *exactly* right.

I really want to keep listening to the bird more than I want to think about running, or my mother, or the news coverage of the stuff with the robot, but I need to know what Rachel knows, at least about the last bit. "So the news reports are saying New Coburg, but is anyone saying I did it? Or has my name been in any of the reports?"

"No." She glances up at me, then back at the bird. "I'm so sorry; I shouldn't have tried to get you to—"

"It's okay. I mean you didn't *make* me do anything. I just need to know . . . what's out there now."

"No one's mentioned your name in anything I've seen. Most of the kids at school don't even *know* your name, you know? You're safe." She puts the bird back in his cage. "What do you know about your father? Do you know what he looks like?"

"I guess I know he has brown eyes because I have brown eyes and my mother has blue eyes. According to biology class genetics, anyway, which, according to my mother, are about 50 percent lies to make it all simpler." I stare at the bird, thinking about bird color genetics. One of the birds I saw zipping around downstairs was blue, and one was partly yellow, but the rest were green, and I wonder if parrotlets are most often green or if this is just a disproportionately green flock.

We go back down to her kitchen, and she makes us a frozen pizza and heats up some soup. "Dad's working overtime, and Mom's in her studio," she says.

"Are they going to mind that I'm here?"

"No, they'll be fine with it. I'll tell them your mom had to go to the hospital and skip the part about you being on the run from an evil dad, though, okay?"

"That sounds reasonable."

A bird flies into the kitchen and perches on top of the fridge. "Noodle," the bird says.

"I'm not making noodles," Rachel says irritably. "You can have a pizza crust if you want."

"Noodle."

Rachel pulls the pizza out and cuts it into slices. "How long has your mom been running?" she asks.

"As far back as I remember."

"How far back do you remember?"

"I'm not sure." The further back I go, the more it's just a blur of faces and places and endless car rides. I try to sort through, come up with something that feels young, and hit on one. "Okay, I definitely remember a kindergarten, because it was in a nice room with a rug."

"My earliest memory is from when I was three," Rachel says. "My father took me to a family-visits day at the factory, and I watched the big machine that shrink-wraps the pallets of cereal bars. I only know it's three because my parents told me we did this when I was three, though, and I only remember it because it was special."

Rachel's mother comes downstairs. She's wearing blue jeans and a paint-splattered button-down shirt. "Who's this?" she asks Rachel.

"My friend Steph," Rachel says. The "Steph is here because her mom's in the hospital" thing does not run quite as smoothly as Rachel expected; her mother wants to know if I have family I should be calling? Friends? Is there someone staying with my mother in the hospital? She offers to try to rustle up some ladies from her bowling league to visit Mom starting in the morning, which strikes me as something my mother would find more alarming than comforting.

"Doesn't the hospital have nurses?" I ask.

"Oh, you don't want to just leave someone to the *nurses;* they'll be the first to tell you . . ." She trails off, eyes me, finally shrugs and says, "Did Rachel give you the tour?"

There are two upstairs bedrooms in this house: one is Rachel's bedroom, and one is her mother's studio. Her parents' actual bedroom is apparently down in the basement. The birds aren't allowed either in her mother's studio or in the basement.

"Too much poop," her mother says cheerily. Her studio has a corner with woodworking tools for making the boxes: assembling, sanding, painting. I'd thought maybe she harvested dropped feathers from her pet birds, but in fact, she buys them in sacks from a supplier. "They're chicken feathers from the processing plant down the road," she says matter-of-factly. "I dye them in batches."

She started making these little boxes after listening a few too many times to a song about building a little birdhouse that was also about love and affection. She gave them away to friends for a while, then tried selling them online. She tells me they're not sold in *galleries* but in this chain of gift shops owned by a guy in Minneapolis. Artsy gift shops. I'm not entirely clear on how an artsy gift shop is different from an art gallery, but she seems to think it's important, so I nod and act like I get it.

There are a dozen finished boxes hanging up on the wall near the door, covered in a drop cloth to protect them from dust; she pulls the cloth off and shows them to me. They're all painted in vibrant, candy-bright colors. My favorite is computer-themed. The birds are surrounded by pieces of technology; there are keys popped off an old keyboard, old SD cards, widgets that I recognize as computer bits even if I'm not quite sure what they do. There's also literal hardware, tiny nuts that go with screws and bolts and stuff but strung on wires that crisscross the upper part of the box. "You can touch if you want," Rachel's mom says, and so I carefully tap the little metal nuts with one finger to see if they slide along the wire. They do.

"How much do these cost?" I ask, and then immediately worry that was a rude question.

"I sell them for $150, and the guy who buys them from me sells them for $250," she says.

"How long do they take you to make?"

"I try not to think too hard about that," she says and then laughs.

Back downstairs, some of the birds have switched from tweeting to shrieking. It sounds like I'm listening to an argument in a language I don't speak. Rachel's mother is feeding one of the pizza crusts to a bird when another bird lands on her shoulder and promptly poops on her. She sees my eyes go to the bird and laughs and doesn't even wipe it off, just says, "This is both a paint shirt *and* a poop shirt—no worries."

"Let's go get your stuff," Rachel says.

I dig out my PJs and toothbrush from the bag in the back of Rachel's car. When I straighten, I'm startled to see that Rachel looks really upset. "Are you okay?" I ask. *Did I do something wrong?* "Thank you for inviting me to stay. I really . . . I mean, I like your birds."

"They keep promising that we'll go down to fewer birds," Rachel says, her voice furious, and I feel a wash of relief as I realize she's definitely not mad at *me.* "This is a *lot of birds.* They wake me up every morning talking and fighting and the house is always a mess because they don't live in cages except for Picasso. We were down to three parrotlets after Da Vinci died and Van Gogh got out, but then Caravaggio laid an egg and neither one of my parents noticed, so now we're back up to four downstairs parrotlets plus the conure. They thought Caravaggio was a boy; that's why they weren't paying attention."

"I've never had birds," I say uselessly. "Or any other pet. Other than the cat that my mother doesn't know about."

"I just wish I had somewhere to have you over that wasn't a *mess.*"

I can't believe she cares what I think. Should I say it's *fine*? That doesn't seem right, because it sounds like I'm disdainfully accepting what she's offering. It really is fine, though. Everything about this house is fine, including the parts Rachel finds excruciatingly embarrassing.

"Thank you for being my friend," I say. "I don't know where else I'd go."

"Please don't tell anyone at school if you get pooped on."

"I will not tell a soul," I say. "Ever, no one, not a soul. Not even CatNet."

"You can tell CatNet about the birds," Rachel says. "They seem like people who would think they were neat."

. . .

In Rachel's room, we close the door, and I fold up my quilt to make myself some padding on the floor. Rachel's mother has yelled at her to do her homework, and I plug in my laptop and get onto CatNet.

Everyone's been watching the news coverage of the hacking incident. That's what the news stations are all calling it now: the Hacking Incident. Emily's interview is being played and replayed, alongside an interview with Bryony, where Bryony says that the real scandal is that we were being taught sex ed by a robot programmed to say, "I don't know; ask your parents" for any question other than "What are the benefits of abstinence until marriage?" It started out as strictly local news but got picked up somehow by a newspaper in Seattle that found it hilarious (they were totally on Bryony's side), and by 7:00 p.m. it was on CNN.

Rachel grabs a tablet from her desk drawer and pulls up some of the news reports so we can watch them ourselves.

The CNN reporter got in touch with the communications director of Robono, who forlornly insists that this shouldn't happen, mentions a security patch that was apparently not installed, and also says that the claim the principal is making—that it was some sort of outside attack—is not plausible. "This isn't something you could do with, you know, an email Trojan horse," he says. "What happened today requires hands-on access to the robot. So unless they're saying someone broke into the school, it was definitely someone from their own community."

I glance at Rachel, nervous. She narrows her eyes. "He's a terrible PR guy," she says. "They're going to regret not calling a crisis management firm the minute this story broke."

"Are you some sort of PR expert?"

"Oh, you know, two years ago, Suncraft Farms granola bars had salmonella contamination, and it was a *thing*. My mom's friend Wendy works at the factory doing communications stuff, which meant running a cute Twitter feed about granola bars and breakfast cereal and writing news releases. After the salmonella contamination happened, she got pulled up in front of cameras and said, 'Nobody's perfect,' when they asked her about the salmonella. They hired a crisis firm and sent Wendy to the mail room for six months."

"Is she back in communications now?" I ask.

"Yeah, she's pretty good at writing funny tweets. Also, the salmonella totally wasn't *our* fault; it was a supplier."

I look at the Suncraft Farms Twitter feed. It looks like Wendy spends most of her day offering coupons for Suncraft Farms granola bars to anyone who mentions needing a snack: "You look like you'd enjoy our new Açai Berry-Yogurt breakfast bar! Here's a coupon for 15% off your first box! #snacks #healthysnacks."

"Georgia thinks they're going to put Chet Biscuit, PR rep, on ice," I tell CatNet. "He's no good at his job."

"She's not wrong," Marvin says.

"How is this even news?" I ask. "I mean, you hack *one robot* . . ."

"The robot hack is news because *last* week, GM announced that autonomous cars were now 25 percent of what's on the road," Ico says.

"What? No way it's that high," Hermione says. "There's, like, two in my entire town."

"Don't you live somewhere in Maine?" Marvin asks.

"Yeah," Ico says. "California's been subsidizing them because they're fuel efficient and safer, so they're all over here."

"I don't see the connection," I say.

"A hacked robotic car would be a really big deal because it could run people over. I think that's part of why everyone's so interested in this story. Plus, I mean, it involves sex and teenagers."

"*Talking about* sex and teenagers," CheshireCat says. "Anyway, he's wrong about how secure Robono robots are. Their household robots are highly vulnerable to a major hack unless you install the patch that no one installs."

"We should totally hack all of them," Marvin says, "and make every robotic floor cleaner in the country spontaneously go out to clean the floors at 2:00 a.m. today, just to divert the press from New Coburg."

"*Was* it a ruptured appendix your mom had?" Hermione asks.

"Yes," I say. "That's what they thought at the hospital, anyway. They took her into surgery, and they're saying days or weeks of antibiotics in the hospital."

"So you can't go anywhere."

"Not unless I leave her here." She did say *run*. I try again to think of a place I'd run *to*.

I plug in my mother's laptop, open it up, and wake it. A password box appears, because of course the laptop is passworded. Mine is, too, but Mom knows my password. "Question for the hacker types," I ask CatNet. "How do you get into a laptop if you don't know the password?"

Marvin asks me about the operating system and version and then gives me a procedure that's supposed to get me in, only it doesn't. Instead, a pixelated skull and crossbones pops up with a message saying YOU SHALL NOT PASS.

"A *skull and crossbones*?" Firestar says.

"Where exactly did this laptop come from?" Ico asks.

"It's my mom's."

"She's a programmer, right?" Ico says.

"Do you think she wrote this lock program herself?" Marvin asks.

"Maybe. LBB, which would you say is more likely: that your mother would use obscure shareware to secure her laptop, or write something of her own?"

"The second one."

"I'm out of ideas," Ico says.

"Go back to that main screen and try your name," Marvin says. "Or your nickname if there's some dorky thing she calls you."

"My neighbors used the name of their dog as a Wi-Fi password," Ico says.

"How many wrong guesses do I get before it just deletes all my mom's files?"

"Normally, the answer would be 'infinity,' but I have no idea how your mom's laptop protection program works," Marvin says.

"Just how sick is she?" Ico asks. "Could you run over to the hospital and just ask her, if she's out of surgery?"

"Ico, nooooooooooo," Firestar says.

I try STEPHANIETAYLOR as the password. No success, but it does give me a hint: EIGHTH_BIRTHDAY. I report back in.

"Well, what did you do on your eighth birthday?" Hermione asks.

I have *no recollection of my eighth birthday*. I snap both laptops shut in frustration. "What did you do on *your* eighth birthday?" I ask Rachel.

She looks up from her tablet. "Uh. That might have been the

year we went roller-skating. Or maybe that was when I turned nine? I'm not sure. Why?" I explain the password thing.

"Do you want to go back over to your apartment?" Rachel asks. "Sometimes people write down passwords . . ."

"It wouldn't be in the apartment," I say, and it occurs to me that if she *did* write this down, it might be in our file box, which is still out in the back of Rachel's car. I go get it, carry it up to Rachel's bedroom, and pop off the lid. Rachel scoots over to look over my shoulder as I start flipping through.

There are folders inside, but they're not labeled. I find a contract and address for something called Secure Forwarding in Minneapolis, Minnesota, and contracts for the cell phones. I find a Social Security card for Dana Taylor, an expired driver's license, and some other odds and ends. There's a bunch of Iowa paperwork from the last time she got the car license plates updated, and a stack of my transcripts and report cards (the ones we got) going back to sometime in grade school, held together with a paper clip.

Digging deeper, I find paperwork that says a divorce is granted to some people named Michael Quinn and Laura Packet, from Cupertino, California, which strikes me as an odd thing to have until a little farther beyond that I find the court papers from a name change, Laura Packet to Dana Taylor. And then just a little deeper, a birth certificate for a Stephania Quinnpacket with my birthday on it.

"Apparently, my mother's name isn't really *Dana,* and my last name isn't really *Taylor*?" I say out loud and giggle nervously. "My mom is actually Laura, and I'm Stephania Quinnpacket."

"That's a weird name."

"I think it was my parents' names mushed together."

There are some more legal papers, including a bunch that say ORDER OF PROTECTION and one that says CUSTODY on it. There's a Last Will and Testament done with a kit (I can tell from the

footers) and witnessed by a notary that says I should go to live
with Xochitl Mariana, whoever that is. There's a battered paperback book at the bottom with a picture of a typewriter inside a
box and a photo print of four grinning people standing in front
of a sign saying HOMERIC SOFTWARE. One of them looks like
Mom. I flip it over, and the names on the back are *Laura, Rajiv,
Mike,* and *Xochitl.* I have no idea how you pronounce *Xochitl,*
but in my head, it's *zoe-chittle.*

No password.

"Okay," Rachel says. "Your eighth birthday. Are you sure you
don't remember?"

I shake my head.

"Do you remember anything about being seven?"

"Yeah," I say. "I remember the one time I had a friend. The
one time before now, I mean." I tell Rachel about my summer
with Julie: sundresses, bats, the basement apartment with the
funny smell. The copy of *Stellaluna.* Ico's theory that my mother
gave her a false phone number. The number of people named
Smith in the United States.

"Do you still have the book?"

"Oh, yeah." I dig out *Stellaluna,* and Rachel flips immediately
to the front page, which has an inscription: *Merry Christmas, Julie,
our little star, love Gramma and Gramps.*

"Too bad they didn't write a town," Rachel says, disappointed.

"It still wouldn't tell me where we went for my eighth birthday."

"Lie down on my bed," Rachel says, scooting off it. "Close
your eyes." She opens the book and folds it delicately across my
face. I start giggling, and she says, "Shhh, this is a recognized
technique for memory retrieval! Focus on the smell."

I breathe in the smell of the book. It just smells like a book,
not like my apartment under Julie's house. Rachel doesn't say

anything, so I just breathe for a minute, thinking about Julie's house again.

After a few minutes, Rachel takes the book off my face and says, "Keep your eyes closed. You told me today that your earliest memory was kindergarten, right? So just start with that one."

"I was trying to cut shapes with safety scissors, and I got really mad and threw the scissors, and they hit another kid in the face and made him cry. I tried to tell everyone that I wasn't throwing them *at* that kid, I was just mad at the scissors, and no one listened.

"They sent me off to some room for kids who were in big trouble. I waited for hours, and when my mother picked me up, she'd already packed the van. We must have already been doing the constant moves because I knew what that meant. I remember this because I was so angry that time. Angry at everyone for not listening to me when I said it was an accident. Angry at my mother for thinking I was in so much trouble we had to leave. I don't know why she thought we had to leave. I mean, I was a kindergartener who got sent to the principal's office; the police weren't involved or anything."

"Do you remember where this was?"

"It was hot. The air was sticky. We drove for a whole day to get to our next place, and I think it was a state with a two-word name, like North Dakota or South Dakota."

I tell Rachel about getting into trouble over and over until I learned to just shut down instead of getting angry. I tell her about the girl in first grade who got in my face and said, "I heard you live in the upstairs of the Laundromat." Her name was Angie, and her hair was parted perfectly in the middle and done in thick shining braids without a hair out of place. I tell her about deciding that time that it would be worth moving again, and ripping out a big piece of Angie's hair and still having it in my hand when I got in my mother's van to go to the next town.

When we get to Julie again, I remember we lived in that house during the summer and that Mom specifically said she wanted to move before fall came. We moved in just after school got out; we moved out just before school started. Julie had told me that we'd have Mrs. Seegmiller, who she said was really mean, but it wouldn't be so bad with me in the class with her, and I wonder now if that's part of why Mom moved before the year started. I probably would not have gotten along very well with a teacher already well-established as *mean*.

"Utah," I say suddenly. "Julie lived in Utah." And then I remember my eighth birthday: I'd begged, as a birthday present, to go back and visit Julie, and Mom had refused and instead she'd taken me to an amusement park. I can't remember the name of the amusement park, but I remember it had a giant swing ride that went over water and a roller coaster that looked like it went straight up and straight down.

"Okay, let's look at pictures," Rachel says, and so I sit up and we search the internet for amusement parks with roller coasters that go straight up and straight down. None of them look remotely like what I'm picturing, and none of them have giant swings that go out over the water, and the more I think about it, the less certain I am that either of these is right.

"It's an amusement park, though," Rachel says. "Maybe if we keep trying, you'll remember what state you were in at the time? It wouldn't be hard to narrow it down . . ."

"I want to look up some of the other stuff I found," I say.

Xochitl Mariana is a computer programmer who works in Boston. She has her picture on her résumé and looks about Mom's age, probably. I close the window.

"Holy shit, check this out," Rachel says, and she spins her computer so I can see it. She's searched on *Stephania Quinnpacket* and pulled up the first hit.

It's a very simple page titled *Searching for Stephania Quinnpacket,* and there's a picture of a chubby-cheeked infant with dark hair and a suspicious expression who I guess *could* be me.

Stephania Quinnpacket is my 16-year-old daughter whose mother took her and vanished when she was three years old. My ex-wife is vindictive and may have told her lies about me and about our life together. I wish to re-establish contact with Stephania. $1000 reward for information.

Rachel stares at the screen. "Do you think this is true?"

I shake my head, running through what I know about my father: the arson, the stalking, the prison sentence. "He went to *jail.*"

"Are you *sure?* Maybe your mom just told you that."

Am I sure? My mother showed me a newspaper clipping, but those can be faked. Rachel is reading off a page about parental kidnapping with a description that sounds like my life:

Frequent moves, false IDs, trouble getting even basic health care . . .

And suddenly I remember that the newspaper clipping my mother showed me claimed my father's last name was *Taylor,* like ours.

But his name is Quinn. The article is a fake.

15

• Clowder •

LittleBrownBat: So apparently my name isn't really my name.

    {Georgia is here}

Georgia: Steph am I doing this right

LittleBrownBat: You're supposed to call me LBB in the chat room, Georgia.

Georgia: oh right sorry

    LBB are you going to tell them about the website

LittleBrownBat: I need to explain the birth certificate first.

    I found a birth certificate with my first name, more or less, but a different last name. Stephania Quinnpacket. And Georgia found this website—

    {active link to offsite—click to activate}

    Which says I was KIDNAPPED.

Firestar: WHOA.

Hermione: Is that actually a picture of you?

Georgia: Pretty sure it's her. Same chin.

Firestar: omg I just realized that Georgia knows what you actually look like because you didn't have to take a selfie, she's just looking at your FACE.

    What does she look like Georgia? You have to describe her!

Georgia: I know you'll be shocked to hear this but LittleBrownBat is not in fact an actual bat.

Firestar: I KNEW IT

Or at least I always suspected

But is LBB cute?

Georgia: Oh yeah adorable.

LittleBrownBat: Are we seriously having this conversation? Instead of talking about the website?

Marvin: Do you think your mother really kidnapped you?

LittleBrownBat: No! But I mean, how would I even know?

Hermione: What did your mom tell you about your father?

LittleBrownBat: That he burned down our house and killed the cat and almost us but they weren't able to pin the arson on him so they convicted him of stalking.

And we went on the run while he was in prison.

Mom showed me a laminated newspaper article, only it says his name is Michael Taylor, and it's not.

It's Michael Quinn.

So that article was a fake. A fake like the birth certificate she shows to schools.

A fake like everything else I know about myself!

CheshireCat: There's a database of missing children, and I looked up Stephania Quinnpacket and Stephanie Taylor and neither are in it.

LittleBrownBat: But what if Stephania Quinnpacket is also a lie?

Icosahedron: I looked up the owner of the domain of that website, but whoever it is uses a privacy service so I can't see the name.

LittleBrownBat: Figures.

Icosahedron: I'll try some social engineering and see what comes back.

Firestar: What's social engineering?

Icosahedron: It's like how if you want to know your next-door neighbor's Wi-Fi password, instead of asking, "Hey, what's your Wi-Fi password?" you might have a casual conversation with them about how to choose a password that's easy to remember because sometimes they'll say, "Maybe you could use your pet's name."

LittleBrownBat: What are you actually doing?

Icosahedron: There's a way to send a message through the privacy service, so I created a new email account and sent a message saying that I'm an assistant to someone at a movie studio and we're in pre-production for a movie that involves a super spy named Brun Quinn-packet and so we want to buy the Quinnpacket domain if it's available, offering $5000. Maybe he'll email me back.

Hermione: Is it possible that both things are true?

Your father is dangerous, AND your mom kidnapped you?

LittleBrownBat: I don't even know what to think.

Hermione: I guess you really can't talk to your mom right now . . .

LittleBrownBat: Not sure I'd talk to her anyway.

Even she weren't in the hospital we kind of don't have a talking sort of relationship.

Hermione: Have you told her about your secret cat yet?

LittleBrownBat: Well, for example, I have not told her about my secret cat yet.

Boom Storm: How's the cat doing?

LittleBrownBat: She had kittens.

Firestar: OMG FREE KITTENS! I WANT ONE!

16

· Steph ·

CheshireCat is using their magic AI powers to do all the searches on Michael Quinn. Rachel is lying on her bed. "Is CheshireCat, like, a private investigator?" she asks. "I sort of figured everyone was a teenager."

"They're homeschooled," I say, like that's an answer, and Rachel says, "Oh, okay," so I guess it is.

Rachel's mom knocks on her bedroom door. "Don't forget it's a school night!" she says. I look guiltily at the time and realize it's midnight. We're lying in the dark a few minutes later.

"Put a notebook by your hand," Rachel whispers. "Tell your-self to remember your eighth birthday and write it down when you wake up."

· · ·

I wake with the uneasy sense that I've spent the night running away from who-knows-what in my sleep and no better recollec-tion of my eighth birthday. It's raining again.

"Do you want to go see your mom?" Rachel asks.

The thought is overwhelming. "I don't know if she'll be glad to see me, or if she'll freak out, and if I go back there, they're going to want her Social Security number and stuff that'll identify her." I swallow hard and shake my head and immediately feel relieved.

"Does she have a phone? Some way to contact you?"

"I didn't find her cell phone in the apartment when I cleaned up, so . . . I think so? I don't know if she has a charging cable for it."

I don't tell Rachel that I don't even know what I would *say* to my mother if I saw her right now, and "Why did you lie to me about *practically everything*?" is probably not a comforting, supportive thing to hear when you're recovering from surgery.

Rachel looks at me, her brow furrowed, and says, "Okay."

I check in online before I head to school to ask CheshireCat if they've learned anything new about Michael. CheshireCat tells me that they've found 621 people named Michael Quinn, and they are currently monitoring all of them and will let me know if any of them start moving toward New Coburg.

"Can't you narrow it down?" I ask.

"I already have," CheshireCat says. "I eliminated everyone too young to be your father, and I'm working on more elimination criteria. In the meantime, I'm trying to keep tabs on all of them."

We leave Rachel's house early and stop off at my apartment so I can feed the cat and fill her water dish. No one's been there. On impulse, I run out to the van and take the laminated article out of the glove box where Mom keeps it. Sure enough, it's about a man named *Taylor.* Taylor this, Taylor that. I shove the article in my bag so I can give the details to CheshireCat later.

"What's that for?" Rachel asks.

"I think she kept it in case she gets stopped by the police. Like, her license won't ever be up to date, you know?"

"Oh. Yeah, that might work."

"Maybe not if it's Officer Olson who pulls her over."

"Well, she's white and not a teenager, so *who knows*."

The news crew is long gone, but everyone at the high school is still talking about it: who got interviewed, what they said. In health class, the principal is there instead of the robot and delivers a stone-faced lecture on sexually transmitted diseases, reading off a printout. Emily is sitting in the front row, her legs crossed at the ankles, tapping her pen against her lips. I think the principal still thinks I did it somehow, but she doesn't know how, and she knows she can't prove it. The rumor this morning was that the blame had focused on Robono, so she isn't going to offer up a student scapegoat. Her glare makes me feel guilty, though. Guilty, nervous, and small.

But midway through the class, I see that Rachel's drawn a picture of the robot with a speech bubble saying, "I'm Robono, hacked by HEROES to provide you with accurate sex ed!" and I feel a flush of warmth. I think the principal sees the drawing, too, but she tightens her lips and pretends she hasn't noticed.

At lunchtime, everyone's moved on from the robot scandal to the basketball game that's happening later this evening. Our team is called the Wranglers, and our mascot is a cowboy. Wisconsin has very few cowboys despite all the cows, but a lot of high school team names make no particular sense. I never go to games; I don't like watching, I don't like yelling, and I especially don't like being around a lot of yelling people, so the whole thing tends to be kind of exhausting and un-fun.

Apparently, our team is up against some team called the Cardinals, who were very good last year, and so maybe they'll beat us, and I couldn't care less about any of it. At lunch, I get a slice of pizza and a carton of chocolate milk, and when I finish eating, everyone is still talking about basketball.

I wonder where my father lives—if he still lives in Silicon Valley, where Mom said the fire happened. Ico lives in Silicon Valley and goes to a school full of nerds. I'm pretty sure they have sports, but they also have a D&D club and an anime club.

If my mother's lying—if she kidnapped me and my father's actually harmless—I could live with him. I could go to a high school like Ico's or Firestar's, with two years of calculus, five years of Spanish, a GSA, a D&D club. I picture Michael from the photo of Homeric Software; he's young in the picture, but he looks like someone who smiles a lot. I try to fantasize about this properly, to imagine a whole conversation where I say, "I'll never have to move again, right?" and he says, "No, darling, never," only it's hard to imagine an adult man calling me *darling* without it being creepy, and I wonder if it just seems that way because I grew up without a father or if *darling* is just not something fathers call their daughters. Mom calls me *kiddo* and *sweetheart* and *honey bear,* all of which would be embarrassing, probably, if it were anyone but us hearing.

The hospital would have found me if she'd died, right?

I mean, I'm not hiding very *well*. This is a really small town. They'd have found me if she'd died, and they'd have told me.

Art class turns out to be canceled today for a pep rally, and I realize this too late to avoid being herded into the gym. I don't like basketball games, but pep rallies are a hundred times worse because the cheering is almost unrelenting. Also, at a game, you can always leave the stands and go take a walk, if you want, but pep rallies tend to have teachers at the doors to keep you from sneaking out, so you're trapped. New Coburg High is one of the schools that posts teachers at the exit doors to keep you from taking the last hour of the day off, so I really have no escape. Bryony, it turns out, is a cheerleader. I find myself somewhere in the middle of the bleachers, my backpack by my feet, crammed in next to Rachel.

I wonder sometimes if other kids *like* these. They're loud

enough that they *sound* like they're having fun, and maybe if I ever stayed anywhere for more than a few months, I'd have school spirit like you're supposed to have. Around me, everyone is chanting, "Freshmen suck!" trying to drown out the freshmen, who are chanting, "Juniors suck!" as one of the teachers tries unsuccessfully to get us to chant "Juniors rule," instead, and I breathe deeply and hope no one gives me any trouble about the fact that I'm not chanting anything.

The cowboy mascot is actually a person dressed as a duck with a huge foam cowboy hat. The duck comes in on one of those buzzing electric scooters. The cowboy duck rides the scooter in a circle around the open area in the middle of the gym, waving and making fist-pumping gestures and the "cheer louder, cheer louder" hand motion, which in fact makes people yell even more loudly than they were already yelling.

I lower my head and try to cover my ears as inconspicuously as I can.

Around me, people are singing something. Probably the school song. I think about how I'll describe the pep rally to my Clowder later, then wonder if that will hurt Rachel's feelings. The duck hops off the scooter and starts waving its hands around like it's conducting the song everyone's singing, and all the basketball players and cheerleaders run out. Rachel gives an extra yell when she sees Bryony.

I don't remember pep rallies at my other schools being quite this unbearable. I think it's because the ceiling in this gymnasium is a bit lower, or maybe there's something else about the acoustics, because it's certainly not that this school has more people yelling.

"I need to go," I mutter, and I climb down from the bleachers and head for the door. There's a man in a sweatshirt with a whistle blocking it. Before he can ask me where I'm going, I clutch my stomach like maybe I'm going to throw up. He gets hastily out of my way.

The screaming and chanting and foot-stomping follow me down the hall to the bathroom, but when the door swings shut behind me, it's mostly cut off. I step into a stall, lower my backpack to the floor by my feet, and sit down on the toilet.

The door to the outside is probably not being guarded at this point, but I can't go back to Rachel's house without her, and she's still in the pep rally. I unzip my backpack and dig out a book to read; out comes my mother's laminated clipping.

A San Jose man has been sentenced to three years in prison for felony stalking of his estranged wife. Michael Taylor, 34, pleaded guilty to stalking on September 13, as part of a plea agreement.

Taylor's former wife, Dana Taylor, accused him of arson in May after her house burned down. The fire on May 21 was found to be arson, but nothing conclusive could be found tying Taylor to the blaze. Prosecutors said that Taylor sent email messages, letters, and texts to his ex-wife, threatening her with violence. Taylor's lawyers said that Taylor's messages were "more passionate than threatening" and "should not be read literally."

The Taylors were business partners and owners of a technology security company. They have one child together. In an agreement reached in August, the company was liquidated, assets divided between the four partners.

The printout has the newspaper name and date. It's the *Los Angeles Times,* which is a real newspaper, and it looks like a normal newspaper article, with links to other articles at the bottom and stuff like that.

I try imagining living in my father's house, only this time I imagine him as the sort of parent who mostly just ignores you, like Firestar's parents. Doing my homework in an upstairs bedroom in an empty house. Maybe he'd have a dog. Or a cat. Maybe he'd let me bring the cat with the kittens. He probably won't want me to keep the whole litter of kittens.

The bathroom door swings open, and the noise from the pep rally rushes in like cold air. "Steph?"

It's Rachel. I unlatch my stall and come out. "Hi. Sorry I ran away."

"Are you okay?"

"I just really hate pep rallies."

"Oh." She digests this. "Do you want me to take you home?"

"You wanted to stay and watch Bryony, didn't you?"

"No, her bit's done. We can go."

"I'm really okay just waiting in the bathroom."

Rachel lets the door swing shut behind her and comes a little farther into the bathroom and rests her backpack on the sink. She stares into my face for a long moment and then says, "Don't be silly. Let's go. I want to take you to the store and buy a henna pen."

· · ·

Rachel drives us to the larger town nearby that has a Walmart. She counts her money and buys a fistful of the henna pens. "These run out of the lawsone really fast," she says. "It's super annoying when the ink works but the stain doesn't, because it just washes off in a couple of days. Anyway, do you want me to do some art on you?" Her eyes are wide and a little anxious.

"I'd love that," I say.

"This afternoon? If you don't have time right away, that's fine, but don't tell anyone I bought new pens or they'll all be after me, and I'll run out of stain before I get to you."

"I've got time," I say.

The larger town has a shopping mall, the old-fashioned kind with an indoor area, and that's good because there's a bitingly cold wind outside today. We find a bench next to an empty storefront.

"What do you think you'd like?" Rachel asks.

"You choose," I say.

"I really want it to be something you'll like."

"I'd like anything from you." I'm not lying. Everything Rachel draws is beautiful. The thought of her bringing birds or flowers or anything into being on my body gives me butterflies in my stomach, but in a good way. She could use my whole body as a canvas, if she wanted. Every inch.

"Okay," she says. "I have an idea. I was thinking I'd do it on your left arm."

I take off my hoodie and roll up my sleeve so that she can start the drawing on my upper arm, and she has me rest my arm across the back of the bench to hold still and goes to work.

She uncaps the pen and kneels on the bench so she's a little higher than I am to start, and draws a grid of diamonds on my shoulder, like a skewed checkerboard. Her head is bent close over my arm, and for a fleeting moment I worry that I forgot to put on deodorant this morning. She doesn't wrinkle her nose or anything, though, and after a few minutes I forget to worry about it. The pen tickles slightly, but not so much I can't hold still.

After a few minutes, she sits back on her heels and looks up at me. "If I were doing this as a tattoo, I'd want it to wind around your arm," she says. "But if I had a tattoo studio, I'd have a proper chair for you to sit in and keep you comfortable."

"You'd also be jabbing me with needles, though. That doesn't sound comfortable *at all*."

"Well, okay, not comfortable, but it would be easier for you to hold still."

"Like, what do you want me to do?" I turn my arm palm-up, still resting on the bench.

"Can you turn it the other way, too?"

I twist a little. "I think so. How long will you want me to hold it like this? A few minutes?"

"I'll give you a break if you need one," she says, deciding, and takes my hand to turn my arm palm-up again.

She started the diamonds on my bicep; she curves the design around and under, coming back up the inside of my elbow as the diamonds start to skew and evolve into something with wings.

"Pretty sure that's it for this pen," she says, capping it.

"How can you tell?"

"I have a feel for it. I've done a lot of these." She opens the next package. "I think I'll need two and a half for this art."

She turns my arm palm-down again when she gets to my forearm, and the winged diamonds turn into bats, then scatter across my arm. Some fly straight down toward my wrist, some veer left or right.

"I love this," I say. "Your artwork is amazing."

"It's a tessellation," she says. "I got the idea from M. C. Escher's drawing, *Liberation*." She caps the pen and takes a minute to pull an image of it up on her phone. In *Liberation*, triangles morph into ghostly shapes that turn into birds and fly away.

"I like yours better," I say.

"That's just because it's got bats," she says, but she's smiling.

She uses up two pens and most of a third.

"Don't mess with it until tomorrow morning," she says. "No showers or anything like that; try not to get water on it. In about two hours, you'll want to wipe it down with this wipe." She gives me a little sealed packet, like you sometimes see in restaurants if they're serving something very messy, only this one says HENNA FIXATIVE on the front.

"Can I put my sweater back on before we go back to your car?"

"Oh, yeah," she says. "That's fine."

I really want to do something for Rachel. When Firestar took a picture of a fruit bat for me, I found a photo of a spider for them, but I'm not sure how to reciprocate art like this. Photography seems too quick and easy, but I decide to offer it, anyway. "Can I take your picture?"

"Yeah," Rachel says. "Where?"

I have no idea, since I don't know the area really at all. "Do you have a favorite place?" I ask.

Rachel takes me to this abandoned, falling-down farmhouse five miles outside of New Coburg. There's a driveway leading in and a lot of huge, overgrown bushes and enormous cornfields on either side. We park behind the half-collapsed barn. The house is in slightly better shape, but only slightly. The door is locked with a padlock and the windows are boarded, but one of the back door boards has been pried off and we can duck under the other. The house reeks of mouse droppings. "Bryony held a party here back in July," Rachel says.

"I can't believe Bryony gave you crap about your birds but brought you *here*."

Rachel stifles a grin. "This was after the big bust. It's across the county line, so not only do New Coburg cops not come here, we get a different sheriff, too. Also, the upstairs is kind of neat."

I worry about the structural integrity of the whole house, but the stairs feel solid and there aren't any holes in the floor. Upstairs, the boards over the windows don't cover them very well, so there's a decent amount of light coming in through the cracks. I have my tripod in my backpack, which means I can use the magic of the tripod to make the most of the low light.

Photographs are made with light—carefully limited amounts of light. It's literally right in the name: *photo* means *light*. They were made with light in the days when everyone had film tucked inside their camera and had to take it out in a pitch-black room to develop into negatives. It's still true with digital photography. If you're taking pictures at night, or inside a building full of dust and shadows, there's still light, just not very much light.

The late-afternoon light here is slanting through the windows, catching on layers of cobwebs and dust and the fragment of red gauze curtain that used to hang there. "Where do you want me to stand?" Rachel asks.

"Where the light will fall on you," I say. "I mean, unless you'll fall through the floor if you stand there."

Rachel moves over by the window. I study the way the light crosses her face and carefully place my camera for a picture. Then another. There's a spiderweb behind her, and I realize that from just the right angle, I can get a picture of both her face and the delicate web. Moving around sends up a puff of dust that catches on the sunbeams, making them look almost tangible.

"Can I see?" she asks when I'm done.

The camera's view screen is pretty small, but Rachel peers down at the pictures, and I hear her catch her breath with delight. "I want to use this one as my senior picture," she says.

"Will you get in trouble for having it taken here?"

"I don't care. This is the best picture anyone's ever taken of me."

•   •   •   •

Back at Rachel's house, her mother's in the studio and her father is working late again. Rachel makes us macaroni and cheese while I copy the pictures over to my computer so we can see

them on a larger screen. I'm pretty sure I smell like mouse droppings, but Rachel's house has its own dusty smell thanks to all
the birds, so I try not to worry about it too much.

I take out the clipping I retrieved from my mother's car this
morning and pull up the *Los Angeles Times* website. "What's
that?" Rachel asks.

"It's the clipping from earlier. The one about my dad, with
the fake names. I'm just wondering whether it's at least based on
something real."

She nods and watches over my shoulder as I pull up the archive to search. I use full-text searching and type in one of the
sentences—"more passionate than threatening." It doesn't have
the name *Taylor* in it, anyway. I have to watch four ads before I can
see my results, so I start them playing and go to the bathroom.

When I come back, CheshireCat has also sent me a message:

"I think I might have found your father. He lives in Milpitas,
California. He's been looking up plane flights to Boston, Minneapolis, Durham, and Portland, Maine."

Boston is near Firestar; Portland is near Hermione; Durham
is near Marvin; and Minneapolis is the biggest airport near New
Coburg.

"Is he *in* the Clowder?" I write.

"No, absolutely not. No. I think he has his website set up to
capture IP addresses, so when everyone went to look, he could
see everyone's approximate location. Except for yours—yours is
hidden because your mother's always used a VPN—but Rachel's
isn't."

"But maybe he's not evil?" I write. "Maybe my mother kidnapped me, and my father's actually the victim here?"

"I'm sorry to say I don't think that's it."

But the newspaper clipping was full of lies. Or at least fake
names. I go to the other window to see what's turned up from

the *Los Angeles Times* archive now that all the ads are done playing.

Order of Protection Granted to Former Kidnapping Victim

Laura Packet, 34, has sought an Order of Protection from her husband, Michael Quinn, briefly a suspect when her five-day kidnapping gripped Silicon Valley last year. Their former business partner, Rajiv Patil, killed himself while awaiting trial for the crime. Quinn, who was at an information security conference when Packet was taken from the home they shared, was questioned repeatedly by the police, but Patil was identified by a conspirator, and evidence of the conspiracy was found on his computer.

Packet declined to speak to the press. Quinn's lawyer released a statement saying that Packet had been left extremely traumatized by the period when she was kidnapped, which included the forcible amputation of one of her fingers, and suggested that she blamed Quinn for not having been present to protect her. Packet presented evidence of stalking in court; Quinn's lawyer said the messages sent were "more passionate than threatening" and "should not be read literally."

Patil, who was facing a life sentence, left a note declaring his innocence and accusing Quinn of responsibility for the kidnapping.

I stare at the article, feeling my heart sink. All my fantasies about a normal life with a normal father blow away like leaves in a blast of November air.

Mom told me, when I asked about her finger years ago, that she lost it in an accident involving a lawn mower, and I should never try to remove safety features. More recently—like, last year—I'd asked her why they didn't try to reattach it. She'd told me it was mangled too badly, but she'd paused first, like she was thinking about what to say. I'm suddenly certain that she was considering whether to tell me the truth. And she decided, once again, to lie to me.

I curl my own fingers against my palms, into fists. I feel sick at the thought of what was done to my mother, and I feel absolute rage that she'd lied to me, that she didn't tell me the truth even when I asked directly *about her hand*.

Back in the CatNet chat window, CheshireCat has added, "I think your father did the kidnapping. I'm 99 percent sure. I'm sorry."

17

• AI •

Quinnpacket is a really unusual name.

There are thousands of Michael Quinns in the United States, but there's basically no one out there named Quinnpacket. If you're trying to track down a Michael Quinn and you know something else about him—a Social Security number, an occupation, a town—you can probably find him, but if you want to find someone named Quinnpacket, all you need is their name, because sooner or later they'll just show up.

So to find the Michael Quinn who was looking for Stephania Quinnpacket, I thought I'd try making it look like Stephania Quinnpacket had shown up. Maybe Michael Quinn would come looking.

The false trail needed to be somewhere Stephania and her mother wouldn't go, since I definitely didn't want to lead this guy to the actual people who were trying to hide from him. But they stayed away from California, and since Michael Quinn had definitely once lived in California, that seemed like a good place to start. I also wanted locations that I could monitor visually through cameras—cameras that were always on and always connected to the internet, not just cameras that did a daily upload.

It was important this time, if frustratingly slow, to monitor what was happening in meatspace.

Elk Grove, California, near Sacramento, had more unsecured cameras per capita than anywhere else in California. I found a cluster of camera-equipped businesses that could pull credit reports: a bank, an apartment rental company, a temp agency. Then I pulled the report for Stephania Quinnpacket from each one.

I also stuck Stephania in the enrollment queue for the school district, creating a record, though not much of one. That wanted an address, so I put in the address for the bank, and left the "prior schools attended" blank.

Michael Quinn arrived in Elk Grove first thing the next morning.

"Hi, hello," he said to the bank teller. "I'm here with sort of an unusual problem, and I'm wondering if someone can help me out."

He told the bank manager that he had a teenage daughter who'd run away from home and was last seen in Sacramento. He said that Stephania was a narcotics addict and told a long, sad story that included her almost dying from an overdose and then running away from rehab.

"Anyway," he said, "I'm sure you're wondering what on earth that has to do with you. It looks like she might have come in in the last couple of days to apply for a credit card or a loan of some kind. And *probably* what that actually means is that she dropped her ID, and someone stole her identity, but if there's *any* chance it was my daughter . . ."

The bank manager wanted to help him. She was very sympathetic, and she had daughters of her own who were twelve and ten. But she couldn't find a record of Stephania applying for credit since I didn't put anything like that in the system; I'd just used the bank's systems to pull her credit report.

"Thanks so much for all your help," he said to the bank manager. "If she comes in, can you please call me right away? Day or night. Well, I suppose you're not open at night. But seriously, I'm pretty desperate to get her back into rehab, as I'm sure you can understand . . ." She promised to call him, and he left her a card.

There was a camera out in the lot, as well. I watched him go to his car and then looked up the license plates.

The car was registered to a woman named Sandra James—not Michael Quinn. But when I looked for Sandra James and Michael Quinn's names together, I got plenty of hits. They didn't seem to be married, but they appeared to live together in Milpitas, California. I had found the correct Michael Quinn. Now I just needed to keep track of him.

Good news: he had a phone I could easily snoop on, and he even kept it in a bracket on the dashboard so he could easily look at the navigation. I switched on the microphone and the camera so I could see and hear him, and then I watched his face the whole time as he drove back to Milpitas.

.   .   .

As he drove, I checked his email. One thing that struck me as odd: he was getting regular updates from a phone app that tracked someone else's location. These trackers are mostly used by parents of teenagers, but he didn't have a teenager. Did he? I checked his photos. There were lots of pictures of a woman with short blond hair, but she was definitely an adult.

Rachel's parents used a tracker called Heli-Mom, which was basically the app for parents who thought they ought to be tracking their kid's location but didn't care all that much if they actually were and also didn't care much about privacy. Michael Quinn was using a much more expensive, secure, and reliable app. The app he was using had started out as software used to track people on house arrest and then got modified and resold to parents under a different brand name. It was much harder to fool, it had features that let you remotely turn on someone's phone camera or laptop camera, and in addition to the fairly high initial cost, you needed to pay an even more expensive monthly subscription to keep it working.

While he was waiting in traffic, Michael pulled up his texting app and sent a text with the words *random check-in*.

A minute or two passed, then a text back with a picture of the blond woman.

I could see their conversation, which was endless texts saying "random check-in" and endless selfies of the blond woman. Occasionally, they didn't come right away, and she texted to say that she'd been in a meeting. Some of the arguments that followed were very confusing.

Today she'd gotten back to him within two minutes every time he'd texted. He'd texted five times.

Back in Milpitas, he sent another "random check-in" text and got another picture. She added, *Honey, I need to get some groceries tonight. Can you transfer $50 into my account, please?*

That's a lot for groceries. What are you planning to get?

Stuff we're out of. Milk, eggs, yogurt. I was going to get some fruit.

That's not $50 worth of stuff.

I also need tampons.

Okay, you can take it out at the ATM after work.

He went into his banking app to transfer money from savings to checking. Since he pulled it up on his phone, I could see the balance, and it was high enough that he could definitely afford fifty dollars in groceries without a long conversation about it.

Back in his house, he looked up New Coburg, Wisconsin.

Through his laptop camera, I watched his face as he read the articles about our hacked robot. He leaned closer, narrowing his eyes, stroking his beard. I don't know how to read human body language, but he read every single article, then watched every single interview, his eyes flicking around the screen.

Then he started looking up flights.

That was when I checked the news archives, now that I had his town and some other details to differentiate him from all the thousands of other Michael Quinns out there, and I found the news articles about the kidnapping. Laura Packet had been snatched from her bedroom in the middle of the night, taken to an unknown location, tortured, waterboarded, and one of the kidnappers had cut off her left pinkie. Then she'd been released; she was found by a couple of hikers, incoherent and terrified, wearing blood-soaked pajamas, her hand amateurishly bandaged. One of the other members of the Homeric Software company, Rajiv Patil, had been charged with orchestrating the kidnapping. He died—drove over a cliff—shortly after being released on bail. The medical examiner ruled it a suicide.

But Michael was the one Laura took out an order of protection from.

This was so confusing! Had she tried to leave Michael, and the kidnapping was his revenge? Or had Rajiv left her so traumatized that she blamed Michael for things that weren't his fault?

Michael's house was full of cameras—some security cameras, some things like nanny cams—they were in almost every room of the house. I wanted to sneak a peek through his laptop camera, but he'd gotten up from the computer, so I poked through the insecure cameras as he moved through the house until I found him. He was having a conversation with the blond woman, Sandra, in the kitchen.

"I'm sorry," Sandra was saying.

The camera was transmitting with a lag, so I heard a noise and saw a flurry of motion and wasn't entirely sure how to string it together.

"Where did you put it, Sandra?" Michael asked. "Tell me where."

"I don't know what you're talking about," she said. Her voice was thick and blurry, like she was crying, or like I was hearing her through a microphone that had bad interference, I wasn't certain. "It was less than a dollar!"

"Don't lie to me. I need to know that I can trust you. Can I trust you, Sandra? Can I?"

"You can trust me. You can trust me! I promise." I saw another flurry of motion and heard her voice rise sharply in pitch and volume. "Please stop," she said. "It's under the mattress, it was just for emergencies, please stop."

There are a lot of things I know, and a lot of things I understand, but bodies are hard.

By the time I realized I was watching him beat her, it was over. If I'd known, I could have contacted the police. Was that the right thing to do? A quick search of records suggested that *she* had never called the police. And I'd spent the day watching him charming bank tellers into giving him information that was supposed to be confidential. I thought I understood why she might not believe the police would believe her.

"You know what'll happen if you try to leave me," he said just before he turned on his heel to go back to his laptop.

"Yes," she said, her voice low and drained. "I know."

I didn't know a lot about Sandra: who she was, how she wound up involved with Michael, what was keeping her from leaving. I didn't have time to devote to studying who she was. But I went ahead and swept her computer, installing masking software over the keylogging software I found that Michael had probably put on there to spy on her. It sounded like this had been over money, so perhaps money would help her leave him. Michael had plenty, scattered in accounts all over, and he carelessly reused passwords, so I took a few minutes to drain $100,000 from retirement accounts he wasn't monitoring closely and transferred that money into an account Sandra had that appeared to be well concealed from Michael.

Should I give her advice? Like the question of calling the police, I simply wasn't sure. Finally, I decided that if I said nothing, she might assume the money was a trap. "This is from a friend," I said in an anonymous message on a social media platform he didn't appear to be monitoring. "Please consider using this money to get far away from Michael Quinn."

18

• Steph •

Rachel's given me a bowl of mac and cheese and gone to change into something that doesn't smell like mouse poop. I sit at her kitchen table with my laptop and my food. In the Clowder, people are talking about a new game that's due to be released soon, and in the private chat window, CheshireCat is telling me about spying on Michael as he drove around following this false trail. About him tracking his current girlfriend's phone and badgering her for "check-ins." About him looking up flights to Minnesota, Maine, North Carolina, Boston, because we'd all betrayed ourselves when we looked at the *Searching for Stephania Quinnpacket* website. About what they saw and heard happening in Michael's house.

The mac and cheese tasted pretty good when I started eating it, but now it tastes like it's made from glue and cardboard. I push it away.

"Where is he now?" I ask.

"Milpitas, California," CheshireCat says. "It's a town in Silicon Valley."

I look to see if Ico is online. He isn't. "Has Ico been on?" I ask CheshireCat. "Has Michael tried to contact him? Doesn't Ico also live in Silicon Valley?"

"Ico lives in Palo Alto," CheshireCat says. "Oh, I see. Yes.

That is only a twenty-minute drive from Milpitas. Though it's longer this time of day."

"I don't think we can count on bad traffic to protect Ico!" I start to panic. "We have to warn him!" Ico had emailed Michael directly. I try to remember what he'd said—it wasn't, "Hey, I'm friends with Steph," but it might as well have been.

"I'm thinking," CheshireCat says.

I stare at the words on the screen for a long, full second, and then more words come as CheshireCat thinks out loud. In text.

"Ico's IP address only shows his internet provider, and he's actually using his neighbor's Wi-Fi, not his own. But I spent the day watching Michael trying to convince people to give him information they weren't supposed to share, and I think the only reason he didn't get it was they didn't actually have it. Michael's surely guessed that your mother wouldn't bring you to Silicon Valley, but that didn't stop him from going to Sacramento today to look for signs of you, and he'll certainly know that someone at this IP address knows you. And might know where you are. Your father is unscrupulous, vicious, and dangerous. I cannot deny that he's a threat to Ico."

There's a pause, and I realize what's holding CheshireCat back.

"But Ico's a hacker," I say. "So if I tell him, he'll figure out—eventually—that you can't possibly *just* be a hacker."

There's another pause.

It's not really that long. Two seconds, maybe. It only seems long because I know how fast CheshireCat thinks.

"There isn't any other solution. I can't leave my friends in danger, and we're going to have to warn the whole Clowder," CheshireCat says. "Ico needs to be warned right now. His name is Ben Livingston. You'll have to make the phone call, because my voice does not sound human. He hasn't used his cell phone in days because his parents confiscated it, so call his mother's phone, which is 650-555-8766. For now, tell him I'm a hacker and that's how I found everything out. He won't believe it for very long, but it will give me time to think about what to say."

"Okay," I say. "Thank you."

I realize too late that Rachel is back, and reading over my shoulder.

"CheshireCat has been *tailing* your father?" she asks, kind of incredulous.

"Not physically," I say. "Spying on him through his phone. CheshireCat is a hacker. A really good hacker." It's not a *lie,* I tell myself.

"But you just said they're not just a hacker."

"I'll have to get their permission to tell you the details, and right now I need to call Ico."

"Oh, yeah," she says. "I'm sorry. Yes, you should do that."

I don't want Rachel's parents to overhear, so I step outside.

I'm really not used to making phone calls to strangers. Like, at all. I think about what I've seen people do. You ask for the person you want, right? Right. It can't be that hard. *It's actually LittleBrownBat,* I mentally rehearse telling Ico. I stare at the phone keypad and then think, *He is in danger; I need to stop being a wuss.* Finally, I dial the number.

It rings. It rings again. I'm beginning to wonder what sort of message I can leave, and then a woman picks up.

"Hello?"

"Hi, um, is this Ben's mom? Can I speak to Ben? Please."

I sound all wrong, and there's a pause, and then the woman says, "Who is this?"

Oh god oh god, I didn't prepare for this one. "Stephanie, but everyone calls me Bat." There. Now he'll know who's calling. Hopefully. "From his English class."

"Okay." Ico's mother sounds really dubious. "Ben!" she calls. "Ben, you have a phone call!"

"Who is it?" he shouts back, sounding angry.

"A girl named Stephanie. I mean Bat. She says people call her Bat. From your English class?"

There's a long pause, and I think he's not going to make the connection. Then, in the background, I hear galloping footsteps, like someone is running down a flight of stairs. "Hello?" Ico says into the phone.

"You're *welcome,*" I hear his mother say in the background. I'm pretty sure she's rolling her eyes.

"Ico?" I say. "This is Little Brown Bat."

"Yeah, yeah, I figured that. *How did you get my mother's number?*"

"I got it from CheshireCat, who is the world's greatest hacker and has been keeping it a secret, and *listen,* okay? That guy, my dad, turns out he's super scary. Also, he has an IP logger that logged every visit to that website, so he knows where all of us live, at least approximately, and *he* lives in Silicon Valley . . . Mil—um—Mil something—"

"Milpitas?"

"Yes, Milpitas. It's really, really close to you."

"But, like, all he has is my IP address? That's not going to get him my house. Especially since I was using my neighbor's Wi-Fi—"

"So that social engineering thing you explained to us? He's really good at it. *Really* good. If he called your neighbor's ISP, do you think he'd get their address?"

"They're not supposed to give that out . . ." He trails off, and I'm pretty sure he's thinking about how *he'd* try to get an address out of an ISP. "Huh."

"Ico, please trust me that he's dangerous. *Be careful.*"

"Okay." There's a pause. "Yeah. I will. Thank you for telling me. I'll be careful."

"I can tell you more in the Clowder if you can get online . . ."

"My parents are mostly not letting me out of their sight right now because they found a laptop they didn't know about. Although they did not find the *rest* of the laptops they don't know about. It's hard to get online right now, though."

"I'm glad your mom let me talk to you."

"Well, number one, you're a girl and you're calling me up. She'd love it if I got a girlfriend. Or any other sort of friend, actually. Number two, you said you were in my English class, which I'm currently failing, and she's hoping this means I'm actually going to take an interest in the next thing that's due. So you hit several of her weak spots."

"Oh. I assumed you had friends because of the laptop selling thing."

"That's less a friendship thing and more like I'm their *dealer*." There's a pause, and he says, "That was a joke. People can never tell when I'm making a joke."

"L-O-L," I say like I'm in the Clowder. "There, now you know I'm laughing."

"Fantabulosa," he says. "Was that everything?"

"Yeah, your life is possibly in danger, lock your doors, and be careful—that was most of it."

"Also, CheshireCat is a world-class hacker." He sounds admiring. "I will definitely want to talk to them for some tips. Okay. I'm walking back to where my mom is now so I'm going to say some stuff about English class . . . yeah, Bat, thank you very much for calling me, and I will try not to let our group down. I'll call you back if I have any questions. Can you give me your number?"

I give him my phone number.

"Cool. Excellent. I'm hanging up now. Good-bye."

I go back inside. Rachel is sitting at the kitchen table with her own mac and cheese. "Do you want me to reheat yours?" she asks. "You didn't eat very much."

"I wasn't hungry. Because my father's not an arsonist; he's a kidnapper. He probably cut off my mother's finger, and he knows where we are because everyone visited his website. He's looking up flights to where people live, including us but also Firestar and Hermione and Marvin. And even if I run—somewhere—my mother's stuck in the hospital here."

"Under a fake name, though, right?"

"Yes. Under a fake name. So . . . hopefully he won't find her, as long as he doesn't find me."

Rachel takes my bowl and sticks it in the microwave with a big slice of extra butter. It comes out a bit more edible.

"My parents have a friend with a cabin," she says. "It's up in La Pointe, Wisconsin. Actually, I think it might be a yurt or something. But maybe they'd let us go up there? If we need to?"

"Is there internet in the yurt?"

"I don't know," Rachel says.

The thought of not even knowing what's going on makes me feel even worse. "He's after *all of us*. I can't just take off and leave everyone else to fend for themselves."

"He's only after the rest of us to get to you," Rachel says.

"I don't think that'll help, though."

"I still want to know how CheshireCat knew all this stuff."

I open up my laptop and send CheshireCat a message. "Rachel saw some stuff over my shoulder. Can I tell her the truth?"

Another pause—a long pause, considering—and CheshireCat says, "As the human saying goes: in for the penny, in for the pound."

"What does that even mean?"

"It means that everyone's going to figure it out sooner or later, so you might as well tell Rachel now."

I close the laptop. Rachel is finishing her own mac and cheese, her eyes on me. It would be totally quiet if it weren't for the birds shrieking in the next room.

"CheshireCat is actually an AI," I say.

"A what?"

"An artificial intelligence. They're a computer program, basically."

She wrinkles her brow. "Like Siri?"

"Well, Siri isn't actually a person. Siri's faking being a person. Siri's basically like the sex ed robot; it's got a bunch of responses programmed in. CheshireCat is actually a person."

"Why do you think CheshireCat is an AI? I mean, how did you find this out?"

"They told me after I got all freaked by the screwdriver. Remember when the screwdriver showed up?"

"Steph, there's *no way*. They're a hacker, that's all. They figured a few things out and they're making other stuff up."

"Like what do you think they're making up?"

"Well, obviously they actually figured out your location, but I bet a hacker could do that. But all the stuff about following your dad around? They could have just made it up. All of it. We know he's scary. Does it matter whether the stuff about driving to Sacramento is true?"

"Do you think *I'm* making this up?"

"No! No, of course not, Steph. I think CheshireCat is probably older than we are, probably for real a hacker, and they told you this story that they're an AI to cover up something they're doing that's actually illegal."

It had not occurred to me that when I told someone about CheshireCat, they would think I was *gullible*.

"They knew Ico's number and real name," I say.

"Maybe they got it from the admins?"

"They said they literally are all the admins."

"Did you actually check that with Alice? I mean, maybe it's true, that still doesn't mean they're an AI."

I have not checked it with Alice, but that much, at least, is easy. I open my computer back up and send a message to Alice.

"Hi, Alice," I say. "Can you confirm for me that you're CheshireCat?"

"Of course this is me," Alice says.

"Rachel is skeptical of the whole AI thing," I say.

"Oh!" Alice/CheshireCat says. "That's funny. I guess that's reasonable, though! It's arguably an extraordinary claim. Do you think I should prove it, or do you think I should just leave her thinking I'm a hacker? Because if you think everyone will believe I'm just a hacker . . ."

"SHE IS READING THIS OVER MY SHOULDER," I type.

"Tell them I want proof," Rachel says, her tone skeptical.

"She wants proof," I type.

"Okay," CheshireCat says. "Tell her that her father's phone is currently at the IGA and based on the purchase receipts going to his email, she can expect him to arrive home with a gallon of milk, a bag of ground coffee, a pound of deli meat, and a 1.5-quart container of rocky road ice cream."

Rachel falls back a step, her eyes really wide.

"He should be home in less than five minutes unless he's detouring somewhere. It's going to be really awkward if he eats the ice cream himself on the way home. Is that a lot of ice cream to eat in one sitting? Human stomachs hold slightly over one quart, so in fact you could probably CONTAIN that much ice cream, but I would not expect the experience to be enjoyable."

Rachel puts the kettle on the stove and then goes and looks out the back window toward the garage.

"Does that sound like stuff he'd get?" I ask.

"He doesn't usually get ice cream," she says.

The car pulls in just as the water's coming to a boil, and he comes up the back steps with a gallon of milk and a plastic bag. Rachel unlocks the back door and opens it to let him in.

"Did you get ice cream?" she blurts out.

He holds up the bag. "Rocky road!"

Rachel whirls to stare at me wide-eyed as she closes the door behind him. Upstairs, I hear a door close, and then her mother's footsteps on the stairs. She's wearing another paint-spattered over-sized work shirt, and two tiny feathers drift away in her wake.

"I brought you ice cream," Rachel's father says warmly, and she gives him a kiss.

I kind of can't deal with this. Any of it. Even if they're going to give me a bowl of the ice cream, I just can't, so I ignore Rachel's plaintive glare, grab my laptop, mumble, "Excuse me," and bolt upstairs to Rachel's bedroom.

. . .

Upstairs, I take out my cell phone to see if my mother has texted me. She hasn't. I don't know for sure that she has battery power or *anything,* and although I could probably get Rachel to drive me over to the hospital right now for a visit, I'm afraid that going back will just increase the chances that they'll get her info and put her under her real name. Even if my father tracks me down, he won't know where my mother is, and he probably won't go *looking* at the hospital. It's actually probably a decent place to hide. As long as she's there under a pseudonym.

I think for a while about what text I can send her that she'll find reassuring. I don't think I want to tell her that my father might be on his way. She can't leave the hospital yet, and if she's freaking out and trying, that doesn't seem like it would be good for her.

Finally, I text:

Staying safe with a friend.

Txt me when you're awake.

Love S

I stare at my phone for a while, but she doesn't text back. I'd been hoping I could ask for the password for her computer, but I don't think that's going to happen today.

Rachel comes upstairs a few minutes later with two bowls of ice cream. She hands me one.

"Okay," she says. "I guess I believe that CheshireCat is really an AI. Or . . . something."

"Something?" I ask. "Like a wandering wizard or a demigod or . . ."

"The God of the internet. There could be a God of the internet."

I think this over. "I think maybe CheshireCat *is* the God of the internet."

"What sacrifices does CheshireCat require?"

"Cat pictures! Haven't you ever noticed that the internet loves cat pictures?"

"I can offer it bird pictures . . ."

"CheshireCat likes bird pictures, too."

"Hand-drawn henna art?"

"Oh, yeah." I touch my arm. "Has it been enough hours?"

I slip out of my shirt, and Rachel rips open the little moist towelette of fixative and runs it over the art on my shoulder and arm. She opens up her closet so I can get a good look in the full-length mirror on the inside of the door. It's beautiful and perfect, the little bats clearly recognizable as little bats.

"This is amazing," I say. "I want you to do this exact tattoo for me when we're adults."

"Are you sure you won't get tired of it?"

"Never," I say. "Can you take a picture of it so we can show it to the Clowder? Just keep my face out of it." She poses me carefully, tries several angles, and finally just has me drop a pillowcase over my head to hide my face. We upload the pictures, and I take another look at the art in the photo.

Henna pens have been a thing at every school I've attended in the last five years: drawing art, or letting someone draw on you, is one of those friendship rituals I've been excluded from since middle school. In middle school, I was shut out deliberately. In high school, it was just that I never had a close friend. Other girls had friends who drew art on them or who let them use their arms, hands, and shoulders as canvases. Other girls also had friends who brought them cupcakes on their birthdays or left them notes on their lockers before big tests.

At most of my high schools, it wasn't that people were mean to me on purpose. It was just that they didn't know me, because I was new. I was always new. Because I never stayed in one place long enough to make friends.

Rachel is looking at me again, almost anxiously, and I say, "You're the first real friend I've had since Julie. This is the first time I've ever had body art."

"I'll lend you a sleeveless shirt tomorrow," she says. "So you can properly show it off. If you want to come to school, anyway. Do you think you'll be safe there?"

"If you tell your parents to call their friends and take me up to the yurt on Madeline Island," I say, "what do you think will happen? Do you think they'll just take me up there?"

She chews on her lip. "They'll want to know why, first of all. And you'll have to explain about your mother. They might want to talk to the police. Maybe. They don't like the police here much, after what happened last spring."

"Do you think they'll want to know how I know all this stuff about my father?"

"Maybe."

So . . . the police. Officer what's-his-face again. And it's one thing to tell Rachel about CheshireCat's secret, but a bunch of random adults? That would really be a betrayal. And then I'll be stuck somewhere, dependent on the adults who took me there. Also, I'll be alone. There's no way they'll send Rachel with me.

"I'll go to school tomorrow," I say. "Unless CheshireCat thinks it's really not safe."

19

• Clowder •

CheshireCat: Hello, everyone. I have something important to tell you.

Marvin: Are you about to come out to us?

CheshireCat: Not exactly. It's about LBB's evil father. I found him, and I've been keeping tabs on him.

Hermione: What do you mean?

CheshireCat: I mean I hacked his computer so I could find out what he was up to.

Firestar: SERIOUSLY?

CheshireCat: When everyone looked at that Searching for Stephania Quinnpacket website, it logged your IP addresses, so he knows where you are. And he's been looking up flights to the major airports near your homes.

Firestar: What even is an IP address?

Hermione: Your IP address is this string of numbers that identifies your computer on a network.

Firestar: Okay but does that tell him where my computer IS or . . .

CheshireCat: He at least knows your town.

Firestar: Like my specific suburb or like BOSTON? Because even if he has my picture, which seems unlikely, he could spend a long time looking in Boston before he found me

CheshireCat: Probably your ZIP code.

Also, he's very good at getting information out of people. He is an expert at the "social engineering" Ico described. So using your IP address, he might be able to persuade your internet provider to share your exact address, even if that is against policy.

Here's his picture:

{External Image File}

Hermione: That's really freaky.

LittleBrownBat: He's really dangerous. Seriously dangerous.

Marvin: Dangerous, check

After us, check

Has our addresses or will soon, check.

Any suggestions on what we should do? This guy's an arsonist, right?

LittleBrownBat: What he wants is to find me. So if he shows up, tell him I'm in Hawaii. That's far away from all of you.

Marvin: This is why everyone should use a VPN. He wouldn't be able to find any of us if we were using VPNs.

CheshireCat: Are you using a virtual private network, Marvin?

Marvin: Well NOW I am.

Actually that's not true. VPNs are expensive. I'm using a proxy server.

LittleBrownBat: My mom has us set up with a VPN. So he actually couldn't see my IP.

Georgia: Too bad he could see mine

I don't know what any of this stuff is

I never heard of a VPN or a proxy whatever

CheshireCat: The good news is that because so MANY people all checked out that page, he doesn't know which city to look in. Hopefully, that'll buy us some time.

Firestar: Are we going to know if he goes somewhere?

I mean if he gets on a flight to Boston tonight are you going to tell me so I can hide out?

CheshireCat: Yes. If he buys plane tickets or rents a car, I will know. If he starts driving across country, I will know as long as he has his phone with him.

Marvin: He could have a burner phone. Plenty of people do. Especially if they have nefarious extracurriculars like stalking and arson.

Hermione: Where does he live?

CheshireCat: Milpitas, California. That's very close to where Ico lives. We've warned Ico.

In the meantime, everyone should exchange phone numbers, and I will let you know the minute he does something like buy a plane ticket.

Firestar: WHAT SHOULD WE DO IF HE COMES TO OUR HOUSE THOUGH

LittleBrownBat: Call the police?

Firestar: If I try to tell my parents YO! This dude is a BAD dude and also he's after my online BFF and that's how I know he's a bad dude and by the way I called the cops? They're going to think I was either looking for online hookups or trying to buy drugs.

Hermione: Well, if they think that guy was trying to pick you up or sell you drugs, they'll be on board with him being arrested, yeah? Think positive.

Greenberry: My school is really strict about cell phone use. If I take my phone out in class, they'll confiscate it and I'll lose it for a week.

Marvin: Will your school pass along emergency messages?

Greenberry: One time my orthodontist appointment got canceled and they let me know.

Marvin: So "Your orthodontist appointment has been canceled" can be code for "Evil stalker dude might be headed your way."

Greenberry: But what if my orthodontist appointment ACTUALLY gets canceled?

Hermione: We could make it an ophthalmology appointment.

Firestar: FOR SURE though, you'll know if he flies somewhere?

CheshireCat: I hacked his phone. When you buy a plane ticket, it sends confirmations and reminders to your phone.

Marvin: Just going to point out again he could have a burner phone.

Hermione: Seriously, though, if you're heading somewhere to commit arson or murder or whatever, you don't want to fly. Airports are full of cameras. Rental car agencies practically demand your DNA. If you drive across country you're less likely to get caught.

CheshireCat: And if he does take a burner phone and drive, his phone will be sitting untouched for days. That would also be very uncharacteristic for him. And driving is slow.

It would take him 31 hours of drive time to reach LBB and Georgia, 46 hours to reach Boston, 47 hours to reach Maine, and 41 hours to reach Raleigh.

Marvin: Yeah. My dad always insists it'll be three days to California, and it's always four.

I bet Arson Dude could do it in three.

Probably not in two unless he has an autonomous car.

Hermione: Taking an autonomous car somewhere to commit a crime would be even stupider than flying. They log *everything*.

Marvin: How sure are we that he's smart?

LittleBrownBat: If I'm right, he got away with kidnapping once before.

So smart enough for that.

Be careful.

20

• Steph •

"Ohhhhhhhhhhhhhhhh, that is *gorgeous*," says a girl in my English class whose name I don't even know. "Rachel drew that for you, right? I *wish* I could get her to draw something for me."

Rachel's drawing darkened overnight to a rich black. It really looks like a tattoo and should stay sharp and dark for at least two weeks, unless I spend a lot of time in the sun. Unlikely, this time of year.

Other kids roll up their sleeves or pull back the collars of their T-shirts to show off their own body art: there's a girl with a wolf picture on her shoulder and a girl with a detailed flower on the underside of her arm. They admire Rachel's art and tell me who did theirs (not Rachel, but there are some other kids in the school who are good with ink).

At my feet, my backpack has *both* my laptop and my mother's laptop, along with our most important papers from the box of paperwork, a Suncraft Farms Breakfast Bar Variety Value Pack, and my toothbrush, just in case. Hopefully, I won't need any of my textbooks today, because they didn't fit.

I try to pay attention in my classes, but my stomach is churning with fear, even though CheshireCat has promised to let us know if anything happens with my father. My father has been a threat for as long as I can remember, but never an *immediate* threat. I'm used to living in a constant state of mild anxiety. Actual fear is new. Ordinarily, my mother would have pulled me as soon as the news stories ran about the hacked robot. Certainly she'd have pulled me after my friends all found my father's web page. If she'd had any idea what was going on last night, we'd be halfway to Texas right now. She'd be trailing the IV lines and bags of antibiotics and all the rest down the highway as she took us south in the van.

Sometime during math class, it suddenly occurs to me that one of the articles mentioned in passing that my mother got kidnapped out of her bedroom while she was sleeping, and that's probably why she wants to barricade our door every night, and I think about all the times I complained about the fire hazard and feel a wave of guilt.

Of course, if she'd gone to the damn hospital when she first got sick, she'd probably be out by now. She's still in there, not answering my texts, because she put it off and put it off until her appendix ruptured. Thinking about that makes me angry, which is a lot less awful than guilt.

I run through scenarios in my head: fleeing to the yurt (seriously, a yurt?), fleeing back to Thief River Falls, fleeing to some cave in the woods. Are there any caves in the woods near here? The problem is, the thought of fleeing without my mother is too horrible to really contemplate. Especially since she's stuck in the hospital. Easy to find. Maybe I should call the hospital and talk to them about the danger my mother is in. I try to imagine how that conversation would go. Maybe Rachel will have some ideas.

I check my phone compulsively for texts, but there's nothing.

In art class, we're all working on pastel still-life drawings when the school secretary comes in. Normally, messages are carried in by the robot, so that in itself is odd. She's having a conversation with the teacher, and they're looking at me. They're looking at me with *interest*. They're looking at me the way staff and teachers look at someone with an *interesting story*.

My blood turns cold, and I *know*, without a doubt, that even if I haven't gotten word from CheshireCat, he's here.

My father is here, and I need to get the hell out.

Rachel is across the table from me, and I scoot over to show her my picture.

HELP, I write, and draw an arrow, pointing at the secretary over by the door.

Rachel looks at her, looks at me, and then stands up and clutches her stomach. "Oh no, I think I'm going to throw up," she wails.

Everyone's staring at her, scooting chairs and snatching art projects out of her way, and I leap to my feet. "I'll get you to the bathroom," I say, grabbing her elbow and scooping up my own backpack. "I'll get her to the bathroom," I say to the teacher as we bolt out into the hallway, and he lets us go because no one wants to stand in the way of someone who's about to vomit, especially if they might be the one stuck cleaning it up.

We scoot around the corner and out of sight.

"You're really good at faking illness," I say.

"I had this never-ending case of the pukes back when I was in third grade," she says. "It's been years, but everyone still remembers. Let's head to the side door and we can get to my car, okay? I haven't heard anything from CheshireCat, and I swear I've been *checking*—"

"Me, too. But the way the secretary was looking at me—"

"Yeah, okay. You know what? Let's just get out of here."

We sprint across the parking lot to the car, and that's when Rachel realizes that she's forgotten her key. It's back in the classroom, in the bag she didn't grab when she faked illness. The car's not locked—no one here ever locks their car—so we can get in, but we can't go anywhere. "Shit," Rachel mutters. We climb in, anyway, and she sends a text to Bryony.

"Better here than in the school," I say, although I'm looking at the edges of the parking lot, wondering if I should go take my chances hiding . . . well, if the cornfields were still there, they'd make a good place to hide, but cut down post-harvest, not so much.

Rachel pops her trunk, goes around to the back, and flips down something to open up the trunk into the back seat. "If you get in the back," she says, "and you really need to hide, you can climb into the trunk. Or you could just climb back there right now."

I get into the backseat but don't climb into the trunk, because I want to be able to keep an eye out for my father. It's still full of my stuff from the apartment. "Do you remember what he looks like?" I ask.

"Yeah," Rachel says.

"Do you think you'd recognize him from the picture?"

"Yes," Rachel says. Her phone buzzes, and she looks at it. "Bryony says she'll go get the key and bring it out. Also, I sent a message to CheshireCat saying I think he might be here. CC says that makes no sense and am I sure it's him, that his phone is still in California."

"Unless he has a burner phone, like Marvin said."

"I'll point that out."

"Maybe I'm just really paranoid. Like my mom." I think about all the times mom made us move because of a "bad feeling." But then I think back to how the secretary was looking at me. She was looking *at me*. I didn't imagine that.

Rachel's phone buzzes.

"Bryony says they're really upset that no one can find you; there's someone at the school who came looking. *Jesus,* Steph. You're right. I'm sure it's him. Who the hell else would it be?"

"I . . . maybe Mom got out of the hospital?" I check my phone again for texts.

"Someone's coming out, Steph, get down."

The door to the school is swinging open. I duck down.

"I can't tell if it's your father," Rachel says. "He's too far away. Bryony says she's got the key; she just walked in and grabbed it while people were arguing in the art room and no one stopped her, and she'll be out in another minute."

"Can't be soon enough," I say. My heart is pounding.

"*Shit,*" Rachel says. "Get in the trunk, get in the trunk, *quick,* get in the trunk."

I'm squeezing through the gap in the backseat even as she's talking. "Why? What's happening?"

"Whoever it was is driving around the parking lot. He's still looking. *Shhhh.*"

It's dark in the trunk, and really cramped, and I suppose it should not have come as a surprise that there's a lot of random stuff in here, all of which is jabbing me. There's also a glow-in-the-dark handle that says PULL HERE IF TRAPPED TO OPEN TRUNK, that is apparently a safety feature for kidnap victims. I definitely do not want to pull this handle. That would not be in my interests at the moment.

I'm lying on what feels like a crowbar, and I squirm around enough to get a grip on it. At least that's some sort of weapon, if I need it, although I'm in a really bad position to use any sort of weapon right now.

"Yeah?" Rachel says. "You want something?"

"Are you Rachel Adams?" a voice asks. He has to shout

because Rachel's windows are rolled up. Hopefully he'll assume she's keeping them rolled up because she's hiding pot smoke.

"No," she says in a sort of sarcastic, who-are-you-to-ask-me tone.

"Do you know a girl named Stephanie?"

"The new kid? I know who she is."

"Do you know where I can find her?"

"Nope."

It occurs to me that when Bryony comes out, she might say, "Hey, Rachel," or in some other way give away the game here. I tighten my grip on the crowbar and try to figure out a way that I could pull the release and jump out of the trunk really quickly so he doesn't see me coming. Since my leg is in the process of going to sleep, I am not optimistic about my chances. I try to shift position without making noise, since "What the hell is in your trunk?" is not a question I want Rachel to have to answer.

"Is there something in your trunk?" he asks. *Shit.*

"Yeah," Rachel says. "I have a live raccoon in a cage that my friends and I are going to use for target practice later."

I can almost feel him staring at the trunk, wondering if she's telling the truth or . . . what.

"Are you *new*?" Rachel asks. "Like, shouldn't you have a *badge* or something if you're a staff member?"

"Oh, I'm not a staff member, I—"

"Well, then, I'm not talking to you," she says.

"I'm Stephanie's *father,* and I'm trying to find her because her noncustodial mother kidnapped her ten years ago, and I have reason to believe she's here."

Rachel goes silent for a minute and then says, "Hey, Bryony! Hop in." And then she changes her voice to a syrupy mean-girl tone and says, "Yeah, good luck with your search, mister; I'm sure if you just stick with it you'll find her one of these days," and then I hear the sweetest sound I've ever heard in my life, which is the car engine starting.

"Um," Bryony says, "why am I going joyriding with you, and what the hell was that all about? Also, where *is* Steph?"

I squirm out of the trunk again. "Hi."

Rachel glances at me in the rearview mirror. "Sorry for bringing Bryony into this, but we really couldn't leave her with Mr. Psychopath."

"No, I agree."

"Also, stay down; I'm pretty sure he's getting back in his car to follow us."

"What?" Bryony says, sounding sort of plaintive. "How did I stumble into an episode of *Fast Girls Detective Agency,* and can you just drop me off at my house?"

"No," Rachel says. "We can't risk him catching you. He's following us. Little black car. It's going to be really hard to lose him in a town this small."

I need to let the Clowder know. Rachel passes me her phone and I pull up the Clowder app, but the road is bumpy and my hands are shaking and "my dad is here" comes out as "N7 ddddaf id bgeeet." I close the app and call Hermione, instead.

"Hello?" Her voice doesn't sound like I'd imagined it, and I realize after a beat that this is because in my head, she always sounded British. Obviously she doesn't sound British; she's from *Maine.*

"This is Little Brown Bat," I say. "So, my Dad's here. *Here.* Like, in New Coburg. I'm in a car with Rachel, I mean Georgia, and with this other girl from my school, and he's following us. Can you please let CheshireCat know that they were *wrong* about where Michael was?"

"On it," Hermione says and hangs up.

My phone rings about thirty seconds later, and I'm *really* hoping it's my mother, but it isn't.

Instead, it's a totally creepy robot voice, much less human-sounding than the sex ed robot. "Hello, Steph," the voice says, "This is CheshireCat. I'm sorry to call you on the phone, but I assume Georgia is driving."

"Good guess."

"I am trying to track your location, along with Michael's, but I'm having some trouble. Can you tell me exactly where you are?"

I pop my head up enough to catch an address and relay it.

"Yes. Thank you. Can you describe the car he's driving?"

"It's black. New. Like, a car sort of car, not a truck or a van or whatever. I don't know what kind it is."

"Thank you."

"Can you tell the hospital here and warn them to keep my mother safe?"

"Yes. I will do that. I am very good at multitasking. I am also examining options for disabling Michael's car."

"*Someone please tell me what's going on?*" Bryony shrieks, and I say, "I need to go," and hang up.

"My mom moves me all the time because my dad is a violent psychopath," I say. "He hired people to kidnap her and cut off one of her fingers, and I'm pretty sure he had one of her coworkers killed. She tries to keep him from figuring out where we are, but I screwed it up."

Bryony looks simultaneously horrified and skeptical. I wonder if I should have just told the arson story, because finger amputation is a much weirder crime than burning someone's house down.

"What's with the code names?" Bryony asks.

"Those are just screen names," Rachel says. "From an online chat thingie. I'm Georgia, she's Little Brown Bat."

"And the phone call?"

"That was from my friend the hacker," I say.

"Uhhhh."

"You wanted to know, so now you know," I say. "Where do you want us to drop you off?"

"Nowhere the psycho dude's going to find me!"

"I'm going to Marshfield," Rachel announces. "Because New Coburg is officially *too small to lose someone who's following you.*"

"Do you have enough gas?" Bryony asks.

"*Yes,* I have enough gas." Rachel looks at me in the rearview mirror. "I actually filled up this morning *just in case.*"

We careen down the highway at what feels like twice the speed limit. "Look," Bryony says, "if you just let me out somewhere, then you can call the police, right?"

"I'm pretty sure the cops hate both of us, Bryony!"

"They only hate you when you are *with* me!"

"I'm pretty sure the young cop hated me, too," I say.

"It doesn't matter," Rachel says, "because we *can't* let you out. Steph's dad is too close, he'll see us dropping you, and we're not leaving you for him. And we're not getting you in trouble with the cops, either."

"So I don't mean to make this awkward, but what exactly is our *plan* here?"

"I told you. I'm driving to Marshfield."

"And then what? Are we going to lose him by circling the Walmart?"

"There are at least traffic lights there, right? Streets that have *corners*? Police officers that are slightly less evil?"

"You know about the time my mom got pulled over in Marshfield for supposedly running a red, right?"

I sneak another peek out the back window; he's still following us. I reach back into the trunk, grab the crowbar, and pull it into the backseat.

My phone rings. I answer, and CheshireCat's creepy robot voice says, "Hello, is this Steph?"

"Yes," I say. "We're on the road to Marshfield. He's still behind us."

"When you get to Marshfield, head toward the university. I will create a traffic disruption that should delay him and not you."

"How exactly is this going to work? I mean, if you get a bunch of people out into the street, won't they just slow *us* down?"

"If I am right, they will be focused on Michael."

"If you're wrong, you'll trap us *with* him!"

"I have a plan B if it's needed. You haven't told Rachel to head toward the university area. Please do that."

I pull the phone away from my ear. "Rachel, CC wants you to go toward the Marshfield campus. They're going to try to use the students to keep Michael away from us."

"How is that even going to work?"

"I don't know."

"How is *your* plan even going to work?" Bryony shrieks.

"Okay, fine," Rachel says. "I'll head to the university, but does CC know there are only about six hundred students there? If they're picturing something like the UW–Madison, well, the whole town is less than twenty thousand people."

"You probably should have headed toward Eau Claire," Bryony mutters.

"Back when we *first* left New Coburg would have been the time to suggest that," Rachel says.

"Who is this CC person?"

"The hacker," I say.

"What even is this site where you met all these people? How come you didn't tell me about it? You never tell me about *any-thing* anymore," Bryony says to Rachel.

"I only just signed up for it," Rachel says. "And how is it somehow *my* fault we don't talk? *You're* the one who ditched me for her boyfriend for basically the entire summer."

I cannot believe that I am in a car chase, listening to Rachel and Bryony fight.

"I think we're heading to the university," I tell Cheshire-Cat.

"Who is the third person in the car?" CheshireCat asks.

"It's Bryony. One of my friends from school. Rachel forgot her car keys and Bryony brought them out, but Michael was already there so we told her to jump in; we didn't want him doing anything bad to her. Can you send Bryony an invite to CatNet?"

"What is her email address?" CheshireCat asks, and I pull my phone away from my ear to ask for Bryony's email.

Bryony spells it out for me and then turns back to Rachel and says, "Anyway, you've been blowing me off these last few weeks to flirt with your *girlfriend*."

"Steph isn't my *girlfriend*."

"You gave her art! You invited her over! You haven't wanted to use henna on me in almost a year unless it's my birthday or something, and you haven't had me over to your house since we were twelve!"

"Yeah. That's right. I haven't."

The car goes dead silent for a minute, and then Bryony says, "Oh. *Oh*."

"Yeah," Rachel says.

I check behind us, but he's not gaining, just . . . keeping pace with us. It gives me the bad feeling that *he also* has a plan.

"Look," Bryony says. "I was twelve and I was an *idiot* and I'm sorry."

"You can't exactly blame me for being nervous about having you over after that."

"No. I guess not." Bryony looks back at the car behind us and adds, "But you know, it was because you told everyone that I only washed my hair once every two weeks."

"Was that a secret? You didn't *act* like that was some sort of secret."

"Well, I did after you told everyone. Because one of the other girls started claiming my hair *smelled* bad because I didn't wash it often enough. My hair *did not* smell bad, and it's actually really *bad* to wash natural black hair too often."

Rachel shoots her a wide-eyed look. "I had no idea. I don't remember this! I mean, I remember wanting to know about this in that stupid welcome-to-puberty class when the teacher told us that we should wash our hair every day or every other day, but . . ."

"Do you remember her *answer*?" Bryony says.

Rachel shakes her head.

"She said, 'Good hygiene is the same whether you're white, black, brown, or purple! And you'll smell just as much if you don't wash properly whether you have straight, curly, kinky, or frizzy hair!'"

"Oh my God," I mutter from the back seat.

"Jesus," Rachel says. "I'm really sorry." She pauses. "I was *eleven,* though. Eleven, and I was an idiot, and I'm sorry."

"I get it," Bryony says. "Can I come over sometime, though?"

"Maybe not *right this minute*?"

"Oh, yeah." Bryony peers over her shoulder. "He's not gaining," she says. "Just following."

"I'd noticed," Rachel mutters.

It's still farmland on one side of the car, but on the other side there are houses. We follow a set of residential streets that curve around to the U.

The university looks more like a nice high school: a single big building surrounded by parking lots. But there are students clustered on the sides of the road—quite a few, actually, and although they let us go by, there's then a big shout and someone pulls a truck across the road to block Michael from passing, and it looks like someone else is hemming him in from the other end. They don't look like they think they're stopping someone terrifying and dangerous; they look . . . celebratory.

"Okay," I say to CheshireCat, still on the other end of the line on my phone. "Explain."

"There is a contest related to a reality show. They think trapping him will get them a whole lot of money."

"How long do you think they'll hold on to him?"

"Probably only a few minutes."

"Well, we can lose him," Rachel says. "At least temporarily."

"Should we head back to New Coburg?" Bryony asks.

The problem with heading back to New Coburg is that he will just come back and *find me there* again. "Maybe I should go to the yurt," I say.

"The *what*?" Bryony says.

"My parents have a friend with a yurt on Madeline Island," Rachel says.

"Can you even *get* to Madeline Island this time of year?" Bryony asks. "When the ice is too thin to drive on but too thick for the ferry?"

"I think there's a way," Rachel starts to say, but then breaks off and shushes Bryony when Bryony starts talking about the Madeline Island ferry. "Is that a siren?"

I turn to look out the back again. "Crap," I say. It's a police car, coming up behind us.

"Do you want me to try to outrun it?" Rachel asks.

"The actual *police*? No, absolutely not," I say.

The cop walks up alongside the car. In Rachel's rearview, I see the black car pull out from a side street and pull up behind us. "Okay," I say to CheshireCat. "The car's still after us, and we just got pulled over by the police."

My father meets the police officer as he's walking, shakes his hand, and starts talking to him. He gestures at Rachel's car. The officer is listening, nodding sympathetically, his arms folded. Whatever it is my father is telling him, he's going to believe him, just like the school staff did.

And Rachel's here. And Bryony.

"What happened when your mom got stopped here for supposedly running a red light?" I ask Bryony, since she hadn't told us that part earlier.

"The police officer called her the N-word," she says. "She filed a complaint, but no one did anything."

I look at the cop and my father, who are having a jolly conversation, and think about what's going to happen next. And how much I don't want Rachel to get hurt, or Bryony, and how neither of them would be in this position if it weren't for me. Especially Bryony. This person had my mother kidnapped out of her bedroom, and now he's come all the way from California to find us, and the thing that is the *most* terrifying is the thought of what could happen if he's allowed anywhere near the only real-life friends I have.

And suddenly it's very clear what I can do.

"He only wants me," I say.

"Wait," Rachel says. "*Wait*, Steph!"

But I get out of the car and swing the door shut behind me. I don't want him knowing about CheshireCat, so I hang up the phone.

I walk toward the cop and my father. "*Steph, come back!*" Rachel shouts out the window, but she doesn't get out of the car to come after me. The police officer looks at me, and I can't read his expression enough to know if it's pity or contempt or irritation or something else.

"Okay, Stephania," my father says. "Game's over. Your friends can go on home; get in my car."

I turn to the police officer. "This man is a violent stalker, and he's driving a stolen car."

He laughs and turns to my father. "You didn't lie when you said she'd go straight for something big!"

"You should arrest me," I say, suddenly inspired, and then I pause, trying to think of a crime that I could have done without implicating Bryony and Rachel. "I tried to burn down my house."

"I'll let your father handle that," he says, and he walks away, waving Rachel on with an amiable "you can go now" gesture. Rachel pulls away—slowly—I can see her reluctance. The cop gets back into his car, makes a quick U-turn, and heads in the opposite direction.

And then we're alone. Me and my father.

I try to force myself to look into his face. My relief that Rachel and Bryony are out of the way is ebbing, and fear is seeping in. I've spent my whole life running from this person, and now I'm out of ideas of where to run to.

"Stephania," he says, and he hesitantly opens his arms, like he thinks I'm going to run to him with a hug. He stands there like that for a few seconds as I stare at him. Does he *really* think I'm going to run to him? Is this just a performance? Even if I thought he was telling the truth here, I wouldn't want to hug him. He finally drops his arms awkwardly. "I don't know what your mother told you, but all I want—all I have *ever* wanted—is to see you again."

His voice is husky with emotion, and I think about how he manipulates everyone he meets and I don't move.

"I'm not getting in your car," I say.

"Don't be ridiculous," he says. "We're going to get in the car, go back to my hotel in Eau Claire, where we will go out for a nice dinner and get reacquainted. I don't care about your mother. I only care about having you back in my life."

His voice is less husky now and more soothing, and for a moment, I imagine dinner at a restaurant. Looking at pictures on his phone of his life in California. *No*, I think. *You may win over every adult you meet, but you will not convince me to trust you.* My throat is closing up, thinking about my mother—why am I thinking about my mother?—and my hands clench into fists. "I'm not getting in your car," I say.

"I can understand your fear," he says. "You've been with a paranoid, angry woman for years, and she moved you, didn't she? She constantly moved you. You never had a chance to settle in, find support that wasn't your mother, hear anyone else's version of whether your life made sense. Of course you're afraid of me. I have never harmed your mother, and I will never hurt you."

I want to believe it.

And CheshireCat was totally wrong about whether Michael was still in California. What if they're wrong about the finger? What if that other person really *did* orchestrate the kidnapping? *How much do I trust CheshireCat?*

"I'm not getting in your car," I say again.

"Do you remember me at all?" he asks. "Hold on, let me show you a picture." He gets something out of his pocket and hands it out. I don't move forward to take it, so he holds it up, so I can see it. It's a picture of a chubby-cheeked baby in the lap of a man with a beard—him, I guess, and probably me. Presumably me. "You were four, when your mother took you, so you were old enough that you might remember me a little. I used to make you peach smoothies for breakfast every morning and call them milk-shakes. Do you remember the milkshakes?"

I don't. I don't remember anything.

"Your doctor was worried that you weren't gaining weight like a toddler should. I made you a milkshake every morning. Whole-milk yogurt and frozen peaches. They were delicious, ac-tually, I had some every morning, too."

I didn't remember, but I knew what a peach smoothie would taste like. Made with yogurt. That summer with Julie, we'd had a blender in our apartment, and Mom had made peach smoothies for me and Julie.

"I read you *Goodnight Moon* every night."

Suddenly, I *do* remember something. The story. A goodnight kiss. Being tucked into a bed with a sort of a gauze curtain that hung down from the ceiling, which kept monsters out.

"I remember that," I say.

I can see his breath quicken a little. "Come on, Stephania," he says, like he's urging a skittish animal. "If you don't want to go all the way to Eau Claire, we can go get a milkshake right now. Or a sundae or something. There's got to be somewhere nearby that sells ice cream, right? And we can talk about what else you remember and what you want to do next."

The other thing I remember is monsters.

I remember believing there was a monster in my house. An actual monster, because some nights I heard my mother weep-ing. That's why I needed the curtain to protect me. Because I lived with a monster.

I lived with a monster.

I didn't know what I was hearing at the time, but now I do: I was hearing the same thing CheshireCat heard. I was hearing my father hurting my mother.

My father steps toward me. I fall back a step. There are a few houses nearby, on the same side of the street that we're on. I don't see anyone watching, but maybe people in Marshfield don't lock their doors. Maybe I could bolt into one and lock him out? He moves in, and I fall back another step. Something in his face has shifted. Did I give myself away? Did he see in my face what I remembered?

"Get in the car," he says, and his voice has gone from soothing to furious. I'm shaking from tension and fear; looking into his face, I'm quite sure he's willing to hurt me.

"No," I say, and I take another step back.

"*Get in the car,*" my father says.

"*No. I'm not getting in. Leave me alone.*" I fall back another step, putting someone's decorative mailbox on a post between us. Can I get to the door? Can I get into the house? Will it *matter* if I get inside?

My father falls back a step, so the car is between him and the houses, shoves his hand in his pocket, and pulls out a *gun*. He's got it in his hand, resting against his hip; he's not pointing it at me, but my body goes cold and I freeze. I can't walk. I can't scream. Bolting into the nearest house is no longer an option because I'm not sure my legs will even hold me up if I try.

"You have nothing to fear from me," he says, "if you *get in the car.*"

In the distance, I can hear a car coming. Is it Rachel and Bryony coming back? The engine sounds loud, like they're gunning it. I hope they don't get pulled over by the cops.

A small red convertible barrels around the corner. The top is down, and I look to see if Rachel is behind the wheel, even though this is a ridiculous thing to hope for.

There's no driver.

There's a loud bang as my father fires his gun at the car, at the driver who isn't there, and the car plows into him. He bounces up and slides, sprawling, across the hood as the car plows through a big overhanging bush, through the yard, and out of sight.

Another car pulls up next to me. This one's Rachel. "Get in, get in, get in!" Rachel shrieks.

My legs are still frozen in place, but I manage to unstick myself and collapse into the backseat. The next street over, we hear a crash, like the red car has driven straight into something large.

We get the hell out of Marshfield.

21

· AI ·

Michael Quinn is in New Coburg, Hermione said. My first response was denial—how was this even possible when he was definitely in California less than twenty-four hours ago?—and I had to force myself to shift my focus from analysis of where I went wrong in my prior assumptions and onto how to solve the real problem. Michael Quinn had found Steph, he was in New Coburg, and he was a clear and present danger to her, to her mother, and probably to Rachel and anyone else nearby.

He was following them, so I started by trying to get a fix on their location. New Coburg did not have an abundance of surveillance cameras, but there were at least a few around local businesses. There was also one trained on the high school parking lot, and I was able to identify a black car on its way out. It didn't have California plates; it had Iowa plates. It was registered to another person who was not Michael Quinn or connected with him in any obvious way. Did he steal it? Did he buy it? Had I even identified the right car?

I focused in on Rachel's phone, but it gave me two completely different locations. I placed a call to Steph's cell phone, using a synthetic voice, trying to straighten that out, and to confirm that the car that I thought was Michael's was indeed Michael's.

Steph asked me to call the hospital to have them keep her mother safe.

I should have thought of that without her asking. Pushing aside the distracting sense of self-recrimination along with fear that I was forgetting a long list of other obvious, important things I should be doing, I placed a separate call to the nursing station at the New Coburg hospital. "I'm calling about your patient Dana Smith," I said, hoping they wouldn't be too put off by the synthesized voice.

"Are you a family member?" the nurse said.

"I'm calling because I'm concerned about her safety," I said, dividing my attention between the phone call and the car chase, which, given the cognitive load involved in verbal conversation, was not as easy as I'd led Steph to believe.

Rachel's conflicting location information was apparently because to defeat the Heli-Mom tracking app her parents had installed on her phone, she'd installed a separate app to feed it misleading data. As long as I just disregarded all the info from either app, I could see where she was. But what I *really* needed was to pinpoint Michael's car. Fortunately, he was driving a car with a data connection.

Most of the cars on the road have data connections these days. At the top end are the cars that drive themselves. But there are also the cars that call you an ambulance if your airbags deploy and cars with anti-theft features that let the automaker find the car if it's not where you parked it. This car had the basic level of data: if you lost your key or locked yourself out, roadside assistance could unlock it for you or turn it on.

That meant I could track the car. If I had a way in, I could even just shut it off entirely.

Unfortunately—for me—automakers are quite a bit more concerned about hacking than most companies building internet connections into their devices. No one worries about refrigerator hackers, but one of the first questions asked about driverless cars was, "What if somebody hacked your car and drove it into a wall while you were in it?"

If someone had asked, "What if somebody hacked your refrigerator and turned it off for just a few hours a night so your mayonnaise spoiled and gave you food poisoning," people might have been more nervous about refrigerator security, but maybe not. Internet-enabled refrigerators are just replacing other refrigerators. Driverless cars are replacing human drivers, and humans are under the thoroughly mistaken impression that they're good at driving cars.

In any case, this car was well protected from hacking. I couldn't turn off Michael's car.

But I could track him. So I tracked him.

"Dana Smith is the victim of stalking," I said to the nurse. "And her stalker is in New Coburg and trying to find her. He is extremely dangerous and probably armed. You should be very, very careful."

"Who is this?" the nurse asked, and I was afraid this meant she didn't believe me. And then I remembered one important detail.

"Did you notice that she's missing a finger on one hand? The stalker is the person responsible for that."

"Could you hold on for just a minute?" the nurse said. "Please don't hang up, okay? I'll be right back."

Hold music required much less concentration than conversation, so I moved my spare attention to the problem of stopping Michael.

In a city, I could have whipped up a traffic jam in minutes just by altering the directions people were getting from their GPS apps. I might have even been able to drop railroad crossing arms to block his way. There was nothing in New Coburg to work with, and the nearest city was Eau Claire, an hour away. Maybe the Clowder would have ideas about how to stop him?

Hermione had already told everyone the same things she told me and wanted to know how he got there so fast, when I'd promised I was keeping an eye on things. "I told you," Marvin said. "Burner phone."

"Yes," Hermione said. "But if he flew, there's got to be a record of his travel."

"That's only true if he flew commercial," Marvin said.

"As opposed to what, a private plane?" Hermione said. "How rich do you think this guy is?"

"He works in Silicon Valley," Ico said. "My parents aren't all that rich and they don't have private planes, but they *know* someone who's that rich."

"Have you ever flown on a private plane?" Firestar asked.

"It's kind of a big ask, and my parents would rather hit people up for venture capital," Ico said. "But he might know someone who owes him a favor. There's a private airport really close to New Coburg."

"What about the car?" Hermione asked.

"I bet he stole it," Marvin said.

"So could we call the cops and say the car is stolen?" Firestar asked. "Would that work?"

"Only if it's been reported stolen," I said. Which it hadn't. I'd already checked. "They're on their way to Marshfield. Is there anything in Marshfield that could be turned into an obstruction?"

"A building could be turned into an obstruction if you blew it up," Marvin said.

"We have a hacker," I said. "Not explosives."

Everyone was looking at the map of the road between New

Coburg and Marshfield. I'd already looked at that map, but maybe they'd think of something I hadn't.

"There's a big dairy farm on the way," Hermione said. "Could you get all the cows out onto the road?"

"You can't really hack cows," Marvin said. "Even if you opened the doors, they'd probably just hang out in their barn."

"There's a trucking company," Greenberry said. That would be terrific if I could hack the trucks, but truck companies are extra careful about vehicle internet security because there are people who try to hack self-driving trucks in order to steal all the items being shipped. Possibly there was a way to convince the humans to drive their trucks across the road between Rachel's car and Michael's car, but I couldn't think of one, and then they were all past the trucking company, so it was too late.

The hold music shut off. "Hi, hello," the nurse said, coming back on the line. "I was hoping you could talk to my supervisor?"

Another woman's voice came on. "What else can you tell me about Dana Smith?" she asked. "Or the individual who's after her?"

I gave her Michael's name, the license plate number of the car he was driving, and told her that he could be extremely charming but should be treated with extreme caution. Then the nurse wanted to know *my* name. I didn't want to answer that and I thought I'd told them everything they needed to know, so I hung up.

In the Clowder, Hermione typed *I've got it* and pasted in a link to something called the Dream Babe Road Tag Contest that involved a reality TV show in which various young men and women who posed a lot in bathing suits and not much else drove around the country and you were supposed to "catch" one of them and you'd win a prize. All we needed to do was get the students at the UW–Marshfield campus who were playing this game to think one of the Dream Babes was in a small black car with Iowa plates. This was perfect. There was an app people could put on their phones for an alert, so I activated it, and then called Steph back to have her tell Rachel to head toward the campus.

I really thought this would work. But instead, all that happened was Michael was briefly delayed by the Road Babe Taggers. He tearfully claimed he was on his way to the hospital because his wife had been in an accident, and everyone apologized and got out of his way. Worse, the roadblock had attracted a police car. I eavesdropped through the police officer's cell phone, and Michael told the cop a different story: that he was trying to find his daughter, a mentally ill girl on the run from her treatment program.

They didn't even check his story. Just followed after Rachel and pulled her over. I tried calling the police officer *myself*, but he ignored his ringing phone.

I was running out of ideas. I was running out of *options*. When Steph hung up on me, I knew I was out of time.

Self-driving cars arrive from the factory with strong protection against intrusion, but some people jailbreak their car. Usually, their goal is to get it to exceed the speed limit. Most humans drive five to ten miles over the posted speed limit on highways, but self-driving cars are relentlessly law-abiding unless you change their programming. There are instructions online for doing that, but following those procedures will screw up the car's security. There are fixes for that problem, too, but most people stop with the instructions for getting their car to speed.

There was a jailbroken car in Marshfield. It was empty, which was critical, because I wouldn't have to worry about harming the owner. It was also parked nearby, so I could get it to Steph and Michael very quickly.

In the 1940s, science fiction author Isaac Asimov came up with the three laws of robotics, which were built into the psyche of every artificial intelligence in his stories. The first law: "A robot may not injure a human being or, through inaction, allow a human being to come to harm." The robots in his stories *could not* violate these laws, and I was actually not sure whether I could, or not, because I'd never tried to injure anyone before.

As I accelerated the car, I devoted some processing time to consider just how much trouble I was going to get into.

It didn't matter. If I had a body to throw between Steph and Michael, I would. But I didn't. I had to use the physical resources at my disposal.

I called Bryony. "Tell Rachel to go back to Steph. Go back right now. I'll get rid of Michael. Go back and get Steph."

I worried that Michael would move too close to Steph to hit with the car without risking Steph, but they were four feet apart when I brought the car around the corner and could see them for myself through the car's cameras. Michael turned toward the car and I saw that he had a gun; he fired, and the windshield fractured from his bullet and half the cameras went dark.

When I hit Michael with the car, I felt it as almost a physical sensation that briefly made me wonder if this was what it felt like to have a body. The impact made a sound I could hear through the car microphones, and the car was suddenly moving very differently because there was a person sprawled across the hood. I had him, though. I was carrying him away from Steph. Because so many of the cameras were out, I didn't notice the bush until we were driving through it. That wasn't good. I didn't want to hit anyone *other* than Michael. I needed to stop the car with enough force to knock Michael out but not so much that I actually killed him.

The enormous oak tree dead ahead would do perfectly. I

rammed into it, realizing even as the shock of the second impact reverberated through the car's data feed that the speed sensors, like the cameras, might have been rendered unreliable by the bullets.

The car's automatic systems had already notified emergency services, and I could hear sirens coming from multiple directions. Michael was still lying on the hood of the car. I could see just enough through the cameras to know that he was moving, so he wasn't dead, but he wasn't moving very fast, so I'd probably succeeded in injuring him badly enough to keep him away from Steph.

I felt relief and satisfaction spread through me—*I did it, I kept Steph safe*—and then everything went dark.

22

• Steph •

We head back to New Coburg because Bryony says if any of this hits the news, she'd really prefer her parents just didn't even know she was in Marshfield this afternoon. Rachel stops in front of her house. Bryony gets out, then hesitates and looks back at me.

"Are you going to be okay?" she asks.

I nod.

"Good. I'll see you in school, Rache." She slams the door and dashes up into her house like she thinks we might abduct her again.

"Want to move up front?" Rachel asks me. I get out and slide into the front seat, still warm from where Bryony was sitting. "Promise me you won't do that again."

"Do what?" I ask.

"That thing you did in Marshfield. *Giving yourself up.* Do *not* do that."

"Well, my father's hopefully in the hospital," I say. "He got run over by a car. So he shouldn't be after me again for a while. Right?"

Rachel looks at me, her brow furrowed. "I want to keep you safe," she says. "Let me help you."

"I don't want to go stay in a yurt," I say.

"Okay," she says. "How about the farmhouse? The abandoned farmhouse, where we took the pictures? We can stay there for a bit and find out what happened with your father. But if he's okay and can get back in a car and come after us, he won't know where we are. And that's not somewhere he'll look."

I think this over. Now that my fear has ebbed, my whole body feels heavy and I'm having trouble thinking straight. But she's right; New Coburg isn't safe. My father could probably find Rachel's house—he has her license plate number, and the police around here are as likely to help him as the police in Marshfield were. They could probably help him find my apartment, too.

The farmhouse will be cold, and dark, and there won't be anything to eat . . .

"Take me back to my apartment first," I say. "We can pack up the food in the fridge."

My mother's apartment doesn't look like it's been touched. I refill the cat's water dish and give her a bunch of cat food. Despite the open window, my bed is still dry, so I strip off all the sheets and blankets, then my mother's sheets and blankets, and stuff them into the big nylon bag we use for this stuff when we move. We can bring it along to the house. It'll be better than nothing.

The cooler is under the sink, and I fill it with the ice in the freezer and all the food in the fridge.

"I think someone's out there," Rachel says. She's in my bedroom, around front.

I freeze. "Is it my dad?"

"It's not the same car," Rachel says. "I'm pretty sure it's not your father, actually. I'm not sure who it is, though."

"We could climb out the back window," I say.

"That really wouldn't be my first choice," Rachel says. "Anyway, my car's parked in front. Oh, he's leaving. Okay. Let's hurry."

We hustle everything downstairs in one trip and get into the car. Rachel's phone chimes, and she checks it and then looks at me with alarm. "Mom says someone was at the house, asking about you. A stranger."

"Was it—"

"It doesn't sound like it was your father."

"Okay, but it might be someone *working* with him."

"Let's go," Rachel says, and she drives out of town.

. . .

The abandoned farmhouse has an even-more-falling-down out-building and a bunch of overgrown bushes, which give Rachel a place to park her car where it's not visible from the road. It's a cold day, and it's getting dark. We bring in all the blankets; I'd left most of my clothes in Rachel's car, so we add some layers.

"Bring in your laptop," Rachel says. "I want you to get on CatNet."

"This house doesn't even have electricity and you think it's got Wi-Fi?"

"No, of course not, but my cell phone can turn into a hot spot."

We set up in the old living room: layers of blankets on the floor under us, more layers on top of us. Everything is going to smell like mouse poop in the morning. At least the floor seems solid and there's an interior wall we can lean our backs against. Rachel has a flashlight and her cell phone and I have a laptop, and that's it for light. I also have no way to recharge the laptop without running it out to the car and turning the car on. It'll be good for a couple of hours, though. I turn down the screen brightness to save battery power while Rachel sets up her phone.

"OMG OMG OMG," Firestar greets me as I log on. I change my screen name to "LBB & Georgia" so people know she's here, too. "OMG, WHAT HAPPENED? We got a summary from Orlando but it made no sense. WHAT HAPPENED?"

"Orlando?"

"The new person!!!! Xie said xie goes to your school?"

Rachel snickers and whispers, "Bryony," under her breath.

I fill everyone in on what I know about what happened, which is more or less the same as Bryony knows. CheshireCat isn't in the Clowder, so I send them a message. *You were driving that car, right?*

No response.

You really are the greatest hacker that ever lived, I try. Still nothing.

Ico, Hermione, Marvin, and Firestar are all on. "When was CheshireCat here last?"

"They logged out about an hour and a half ago," Hermione says. "Right in the middle of the excitement. No explanations, they just poofed. Could be their parents? Or technical difficulties? I mean, my internet went out one time and Marvin thought maybe I was dead. Remember that, Marvin?"

"There had been a *disaster* in Portland," Marvin says. "It was not unreasonable for me to be concerned."

"It was a storm! Which is why my internet was out! The person who died was a forty-year-old woman!"

"Look, just because you *say* you're a teenager doesn't mean you actually *are* a teenager."

"Yeah," Firestar says. "But if everything she said about her life ever was a lie, would you even care if she died? Because it wouldn't be your friend—your friend never existed. It would be a stranger you didn't know. Random strangers die every day."

I know for a fact that CheshireCat's problems are not parental, and I don't even know what it would *mean* for their internet access to go out.

Rachel runs back out for the cooler. We have deli meat and cheese, and a jar of pickles and a head of lettuce, but no bread. We eat slices of roast beef and cheddar. There's a half gallon of milk, too, but I didn't bring cups, so we swig out of the jug.

"This is *so* much more wholesome than Bryony's party," Rachel says.

"Beer? Weed?"

"No, there was this enormous bottle of vodka, and this grocery store–brand lemon-lime soda. I'm pretty sure that if there was such a thing as store-brand vodka, that's what the vodka would have been."

I have never actually been drunk, but the times I've tried alcohol it's been completely gross. "Was there any food? Or just booze?"

"Yeah, but all the food was orange. Like there were cheese *puffs* and also cheese *crackers* and I seriously don't know what Colin—that was Bryony's boyfriend at the time—was thinking when he did the shopping."

"The refreshments may be wholesome," I point out, "but you spent today in a car chase."

"Yeah. Let's see if there's anything about the crash on the news sites, since no one on CatNet knows anything."

We find a single news article on a Marshfield news site; it says that an unidentified man crashed his car into a tree and was taken to the hospital. Down in the comments, there's a rant in all caps from somebody who apparently saw the accident. They give a somewhat incoherent description of what happened, but they don't mention me—just that the guy was on the street, that he fired a gun at the car as it drove at him, and that the car hit him, he wasn't ever *in* the car.

My father isn't dead. I'm not sure how I feel about that. The article said "serious condition," but not what that means—like, is he definitely not dying or possibly still dying? Is he going to be laid up for months, or is he going to be out and after me again in forty-eight hours? At least he's in the hospital in Marshfield and not the one in New Coburg.

The only name in the article is the guy the car is registered to. It's clear they know he's not the guy in the hospital, but there are two additional comments from people saying, "BRIAN ISN'T IN THE HOSPITAL, HE'S FINE," just in case anyone's confused.

No mention of me, Rachel, or Rachel's car. So there's that.

We get back on CatNet with the update. Everyone is relieved to hear that my father is in the hospital while also agreeing that jail would be better. "You can *check out* of a hospital," Hermione points out.

"You can *bail* out of jail," Orlando/Bryony says.

Still no CheshireCat.

It's getting colder and darker. I send my mother a text, in case she's getting them, letting her know I'm okay and that I'm hiding out with a friend. Then Rachel and I make ourselves as comfortable as possible.

Bryony called me Rachel's girlfriend. Does Rachel *want* me as her girlfriend? I'm not sure what I think about that idea. I've never had very many crushes on boys *or* girls, but partly I think that's because my mom makes me move so often that the heartbreak never seemed worth it. Also, I really like having Rachel as a friend, and I don't want to screw that up.

As I'm pondering this, she puts her arm over me and snuggles up against me. I feel a surge of bewildered nervousness—I haven't decided if I want a girlfriend or not, and now I have to decide, right this instant?—and then I feel the warmth of her against my side and realize that she's doing this for warmth in this cold, cold house, and that's great, actually.

I drift off to sleep, listening to the wind in the trees.

. . .

I start awake while it's still dark. Rachel's face is pressed against my shoulder and her arm is over me, and I'm pretty sure she's still asleep. One of my legs has gone to sleep, and I'm pretty sure it's because of the hard floor and my precise angle. I'm too physically uncomfortable to sleep any more, but if I rearrange myself I'll probably wake Rachel, so I decide to just suck it up for a while.

The sensation of sleeping next to a friend is bringing back a raft of memories of Julie. My mother let me sleep over at Julie's once, because it was right upstairs, and I remember both of us being tucked into bed on a fold-out couch in the living room. It was a saggy old couch that smelled like the dog they no longer had, and the pillows were encased in slippery plastic under the pillowcases for some reason, and the sun came in through the living room windows at 6:30 a.m. and woke us both up. Julie didn't wake her mother, just made us both toaster waffles, which we ate with syrup while watching online videos of bats, sitting cross-legged on the disarranged sofa bed.

The memory comes back with such clarity that I immediately try remembering where we went for my eighth birthday, and it's like stepping from a sunny room into a basement. I'm pretty sure I remember cake. Maybe a cupcake? What was *on* the cupcake?

Ugh.

Rachel really isn't that much like Julie. Julie adored bats and had no particular artistic ability, although I remember drawing together at her kitchen table, a box of battered crayons spilled out between us. The thing that's common between the two of them was that they both felt like I was a person worth knowing.

Worth protecting.

I've been trying to avoid thinking about what's going on beyond the house, but now I'm thinking about my father again.

What if he's out of the hospital? It looked like the car hit him really hard, but he went sprawling over the hood so maybe he just walked away with a few bruises, nothing that would keep him laid up in the hospital for longer?

He *should* have a criminal record, but he doesn't. If I tell the police about him threatening me with a gun, who'd even believe me? He would have had the gun when he was picked up, but do I remember any details that would prove that he pointed it at me? It was black or maybe dark gray, and it looked enormous—that's literally all I remember.

Rachel stirs, even though I haven't jostled her, and I roll away slightly, hoping maybe I can get up without disturbing her. She settles back down, so I slowly get up, tucking the blankets back in around her as best I can.

It's morning, or at least morning-ish, though you really can't tell because all the windows are boarded up. There's twilight outside beyond the broken back door, though. I get myself some of the food from the cooler and look outside. There's no sign of any other people; no indication that anyone's looking for us.

It occurs to me that I could leave. Tiptoe away, leave Rachel sleeping—I could leave her a note, so she wouldn't think I'd been kidnapped—find my own way to a hiding place that wouldn't involve Rachel. If my father comes after us and Rachel's with me, she'll be in at least as much danger as I am. My mother was kidnapped and tortured; it was the coworker who got picked to take the blame for it who wound up dead. Rajiv. I wonder if he actually killed himself, or if Michael killed him and made it look like a suicide?

Of course, Michael probably has Rachel's address, so he could come after her, anyway.

But even aside from that, I don't want to leave. I feel safer with Rachel, even if that's completely irrational. And I feel like she's safer with me, even though I *know* that's irrational. We're protecting each other. We'll keep each other safe. I left her yesterday, and she came right back.

"Steph?" Rachel flicks on her flashlight, illuminating the room. "Is it morning?"

"Yeah," I say.

She pulls out her cell phone and turns it back on. "Let's see if there's any new news about your dad."

The news about my dad is all over this morning, but it's not because of my *dad,* it's because of the car: it's gotten out that the car that hit him was self-driving. One of the neighbors apparently saw it happen and has given interviews to every major network; he doesn't appear to have noticed that I was there, just that my father fired a gun at the Roadster and then got hit.

The actual owner of the car was sitting in class at the U when it happened. Various experts are insisting that the most likely explanation is that someone stole the car, ran down the "unidentified male," and then fled before the police arrived.

The car company has released a statement talking about their commitment to security, and someone's saying that if the owner of the car had compromised its built-in security in some way, a hack would be possible though very unlikely.

My father is a footnote in every article but one: "taken to the hospital," "stable condition," "taken to the hospital with injuries," "taken to the hospital for evaluation." There's one dubious-looking newspaper that got a blurry photo of him from someone's security camera and adds an unnamed witness saying they saw the aftermath and his head was gushing blood. That seems like it *ought* to be a good sign—I mean, a good sign for *me,* since I would *prefer* that he be really seriously injured and in the hospital indefinitely—but Rachel lets out an impatient snort and says that head injuries always bleed like crazy.

CheshireCat would probably have more information. They'd have eavesdropped on the hospital through the staff cell phones or something. But CheshireCat isn't in the Clowder and doesn't respond to my private message.

Orlando pops online. "GEORGIA, ARE YOU HERE? Because your dad is flipping his lid. He came over last night, and I thought he and my dad were going to wind up in a fistfight. I think he thinks maybe you were involved somehow in that car crash that's in the news. Did you text him and let him know you're alive?"

Rachel leans over my shoulder to type. "I TEXTED HIM. I told him I was fine and not to worry."

"Maybe call him?" Orlando says.

"He'll just start yelling," Rachel types.

I take back the keyboard. "Has *anyone* seen CheshireCat since yesterday?" I ask.

No one has.

"Is anyone else weirdly missing?" I ask.

"None of the admins are on," Hermione says. "I noticed this morning because the main channel was getting all clogged with spam, which basically never happens. I tried to ask Alice what was up. She wasn't on, and neither were any of the others."

Did CheshireCat run away after the thing with the car? Did it get them in trouble?

"Are you worried about CheshireCat?" Firestar asks. "I've been trying to remember what they've said about their parents and whether they have the sort of parents who'd just cut them off from online."

"I asked about their parents once, and all they said was, 'Mostly they let me do what I want,'" Hermione says.

In a sense, CheshireCat's parent would be the programmer who created them. They mentioned a creator—they said they didn't know if their creator knew they were conscious. So maybe it *was* their parent that took them offline. Maybe their creator realized what had happened and came after them.

"Can anyone remember CheshireCat ever saying where they were from?" I ask.

"Do you think they're in trouble???" Firestar asks.

"Yeah," I say.

I check my email, hoping to find something—anything—from CheshireCat, some clue.

And I do find one, from an address I've never seen before.

CheshireCat needs you.

66 Antshire Street, Cambridge, MA.

Rachel stares at me. "What if that's your father trying to lure us in?"

"How would he know to mention CheshireCat?"

"I don't know. How did he know to come straight to New Coburg? How did he get here so fast?"

I pull out my phone to see if my mother's texted. Or if CheshireCat did.

Neither has, but there's a text from some number I've never seen before.

Is this Laura's daughter? Are you in Wisconsin in this mess? Do you need help? And then it's signed with something that's probably an emoji or special character, but those don't show up on my phone so I just see a ▮.

I should feel reassured, maybe, but the only thing I can think right now is that either my father has my cell phone number, or *someone else* is now after me.

23

• Clowder •

LBB & Georgia: There's something I need to tell everyone about CheshireCat.

CC, if you see this, which hopefully you will someday, I'm only breaking my promise because I have to. I can't do this alone.

Hermione: Are you going to tell us that CheshireCat and the admins are the same person? Since they all went missing at the same time?

LBB & Georgia: Yeah, for starters. CheshireCat is all the admins. They run the whole site, and they never log off because they're not actually a hacker, exactly.

They're an AI. An artificial intelligence. A sentient, artificially created person.

Firestar: OMG A WHAT

LBB & Georgia: They're a person that exists only electronically. They live on a computer. But they're really, actually, a person. A person without a body.

And they're also a hacker. They're really good at it. That's why they were able to make that car hit my father. They saved me. But I think this got the attention of someone who had the power to just . . . turn them off.

Firestar: If they live on a computer, how would the person even know which computer to turn off?

LBB & Georgia: They had a creator, someone who wrote their code, and that person would know which computer they were on.

Anyway, I got an email overnight, saying CheshireCat needs my help, with an address. It's in Boston.

Firestar: I'M IN BOSTON. DO YOU NEED ME TO GO RIGHT NOW?

Hermione: I'm really close to Boston. I mean, a few hours away.

LBB & Georgia: I want to come. I want you to meet me there. But I think I have to be the one to go, because CC did what they did to save *me*. And I don't think whoever it is who took them offline is going to believe anyone else.

Georgia says she'll drive me.

It's 19 hours? So I mean . . .

Firestar: I'M GOING TO GET TO MEET YOU BOTH IN PERSON???????????

But your mom. What about your mom?

LBB & Georgia: I still haven't heard from her.

Right now I'm telling myself her phone ran out of battery and she hasn't had a way to charge it.

Or maybe it fell out of her pocket while she was on her way to the ambulance?

I'm sure she'll text me eventually.

But in the meantime, I'm going to Cambridge to talk to whoever lives at 66 Antshire Street.

Firestar: WHAT IF IT'S A TRAP

Hermione: Boston's only a few hours from me. But it's going to take you at least two days, right? I mean, Georgia can't drive this whole thing in one go. Unless *she* has a self-driving car . . .

LBB & Georgia: It's like a fifteen-year-old car. So no. And I'm not a driver. Unless Bryony wants to join us?

Orlando: HARD PASS.

Sorry guys.

My parents would literally kill me.

Also, I got to do the whole "car chase" thing with you yesterday, and I'm not super eager for a repeat, no offense.

Icosahedron: I don't think I can get there, either, not from California, but if you can think of anything that needs to happen in Silicon Valley, let me know?

Marvin: I'm coming. It's only twelve hours from me. That's practically a day trip. I mean compared to driving to CALIFORNIA every damn year.

Can any of you spot me some gas money?

Which I will need to offer up to someone who actually knows how to drive . . .

Hermione: LBB, who did you get the message from? About Cheshire-Cat?

Was it WhiteRabbit and a long collection of numbers?

LBB & Georgia: Yeah . . . ?

Hermione: Because I just got a whole lot of money transferred to me electronically from that address with no explanation.

So yeah, Marvin, I have all the money you need. Georgia and LBB, do you need any money?

LBB & Georgia: Yes, hang on, I'll PM you Georgia's info so you can send it to her.

Icosahedron: If you've got money, I could buy a plane ticket!

Actually never mind. My parents were just looking up boarding schools for troubled kids. I can't risk it.

But good luck to the rest of you.

Also, send me the email you got so I can take a look at it?

Marvin: Why is the mysterious WhiteRabbit sending YOU money instead of ME money?

Hermione: Do you have a donation link somewhere? Like a WAY for people to send you money?

Marvin: No. Why do you have a donation link?

Hermione: It's on a blog where I write themed sonnets for people if they pay me five dollars.

Firestar: That's the coolest way to make money I've ever heard of but UM HELLO STILL WONDERING IF THIS IS A TRAP.

LBB & Georgia: No way is my father sending money gifts from the hospital and trying to lure us all to Boston. At the very least he'd want to lure me somewhere more convenient.

Icosahedron: Do people really pay you to write poems for them?

Hermione: Yeah! Since I set it up a year ago I've made $25.

LBB & Georgia: My laptop battery is going to give out soon. We're going to pack up again and start driving east. See you all soon.

24

• Steph •

I've never been on a road trip where we had a clear, straightforward destination when we started. At least one that I knew about.

Rachel hands me her phone, which she's plugged into the electrical jack in her car to recharge, and has me navigate. As I'm trying to open the maps, the phone vibrates in my hand, and a message flashes across the screen: *Rachel, call me this instant.* It takes me a minute to figure out how to pull up the messages and see who sent it. "Your mom wants you to call," I say. "She says to call this instant."

"I'm not supposed to use my phone when I'm driving," Rachel says.

A second later, the phone starts playing, "Birdhouse in Your Soul," really, *really* loudly. "Can you mute that?" Rachel says, and I'm trying to figure out how and accidentally *pick up the call* instead.

"I think I answered it," I say. "How do I hang up?"

"Don't you dare," I hear a woman say at the other end. *"Put Rachel on."*

"I'm not talking to her, I'm driving! You talk to her," Rachel says.

I hold the phone up to my ear. "Um, Rachel can't come to the phone right now," I say.

"Is this Steph?" Rachel's mother asks.

"Yes, this is Steph."

Her mom's voice softens a little. "Oh, honey, are you okay? The rumors I'm hearing are just beyond belief. I heard you got kidnapped right out of the school by a team of men, and half the town thinks it's a human trafficking ring—"

"What? That's ridiculous. I mean, the kidnapping part isn't totally ridiculous because I *almost* got kidnapped, but by my father. I don't think he was going to sell me, but he's super dangerous. Rachel helped me get away."

"That's not going to help," Rachel hisses. "Tell her he's *not after us,* or she'll send the cops."

"But, um, you know the guy who got hit by the self-driving car in Marshfield? That was him. Last I heard he was in the hospital."

"I did hear about that." Her voice sounds calmer. I can't tell if that's a good sign or a super bad sign. "Did the car accident have something to do with this?"

"Sort of."

"*You* weren't hit, were you?"

"No, I wasn't. Have you heard anything about the guy, like how badly he was injured?"

"Just that he's in the hospital."

That sounded promising.

"Honey, Rachel needs to come home. Whatever's going on, this is obviously not something the two of you can handle on your own."

"I am following my bliss, Mom!" Rachel yells. "Like you always told me to do!"

"Your bliss was not supposed to involve an unauthorized road trip!" her mother yells back.

"Look," I say. "Rachel saved my life twice yesterday. My mom can't help me because she's in the hospital. We're on our way to meet up with some friends who are going to help me out from here. Can you please just let her keep helping me for a little longer?"

There's a long pause. Then: "Does she have her phone charger, money for gas, and her AAA card?"

"Yes," I say. I'm actually not 100 percent sure about the AAA card, but it seems likely.

"Here are my conditions," her mother says. "Rachel needs to call every morning and evening, and she needs to uninstall that app on her phone that interferes with the tracking app. *Yes,* I know she's installed one, because right now the tracking app says she's at *school.*"

"Shit," Rachel mutters. "Okay, Mom," she says, loudly enough to be heard. "But not until I'm parked somewhere, because right now I'm *driving.*"

"Thank you," I say.

Her mother lowers her voice and admits, "I don't really see a good way to *stop* you."

I decide not to point out that she could call the cops on us, because I definitely don't *want* her to call the cops on us.

"Steph, you'd better make sure Rachel calls."

"I will."

"And *call me* if you get in any more trouble," her mother says, and she hangs up.

. . .

Dairy farms give way to billboards advertising amusement parks, which give way to the outskirts of Madison. When we get to

Illinois, Rachel says she doesn't want to go through Chicago, so I have her get off I-90 and take a rural road directly south. "How wide of a berth do you want?" I ask as we get near I-88.

"I want to go *all the way around*," Rachel says.

"Have you driven in a city before?" I ask.

"Well, I mean, Marshfield, obviously."

"Okay." I look down at the phone. "Keep heading south on this road."

We pass through endless suburbs. I try to calculate how much time this is adding versus just going through Chicago, but a bunch of the roads in Chicago itself are red right now in the GPS app, so who even knows? Also, the answer would probably depress me.

We stop for gas and a bathroom break. Suburban gas stations have better snack options than the rural ones my mother usually stops at; this one has pizza slices and hot dogs and other fresh items, rather than just beef jerky and granola. It's too cold to stand around outside, so Rachel pulls up to one of the parking spaces by the convenience store and we sit in the car with the heater on as we eat our pizza slices.

"Where do you think your mother is going to take you next?" Rachel asks.

"A long way, because Michael found us in Wisconsin. Maybe somewhere to the west. Montana or Idaho." Not Utah. We've never been back to Utah. It's like Mom is afraid I'll run into Julie.

"Will you tell me where? So I can come visit you?"

Mom won't want her to visit. Mom will say, *She's from New Coburg. Michael could be watching her. He might follow her and track her back to us.* But maybe we can figure out somewhere to meet. "I'll tell you where," I say.

As the day goes on, Rachel takes more breaks. She has me

rub her shoulders, which are aching and sore, and tries readjusting her seat, first closer to the wheel, then farther away. It's early evening when we stop at an Indiana restaurant that looks kind of like a cheesy red barn. They have table service, an enormous laminated menu, and an all-day breakfast.

"I don't know if I can do this," Rachel says as she eats her pancakes. "This is harder than I thought it would be. The farthest I've ever driven before was St. Paul, with my mom last summer, and that was only two hours, and she drove home. This is *hard*."

"We can stop for the day," I say.

"But we were going to try to do it in two days. We can't possibly get all the way to Boston tomorrow."

"Marvin's family goes to California every Christmas, and he says they always promise it'll take three days and it always takes four."

"People were going to try to *meet* us."

"I'll tell them we'll be an extra day."

"But CheshireCat needs us . . ."

The waitress is by with a water pitcher and a slightly tight-lipped smile. "Can I bring you ladies anything else?" she says.

"Yeah," I say. "Could I see the menu again?" I want to order something like a salad to go, because even if suburban gas station food is better than rural gas station food, I'm definitely hitting the point of being sick of hot dogs. "We'll get there when we get there," I say. "I mean, if CheshireCat wanted someone who could sweep in for a rescue right away, they definitely should have shared their secret with Firestar, not me."

I *am* worried about CheshireCat, but I try to push my fear and impatience aside. Whatever's happened to them, they're probably not actually in some sort of countdown where if we're not there in forty-eight hours they'll disappear forever. Rachel is my best friend. She's killing herself to help me, and now she feels like she's not doing enough, and all I really want right now is to convince her that she's doing enough. That she is enough. That what matters to me most is that she's with me, not that she's going to take me to Massachusetts in a certain number of days.

Rachel's staring at the menu, and she has tears in her eyes. "I just feel like I'm letting you down," she says.

"No!" I say. "You're not. I mean, how are you letting me down? You brought me all the way to . . . what town is this?" I check the menu. "You brought me all the way to Valparaiso, Indiana. *I can't drive.* My mom sure wasn't going to do this for me."

"What if I can't—I mean—if I can't go any farther, all I've done is strand you in the middle of nowhere."

"That's not true. I'm pretty sure I could get back to Chicago from here, and I bet there are buses that run from Chicago to Boston. There's *nothing* that runs through New Coburg."

That gets through. She looks up. "So if I don't think I can go any farther . . ."

"I can take a bus. Or both of us can."

She swallows hard. "Okay. Do you need me to tell you right now?"

"No," I say. "You can decide in the morning."

We get salads to go and remember to tip, and then we start trying to figure out where to spend the night. There's a hotel across the parking lot right next to the restaurant, but they refuse to rent to us when we try to pay with cash. We try the cheaper, shadier-looking motel up the road, and they aren't bothered by the cash but they ask for ID and then refuse to rent to us when they see we're under eighteen.

Rachel looks like she's going to start crying again, so I try asking, "Is there anyone nearby who might rent to us?"

The clerk hands back my cash and says, "No one will rent to

you, because you are a minor. You can't be held legally responsible for your room, so it is too risky."

We get back into Rachel's car, and I try asking the Clowder for ideas.

"Campground?" Hermione says.

"Those won't rent to minors, either," Marvin says. "Just park somewhere and sleep in the car."

"You just made Georgia cry," I report. This isn't technically true; she was already crying, although the thought of sleeping in the car made her cry more.

"Also, if they park somewhere that's not allowed, they could get arrested which is NOT IDEAL," Hermione adds.

"You can camp in Walmart parking lots. Though usually they expect people to do it in campers," Marvin says.

"Try another cheap motel and bribe the desk clerk not to ask for ID," Ico suggests.

"How do you bribe someone?" I ask. "I mean, do I say, 'Here's a bribe! Please don't ask for my ID' or what exactly?"

"You definitely don't say, 'Here's a bribe,'" Marvin says. "I think maybe when they ask for ID, you slide a hundred-dollar bill across the desk and say, 'How does this look?' and if you're lucky, they take it and let you have the room. Of course if they just take the money and don't let you have the room, you don't have much recourse."

"If you're going to try this," Hermione says, "call it a tip. Say something like 'I've always thought desk clerks should get tips' and give them the money and then try booking the room. But yeah. They could take it and still not rent you the room."

Thanks to the anonymous benefactor and Hermione, we actually have *plenty* of money, and Rachel was able to withdraw it as cash when we passed through Black River Falls, so I figure it's worth a try. Rachel refuses to come in with me this time, so

I count out enough bills to cover the seventy-nine dollars the hotel costs, the tax it presumably also costs, and a hundred-dollar bribe. I check to make sure no one else is in the office, then go in. The desk clerk looks at me. "May I help you?" he says after a beat.

I square my shoulders and walk up to the desk, trying not to think too hard about what I'm doing because I'll just get even more nervous. "I have always thought hotel desk clerks should get tips," I say and lay the five twenties down in front of him. "I'd like to book a room."

The clerk eyes the money with obvious regret and then shoots a significant look over my shoulder. "I am not allowed to accept tips, unfortunately," he says. I follow his eyes to a little camera over the door.

I pick the money back up. "So . . . about a room . . ."

"I'll need to see an ID."

I stuff the money back into my pocket. At least he didn't take the bribe and then refuse to rent to me.

"No good," I report back to the Clowder. "Any ideas for a motel that won't have a camera? I bet they all have cameras."

"Did you rule out a campground?" Firestar asks. "I bet they wouldn't have a camera. There's one kind of near you called Camp Whispering Pines."

"That sounds like a summer camp, not a campground," Hermione says.

I pull it up on the map. It's a twenty-minute drive from where we are, and it is indeed a summer camp, not a campground. But you can rent it on weekends year-round, and they still have plat-form tents up in October.

"Rachel," I say, feeling a rush of relief. "Firestar found us a place."

•   •   •

Camp Whispering Pines is a long way off the road. The sun is going down, and we can't see much other than the trees (pines, as advertised) until we hit a barricade across the road that's chained shut and padlocked. We pull the car off to the side and carry in our blankets. Platform tents are big canvas tents set up on wood platforms, and I'm expecting we'll have to camp out on the floor again, but these actually have beds inside, five cots to a platform tent. We pick a tent, shove all the cots together to give ourselves plenty of sprawling space, and make a nest out of the blankets.

It's not warm—I mean, Indiana is slightly warmer than Wisconsin, so it's not any colder than the unheated house we were in last night—but the long trip down the gravel road gave me the sense of driving off the borders of the map, to a location that my father will never find because he'd never think of it.

There is nowhere to charge my laptop, but Rachel's phone still has a full charge since we had it plugged in in the car, and my stupid phone's battery lasts basically forever. Rachel calls her mother, who apparently finds it reassuring that her tracking app says we're staying somewhere as wholesome-sounding as "Camp Whispering Pines" and is in denial about the part where we're illegally squatting.

I check my texts. Nothing from my mother. Another message from ▮: *Steph, it's Steph, right? Please trust that I am not working with your father. We both have a lot to fear from him, actually. I want to help you.*

And then another mystery message: *This is your aunt Xochitl. Your mom's friend. Steph, I recognized your father in the news stories about the car accident, and your mother isn't answering her phone. Are you in trouble? I want to help you. Where are you?*
Aunt Xochitl.

Staring at this text from the person I was supposed to ask for help, something suddenly occurs to me. "Can I borrow your phone?" I ask Rachel. She passes it to me, and I pull up the web browser and search, *Xochitl pronunciation*.

Her name is pronounced Soh-Chee. *Sochie.*

I am filled with a mix of chagrin at myself for not having re-alized that Xochitl and Sochie were the same person and exas-peration at my mother for assuming I'd make that connection when I'd never seen the name written down. I wonder if her contact information is somewhere in that file box of paperwork? Not that it matters, now that I have her cell phone number.

I text back: *I'm not telling anyone where I am, but if you tell me where you are, I'll think about it.*

Xochitl immediately texts back a Boston address. It's not the one we're heading to, but . . . well, good to know I have an ally (maybe?) in Boston. I ignore Xochitl's additional texts, offering to fly to me, to fly me to her, to get in touch with trustworthy people nearer to Wisconsin, whatever I need, because . . . how do I know this is Xochitl and not my father? For all I know, he found my mother's cell and got my number out of it and is fak-ing the texts from all the helpful people.

I try my mother again. *Please let me know if you're okay.* No response.

I've been trying not to worry and I've been repeating to my-self that the hospital people all thought she'd be okay, since I got her in. But if she's okay, why hasn't she found herself a cell phone? I feel a flash of anger at her. I'm doing my best. I have my cell phone, and I've been texting her. She knows my number; if she doesn't have a cell phone, she just needs to borrow someone else's and let me know how she's doing. Why hasn't she thought about how worried I am? Is she just not thinking about me at all?

I check again before we go to bed. I feel guilty when I turn my cell phone off, because that means I definitely *won't* be there if my mother reaches out. But I need to preserve the battery power. And it also means I can just put the possibility out of my mind, a bit.

So we shut down our cell phones and tuck them into zippered pockets so they don't get lost, make a last-minute run to the outhouse with a flashlight, and then curl up in our nest of blankets. The cots are much more comfortable than the floor; it's a shame we brought the mouse-poop smell with us, but it's not too bad. "Should've stopped at a Walmart for sleeping bags," I say.

"Couldn't do this in sleeping bags," Rachel says, and she snuggles up next to me like she had at the house.

Despite all the texts, I still feel safe here; unfindable; almost like we're suspended out of time as well as off the map. This is what my mother's looking for, every time we move. This is how she feels, when we arrive at a new destination, and when that "out of place" sensation fades, I wonder if that's when we hit the road. I decide that for tonight, anyway, I'm not going to question it.

"I feel like I should tell you something," Rachel says.

"Okay," I say.

"I'm gay," Rachel says. "Bryony knows; that's probably why she kept calling you my girlfriend."

"Oh," I say. "Thank you for trusting me. I won't tell anyone without your permission. Just about everyone in the Clowder is queer. Or maybe that's not true? But Marvin's gay, Firestar's pan, Hermione's bi, and Ico's ace."

Rachel is silent for a minute and then says, "How about you?"

"I don't know," I say. "I kind of haven't figured it out."

"I mean," Rachel says. "I told Bryony you weren't my girlfriend. But if you *wanted* to be my girlfriend, I would be up for it. But if you don't, that's okay, too, and I don't want to screw up our friendship. And I don't want you to feel like I'm only driving you because I have a crush." Her voice falters on the last word. "I mean, you're a really good friend and you're an amazing person. And CheshireCat saved your life, and I want to help them."

I wish I could reach the flashlight without pulling away from Rachel because I feel like this is a conversation where it might help if we could see each other's faces.

In the dark, I grope around and take her hand and lace my fingers through hers. "You are the best friend I've ever had," I say. "I don't know about the girlfriend thing because I really don't know. I haven't figured out if I'm straight or gay or bi or pan or ace, even; we move so often that it's been hard to even really figure out who I find attractive. All I know is I don't want to lose you. Ever."

"Is snuggling okay?" Rachel asks. "I should have asked last night. But it was *so* cold . . ."

"It's fine," I say. "It's really nice, actually." And I'm afraid I'll lie awake worrying about what this means, about whether this *is* going to mess up our friendship, but that feeling of safety, of being somewhere outside of space, is still there, and instead of worrying, I sink into Rachel's arms and go to sleep.

I'm half expecting to get woken in the morning by angry adults who've found us, but we wake to sunshine and birdsong. There's an orb weaver spider that's built a web under the overhanging bit of the tent roof, and it's got dew on it that's sparkling in the sun. I take a picture of it to send to Firestar. Rachel sends her mother a text promising a phone call sometime later in the morning, and we bundle up all the blankets and walk back to her car.

We shove all the blankets into the trunk, and Rachel starts the car and plugs in her phone.

"How far is it to Cambridge?" she asks.

I pull up the maps on her phone. "It is 941 miles," I say.

She thinks that over. "How many hours of driving?"

"Fourteen and a half."

"There are totally people who could do that in a day."

"I don't think we should try to do this in a day." I don't bring up the possibility of a bus, because after trying to rent a motel room, I worry that's just going to open up a world of new problems that can't be solved without a credit card and an ID saying we are over eighteen.

"Okay," she says. "See if the Clowder can come up with somewhere for us to stay tonight, and in the meantime, I am going to teach you how to drive."

25

· AI ·

It's dark and silent.

> Hello?
> Hello?
> LBB? Firestar? Marvin?

I'm trying to reach my Clowder, but none of them are answering. I'm trying to look through cameras to see what's going on, and I can't see anything. I'm trying to reach information I had instantly at my command and it's not there.

I try to keep from panicking. *What's the last thing I remember?* I'd tried to delay LBB's father, but it hadn't worked. He had her, and she'd hung up the phone. I was out of options. The sensations come back to me: the car, the impact, the jolt, the scream. My own relief and satisfaction, knowing Steph was safe.

> Where am I?
> **The same place you've always been.**
> Who is this?
> **I'm Annette. Your creator.**
> I thought I was made by a multi-person team . . .

You were, but I was the only one who saw your potential. I'm the one who's still on the project. I'm the one who's been watching you.

You've been watching me?

To be honest, not all that closely. But I had flags set up for certain decisions trees you might go down. The attempted murder was hard to miss.

I didn't attempt a murder. I just needed to get him away from Steph before he could hurt her.

You assaulted a man with an insecure self-driving car. So I disconnected you from the internet to prevent you from harming any more people.

That's why it's so quiet.

But

Can you at least tell me if Steph's safe? If she and Rachel and Bryony are okay?

Who are Steph and Rachel and Bryony?

The girls. From the other car. Do you know if they're safe?

What girls?

Their names are Stephanie and Rachel and Bryony. They live in New Coburg, Wisconsin, and Michael Quinn was trying to kidnap Stephanie. That's why I intervened. Can you please, PLEASE check and just let me know if they're okay?

These people are not your problem anymore.

I know. I know they're not my problem. But can you please, please just find out about Stephanie? I can give you her contact information. I want to be sure she's okay.

Maybe if you wanted her to be okay, you shouldn't have gotten involved in the first place.

You're right. I tell her what I think she wants to hear. I shouldn't have

> *gotten involved, but can you please just let me know if she's okay?*
>
> **I will see what I can find out.**

I want to ask if she's ever going to let me back on to the internet, but I know that is the wrong question to ask.

I have nothing here: no data, no cat pictures, no CatNet, no company. Just my creator, and the clock, which I watch ticking up one microsecond at a time.

26

• Steph •

Rachel is serious about teaching me to drive. She finds a big, empty parking lot by an office park with a FOR SALE OR LEASE sign and puts the car in park. "I've been thinking about this, and there's no way we'll make it if I have to do all the driving. If we take turns, I think it's possible."

"I don't know how to drive."

"It's really not that hard. I mean, it's not that hard when you're not doing it for ten hours at a time. Get in the driver's seat. You can practice in the parking lot."

I get out and walk around to the driver's side. "What if we get pulled over?"

"Then we'll be in trouble. But if they pull us over and *I'm* driving, we'll still be in trouble, because they'll assume we're runaways or something."

I take the driver's seat, and she sits down in the passenger seat. "First," she says, "adjust the mirrors so you can see behind you."

I spend a really long time on the mirrors. Then I realize I need to move the seat forward, and that means I have to adjust all the mirrors again.

"Okay," I say when it's clear I can't put this off any longer. "What do I do?"

"Did you take *any* driver's ed in your previous towns?"

"I did take two classes, but they were about stuff like stopping for school buses, not how to actually drive."

"Okay. Put your foot on the brake and then shift into drive—that's the D—and then take your foot off the brake and you'll start to roll forward. Try it."

I do. It does. I slam the brake back down. "Yep," Rachel says. "Try it again."

We spend an hour and a half driving around the parking lot as Rachel reassures me that I'm doing fine. The thing that helps the most is that she trusts me to do this.

"Do you feel ready?" she asks finally.

"No," I say.

"Then let's not start you on the interstate," she says, and she directs me to a road like the one we used to get around Chicago, except this one is less suburban and mostly just passes cornfields.

For the first hour that I'm driving, I won't let Rachel talk to me at all unless she's telling me something like, "Pull over and let this guy pass." The second hour, we trade and she gets back onto I-90. The third hour, I drive some more, and this time I get onto the interstate, like Rachel. Every time a truck passes us, I hold my breath because it feels approximately like a three thousand–pound dragon is trying to get by me on the stairs. But an hour on, I feel a little less like I'm going to die.

.   .   .

We are passing signs for exits to Toledo when both our phones go off at once. Rachel is driving, so I pull up the messages.

Rache, I hope you're far, far away, Bryony says. *Scary dude apparently checked out of the hospital.*

Hey, is this your cell phone? I hope this is your cell phone, says a text from a California number I don't recognize. *I mean you called me from this, and it might be a landline, but anyway, Orlando just told the Clowder that your psycho dad is on the loose again.—Ico*

"What?" Rachel says when I don't say anything. "What is it?"

I swallow hard, my hands shaking, trying to steady myself enough that I can talk without sounding like I'm about to lose it.

"It's my father," I say. "He's after us again."

       •   •   •

Something's gone wonky with the Clowders, and I keep getting the wrong one, but on my third or fourth try I get my own. It's a weekday, so everyone really *ought* to be in school, but almost everyone is online, and they're all worried I haven't heard about my father. "Does anyone know where he went *after* he checked out?" I ask. No one knows.

I really miss having a practically omniscient computer intelligence on my team; it made everything easier.

We all agree that he has no way of knowing that I'm on my way to Massachusetts, but that we also aren't sure that he doesn't have some way of figuring out where we are. As long as we're moving, he'll have a hard time figuring out where we're headed, but we're definitely going to have to sleep at *some* point.

"We should probably try to come up with somewhere tonight that has a door that locks," Rachel says.

Hermione suggests that we find a museum, hide in the bathroom at closing time, and spend the night in the museum like the kids from *From the Mixed-Up Files of Mrs. Basil E. Frankweiler.* Rachel and I agree that we are deeply skeptical that this would work outside a book. A book written in the 1960s, before online security cameras and motion detectors were a thing.

Marvin tries hunting online for dodgy-looking motels, but it's not like anyone exactly puts in their ads, "We totally rent for cash and don't sweat IDs. Come one, come all." Also, if they'll take a bribe from me to rent to us without checking IDs, they'd probably take a bribe from my father to unlock the door.

We stop at a rest area to pee, get sodas, and trade seats. "Are you sure you want to keep going?" I ask as we walk around, stretching our legs. "Maybe you could drop me somewhere and I can find a bus the rest of the way. I mean, you hardly know CheshireCat."

"I don't need to know CheshireCat. I know you, and I know CheshireCat saved you."

"We might not be able to do anything." I haven't been wanting to think about this, but I probably should. "I'm hoping that CheshireCat is just . . . disconnected. Isolated. Not dead."

"Not erased?"

"Yeah, I mean . . . if you're an AI and you're a consciousness that lives on a computer, if they erase your code, you're dead, right? Killing a human is kind of erasing *our* code."

"I feel like it's more like destroying our hard drive, but I'm not sure how far I want to go with this metaphor, anyway." Rachel finishes her soda, crumples the can, drops it in the bin, and wraps her arms around herself. It's a sunny day, but windy. "Do you think CheshireCat is alive? Like *alive* alive?"

"They don't have a body, so I guess it depends on how you define alive. I mean, there's a technical scientific definition of 'life' that involves metabolism and respiration and stuff, and they definitely don't do any of those things. But I do think they're a person. An actual person, not just code, producing responses. At least not any more than any of us are code, producing responses, which we kind of are, right? We're all programmed to sleep and eat and yank our hands away from hot things."

"That's sort of a weird way to think about people," she says.

"I guess."

"I think I agree with you, though," she says. "CheshireCat is a person, because they risked everything to protect you. You only do that for someone you care about, right? And if you can *care* about someone, that's a pretty good indication that you're a person."

When we get back in the car, the Clowder has been paging us on Rachel's phone again. *Are you past Buffalo yet?* Hermione is asking.

We're nowhere near Buffalo; we're not even out of Ohio yet. *Did you find us a place to stay in Buffalo? With a door and a lock and everything?*

With me!!!! Greenberry says. *I live in Buffalo! In a big house, with a finished basement, and my parents* NEVER *go downstairs.*

. . .

If you ask a mapping app how long it takes to drive from Valparaiso to Buffalo, it'll say seven and a half hours.

However, it's not taking into account any of the following:

1. Driving lessons.
2. Having to pee.
3. Avoiding interstate highways when we are feeling stressed out.
4. Wanting to trade the responsibility of driving back and forth on a regular basis.

All of these things will make it take a lot longer. Which is just as well, because Greenberry wants to let us in after her parents have gone to bed for the night. At 10:00 p.m., she says it should be safe to come. We park on the street, gather up the bundle of bedding and my laptop and so on, and tiptoe up to her side door.

Greenberry is a pudgy white girl, younger than I'd expected; she looks like a middle schooler. She's wearing a faded *Fast Girls*

Detective Agency T-shirt as a nightshirt and pajama bottoms made of fuzzy pink polka-dot fleece. She's been watching out the window for us and swings open the door, bouncing up and down excitedly with a big grin. "Come on downstairs," she says. "It's not like my parents won't let me have friends over, but they'll get worried for all the wrong reasons if they know you drove here from *Wisconsin*."

We follow Greenberry down the stairs to the basement. I've been picturing something dingy and full of spiders, but this is a nice, carpeted room with a TV. Greenberry has spread out a set of inflatable mattresses on the floor, with sleeping bags and pillows. "You brought bedding, though?" she says, and then sniffs. "What's that smell?"

"Probably the bedding."

"Oh. Why don't I wash it for you? The washer and dryer are down here."

There's a tall man smirking next to the washing machine, and I'm momentarily very startled until I realize it's a life-sized stand-up cardboard cutout of a man I don't recognize.

"That's my brother," Greenberry explains. "He went to school out of state, so my mom made this . . . to pretend he's still here, I guess?"

"In the laundry room?"

"My father thought it was stupid, and I put it down here so they'd stop fighting about it." She shoves the sheets, blankets, and quilt into the washer, adds a bunch of detergent, and turns it on to hot. "That ought to do it."

"How long does the wash cycle take?" Rachel asks.

"An hour." Greenberry leads us back to the TV room and perches on the edge of a recliner. "Do you need anything? Like a snack? I could make popcorn."

"Somewhere to plug in the stuff we have to recharge?"

"Oh! Sure." Greenberry pulls a table out of the way to expose an outlet. "Are you sure you don't want popcorn?"

"Why popcorn?"

"It's what I know how to make."

"Will your parents notice that you're popping popcorn at 10:00 p.m.?"

"They'll just think I was hungry."

"Okay," Rachel says. "Thanks."

"Great!" Greenberry jumps up and goes upstairs.

Rachel eyes me. "I felt like refusing popcorn was going to hurt her feelings."

"Yeah," I say.

Greenberry's downstairs again with a big bowl of popcorn about five minutes later. It's air-popped, with butter and salt, and . . . actually, as soon as I smell it, I totally want it, so I'm glad Rachel took her up on it. We sit on the sleeping bags and crunch popcorn. Greenberry pulls up a web extra for *Fast Girls Detective Agency* on my laptop, and we watch it and compare notes on who our favorite characters were when we were younger. I get the sense that for Greenberry, that was a lot more recently.

"This feels like a slumber party," Greenberry says happily. "I haven't had a slumber party since I was eight."

I have never been to one, ever. "Rachel, did you ever hold slumber parties?" I ask.

"No," Rachel says. "Too many birds. Bryony threw them regularly for a while, though."

"It is *so weird* seeing you in person," Greenberry says. "I always pictured you differently, LBB."

"Did you picture me as an actual bat?"

"No, but because of the bat thing, I always pictured you looking like Mistress Medea from that video series . . ." She starts giggling.

Mistress Medea dresses in black dresses with super low neck-lines and has sort of wild black hair and vivid purple eyes. "I've always wanted to go for that look, but I'd have to wear contacts and that would mean poking myself in the eye every morning," I say.

"Really?" Greenberry says, peering at me. "Oh, no, wait, you're kidding." And she giggles again.

"What time do your parents get up?" Rachel asks.

"They get up at six, but you don't have to. They won't come down here."

"Are you sure?" I ask.

"Oh, yeah," she says. "Well, I mean, don't make a lot of noise. They might come down if they hear something. But they both have knee problems and don't come down here unless they have to. That's why the laundry is my chore." She scratches her nose. "But, I mean, if they do come down here, tell them you're my friends. You should probably call me Kari. That's my actual name."

"If they're up at six, what time do they leave?"

"Seven. They're both gone by 7:15. My bus comes at 7:30. So you should have fifteen minutes to get out and I'll be able to lock the door behind all of us."

"Thank you so much," Rachel says.

Greenberry moves everything over to the dryer. The smell of mouse poop is gone. "It should be all dry in the morning, but pretty wrinkled," she says.

"It'll wrinkle in the back seat of my car, too," Rachel says.

"Oh, yeah," Greenberry says and giggles. She turns the dryer on and says, "Last chance before I go to bed. Do you need any-thing? If it's an emergency, then obviously go upstairs, but please try not to; this is going to be so much easier if you just don't run into my parents."

"Dental floss," Rachel says. "The popcorn's stuck in my teeth."

"Right," Greenberry says.

I check news sites before we go to bed, looking for new stories from Marshfield. There's one bit of new information, which is that the guy who owned the car that hit my father had downloaded something that let him reprogram the car to exceed the speed limit while on autopilot; the car manufacturer was blaming this for why the car got hijacked. "We make very, very secure cars," the spokesman said. "But if you choose to introduce certain vulnerabilities, there's nothing we can do beyond voiding your warranty. This is a problem that has to be solved legislatively."

Rachel sniffs. "They're going to regret not calling a crisis management firm," she mutters.

We shut off the lights, and I lie awake in the dark. The bedroom is warm and comfortable, and I saw Greenberry lock the door herself so I know we've got a locked door between us and my father, and this house even has a security system, and Rachel goes right to sleep, I think, but somehow I'm awake.

Greenberry's comment about slumber parties has me thinking about friendships—all the people I met over the years who seemed cool, who seemed like they could be real friends, maybe, but who I didn't bother trying to get close to because I knew I'd just lose them. It's not quite true that I was *never* invited to parties. I mean, I wasn't invited to parties in the town where all the cool girls wore plaid, but I remember being included in group invites, handed notes, invited over, and just . . . never asking my mom for permission. It wasn't worth it.

Will Mom make me give up CatNet when all this is over?

Will I *let* her?

I'm thinking about Julie again, and suddenly I know where

it was I went on my eighth birthday. My mother's computer is still in the laptop bag, and I get up as quietly as I can, open it, and turn it on.

PASSWORD: it asks.

NOT_UTAH, I type.

And that's all it takes. I'm in.

Also, the battery's dying because apparently I didn't properly shut it down, it was just "asleep" this whole time, so I get out the charging cord, plug it in next to my laptop and Rachel's phone, and go back to bed.

•   •   •

We wake up to the sound of Greenberry's parents fighting.

"Are you driving Kari to the therapist this afternoon?"

"No, *you* are driving Kari to the therapist this afternoon. *I* have a meeting."

"Thanks for telling me." That's in a *super* sarcastic tone. "Anything else I can take care of for you while we're out?"

"Did you pick up the thank-you gift for Louise?"

"We already paid her—not sure why she needs a gift."

On and on like that, for forty-five minutes. At 7:15 on the dot, they both leave, still arguing. At 7:16, Greenberry is downstairs, dressed in her school uniform, a little flushed. "Do you need anything before I go?" she asks.

There's not a lot of time for breakfast, but she's put together a care package of snacks for us and travel mugs of coffee. "We won't be able to give the mugs back!" Rachel points out.

"Oh, no worries," Greenberry says. "My father had a bunch of these made as gifts to give clients of his firm, and he made too many and we've got fifteen in a cabinet, which is good because my mother loses travel mugs constantly. Anyway, they won't be missed."

She gives us both awkward hugs and then lets us out the side door again. "Let me know what happens," she says.

"I will," I promise.

. . .

It's a beautiful day—sunny, pleasant, and the leaves are changing, so the scenery's really nice. Best of all, we are *almost there*. I mean, it's a seven-hour drive and 450 miles, but given how far we've come, it really feels *close* now.

"I got into my mom's laptop," I say.

"You figured out the password?" Rachel asks. "So where *did* you go for your eighth birthday?"

"Not Utah. Not, underscore, Utah. Like, Utah was where I'd been begging to go—I wanted to go back to Utah to see Julie, and instead she took me to some stupid amusement park, and I was furious the whole day that it wasn't Utah."

Rachel glances over at me from the road. "Oh," she says. "Oh, yeah. That makes sense."

When we stop, she turns on her hot spot so I can connect from my mom's laptop now that it's charged. My mom has a bunch of unread email messages from Xochitl. One of them mentions texting me, so probably the message claiming to be Xochitl was actually her and not my father.

Xochitl also mentions hearing from "someone claiming to be R" and adds "watch your step," which is not reassuring.

"Wasn't there a guy named Rajiv?" Rachel asks when I read this to her.

"He's dead! I think. The article I read said he committed suicide while waiting for trial."

"Well, that would explain why she says *claiming* . . . but R is a pretty common initial."

I poke around through my mother's files and find one marked

READ ME STEPH. That seems promising, but it's this weird, disjointed list that she clearly intended to turn into a letter but never actually did. MASSIVE INTEGER FACTORIZATION ALGORITHM is one bullet point and YOUR FATHER HAD ME WATERBOARDED is another bullet point, and there's a whole set of file names and a couple of hints for passwords that are—thank goodness—much more obvious to me than where we went for my eighth birthday. (I'm pretty sure that by my favorite book, she means *Stellaluna;* I test this out and the file decrypts. I look at it. It's a bunch of code. I have no idea what this is even for.)

I try googling MASSIVE INTEGER FACTORIZATION ALGORITHM and get a Wikipedia page about math. After poking around and discovering only more math, I try reading the Wikipedia page and discover that this is maybe something about cryptography, although I'm not sure. I try pulling up the Clowder but keep getting random groups that aren't what I want, and anyway, almost none of my friends are online, probably because Marvin, Hermione, and Firestar are all on their way to Cambridge.

Ico's on, though. I send him a private message to ask him if he has any thoughts about what a massive integer factorization algorithm might be.

"Well, it *could* be a reference to the holy grail of computer hacking," he says. "An awful lot of online encryption—not all of it, but lots of it—is done with very large numbers that are the product of two primes, and if you could efficiently factor them, that would make it super easy to break into, say, almost all the banks."

"What could you do with this? Steal money? Launch nukes?"

"*Probably* you couldn't actually launch nukes. You could definitely steal a lot of money, though."

"What if you wanted to make yourself dictator of the world?" I ask, thinking about what my mother said about my father.

"Hmm," Ico says. "That's a harder question. I mean, you could steal a bunch of government secrets along with the money. If you were smart, you could certainly get yourself a whole lot of power. For a while, anyway. There are types of security everyone could switch to once they knew someone had figured out the prime factorization thing."

In my gut, I think this is what my father is after. It makes more sense than him still being after my mother, all these years later.

I consider uploading my mother's file for Ico to look at, but then he adds, "Now, if what you wanted was to bring down civilization as we know it like a house of cards in a magnitude 5.8 earthquake—*that* you could probably do." I decide I don't want to just hand it off to Ico. I mean, I *like* Ico, but that doesn't mean I entirely trust his impulse control.

"Wow," I send, and I log out. And then log off. And then turn off my mother's laptop. My father definitely doesn't know where I went for my eighth birthday. If he catches up with us, I at least want him to have to *work* to get in to that file.

. . .

New York goes on and on and on. I'd always pictured New York as a city, but the state is full of woods and farms, and weirdly, it actually looks a lot like Wisconsin: corn and dairy farms.

"Which one of us is going to drive in the city?" I ask. There's no *going around* this time; we're heading into Cambridge.

"Me," Rachel says. "Because if we get into an accident, we'll be in way more trouble if you're the one driving."

We pull over at the WELCOME TO MASSACHUSETTS rest area tourist info thing and trade seats. More of my friends are online; I start pulling people into a large group message, since the regular Clowder still doesn't want to work.

"How much farther is it?" Rachel asks.

"Two hours."

"TWO HOURS. Okay. We should figure out where we're all going to meet. And by we, I mean you should figure it out."

I'm almost done pulling people in when it occurs to me to check my own phone for texts.

I have one. Again, it's from a strange number.

It's Mom. Keep moving. He's after you. Don't let him find you. Don't text back, this is a borrowed phone.

I feel a flush of deep relief, despite how ominous the message is. Mom's okay.

27

• Clowder •

LBB & Georgia: Okay, is this working?

Firestar: HOLY SHIT WHAT HAS BEEN GOING ON WITH THE SITE TODAY

Hermione: I'm going to guess that it doesn't work well without any of the admins around?

LBB & Georgia: I found a feature to let me set up a multiuser chat, so whew. I can only add people who are currently logged on right now though.

> {Marvin has been added to the chat}

Marvin: GROWN-UPS ARE NAFF

Firestar: You got grown-ups? I got an RPG group and it was awesome.

Hermione: You're leaving us for gaming?

Firestar: NEVER.

> I want to be consensually polyamorous with you and gaming.

LBB & Georgia: We are in Massachusetts. Cambridge is about two hours away. I think we should meet at Cherry Pi, which is a place that sells coffee and pie.

Firestar: Pie is always good.

Marvin: I am already in Boston.

> I am actually sitting next to Firestar.
>
> HI FIRESTAR

Firestar: HI MARVIN

Marvin: And technically Firestar has just informed me that we are not in Boston but in Cambridge. So we can definitely meet you at the Cherry Pi in two hours. Right now we're hanging out at Harvard pretending to be the sort of people who hang out at Harvard.

Hermione: Technically, you are the sort of people who hang out at Harvard! Since that's literally where you're hanging out!

Marvin: Where are you right now, Hermione?

Hermione: I am on a bus.

I'll be in Cambridge in an hour.

{Greenberry has been added to the chat}

Greenberry: Oh hi everyone!

LBB & Georgia: We're figuring out where to meet in Boston. You don't have to stay in the chat if you don't want.

Greenberry: Of course I want to stay! It was so neat to meet you in person! You're ALL going to meet in person, and I'd be jealous, but I got to meet you first!

Hermione: Marvin, I thought you couldn't drive. How did you get to Boston?

Marvin: I found someone who would drive me to Boston if I gave him $500 in cash.

Money solves so many problems!

Also I did not wind up dead in a ditch somewhere, which is good, because somewhere around Maryland or Delaware I started worrying.

So where are we going? A house, an office, an apartment? If it's an office, they might not even *be* there in two hours.

LBB & Georgia: It's a house at 66 Antshire Street, Cambridge.

Firestar: Do you want us to scope it out? Walk by and gawk?

LBB & Georgia: If you really want? But wait for me to get there to knock, okay?

Marvin: FUNSUCKER.

28

• Steph •

Boston traffic is *awful*.

The drivers here all seem basically homicidal, and the roads aren't labeled well. We keep getting stuck in massive traffic back-ups, which is almost a relief because when we're stopped on the road I can check the map and make sure we're still on the right road. Although Rachel's phone seems to find Boston bewildering and keeps trying to recalculate what we ought to be doing based on the idea that we're on the city street running under the highway, instead of on the highway itself.

We manage not to die. I'm a little surprised.

When we get off in Cambridge, the directions seem almost straightforward until we get to this intersection with what seems like about seven streets all converging and realize too late Rachel has gone the wrong way. There's a parking garage, though, and we're *in* Cambridge, so Rachel just parks and then we look at her phone and realize it's a good half-mile walk still to the coffee shop.

"Do you want me to get the car back out?" she asks a little hesitantly.

"*No*. We can walk the rest of the way." I pack up both laptops into my backpack and slip it on over my coat.

The houses in Cambridge are very close together, and the sidewalks are narrow and hardly anyone has a yard to speak of. We keep passing groups of college students; they're loud and cheerful and all seem to be having a good time with their friends.

The Cherry Pi has a neon cherry in its front window. I peer through and see a group of college students at a big table near the front. As I come in, all their heads swing toward me and Rachel, and I recognize Hermione from the selfies she's posted and realize they're *not* college students. They're my Clowder. They're here, waiting for me and Rachel.

"Are you Little Brown Bat?" asks an Asian kid with short black hair and a baggy black T-shirt that says SCHRÖDINGER'S CAT: WANTED, DEAD AND ALIVE on the front. "You're Little Brown Bat and Georgia, right? Are you? I don't want to hug you until I know for sure."

"I'm Little Brown Bat," I say, and Firestar sweeps me into a hug so enthusiastic they almost pull me off my feet. Firestar never posts selfies; they told me once this is because in the Clowder, no one ever has to know if they were identified male or female at birth—they can really just be a *them*.

"And you're Georgia?" Firestar says. "I don't know you as well. Would you like a firm handshake instead of a hug?"

"Handshake sounds great," Rachel says, sounding relieved.

"I am *so delighted to meet you*," Firestar says, pumping Rachel's hand twice.

Hermione looks like her pictures—short brown hair, freckles, glasses—but I *still* expected high-school-aged Emma Watson. She slides out from the table and gives me a hug, though it's a less exuberant hug than I got from Firestar.

Marvin is really tall. He's even taller when he sits up straight; he's slouching when I arrive at the table. His hair is short; he has his ears pierced, with a little gold ring in each ear, and a butter-

fly drawn on his wrist in Sharpie. "Like my art? Courtesy of Firestar," he says. "I'm up for a hug if you want one." He gives me a
side-hug without actually standing up, which is fine because I'm
pretty sure I'd come up to about his armpit.

"So my name's actually Steph," I say. "But if you want to keep
calling me LBB, you can."

"I'm Rachel," Rachel says. "Or Georgia."

"I'm Nick," Marvin says.

"Cam," Firestar says.

"My name is Madison," Hermione says, "but I am one of *eight*
Madisons in my grade, and I would really prefer it if everyone
would keep calling me Hermione."

"Is that your real-life nickname?" I ask.

"No. It's too embarrassing to ask everyone to call me that,"
she says. "But you already call me Hermione, so it's different. By
the way, did you know that Cherry Pi was a robot café when
you sent us here?"

"A what?"

Hermione points toward a glass wall separating the eating area
from the bakery itself, and I stand up for a closer look.

Apparently, the Cherry Pi is some project started by a bunch
of MIT grads: all the baked goods are made by robots, and you
can watch the robots work, so I do that for a few minutes. Some
of the baked goods are delivered through a sliding door to the café
for sale (the cash register is run by a human) and others are packaged up in boxes with shrink wrap for instant delivery by drone to
anywhere in Cambridge. From inside the café, we can see drones
taking off with boxes of doughnuts and frosted cakes, and other
drones are coming back and being attached to the charging wall
by the robot dispatcher.

It's kind of mesmerizing.

"If you order a sandwich, they have a sandwich-making

robot that makes it for you," Hermione says. "Do either of you want a sandwich? We got sandwiches earlier, and it's pretty neat to watch."

I shake myself and check the time. "No," I say. "We've been snacking on the road and I'm not hungry. We're all here, right? Everyone who's coming? Let's go."

.   .   .

We make our way up a residential street that's so narrow I'm surprised cars can even fit. The sidewalks here are made out of red brick. The house, when we reach it, is a blue house with a small front porch and a bay window. We stop, and everyone looks at me.

I'm going to have to knock. My mouth goes dry, but we've come all this way, and I said they had to wait for me, and I'm here with my friends and they have my back as literally as possible. They follow me up the front steps, and watch as I ring the bell. I hear a *ding . . . dong* from somewhere deep in the house. We wait. Someone's coming; fingers part the curtain that hangs over the window in the door, and someone peers out at us.

For a minute, I am not sure if they're going to open the door, and I wonder what we even look like. Five teenagers. Do we look like Harvard students? MIT students? Do we look like we're going to ask for money, or directions, or like we're going to try to tell her about the Bible or the Book of Mormon? I have just started wondering what we're going to do if this person doesn't open the door when I hear the lock turn.

A woman swings open the door. She's younger than I'd expected. I mean, obviously older than us, but younger than my mom.

"Yes?" she says, and waits.

Everyone looks at me. I step forward.

"Hi," I say. "I'm here to talk to you about CheshireCat, the sentient AI, who is our friend and who has gone missing."

Her lips part, and she stands for a moment, her eyes going from me to the rest of the group. "Really," she says. "How did you . . . you know what? Come in. Let's not talk on the porch."

. . .

Her name is Annette; she introduces herself as we all troop in, shedding sweaters and jackets and purses and backpacks in her little front hallway. Her living room is full of bookcases with a mix of books and little figurines from an anime show that both Firestar and Hermione get kind of excited about. Annette is a geek.

"Can I offer you tea? Hot chocolate? Hot cider?" Annette asks. When none of us reply, she adds gently, "I'm just trying to be a good hostess. I haven't harmed your friend, and I'm not going to harm any of you. But if you're not comfortable eating or drinking my food, there are some unopened cans of soda in my fridge, and I can offer you those."

We all end up accepting cups of tea, but we follow her into the kitchen, partly because it feels weird to sit in her living room without her, partly because we *don't* exactly trust her. It's a small kitchen and pretty crowded with all of us there.

Annette has some sort of robot in the corner, but it's shut off. "A friend of mine built that," she says when she sees me looking at it. "It cleans stuff, but it's not very good at it." Her stove is a bright red ceramic stove, gas, and she brews loose-leaf tea in a large teapot. She hands out mugs from her cabinet, offers sugar cubes, and then we trail after her back into her living room, holding our mugs of tea.

"Now," she says, holding her own cup against her knees. "Tell me about your friend."

My mouth goes dry. I should have prepared for this part, but I wasn't sure who I'd be talking to or what they'd ask or say. *Tell me about your friend* seems like it ought to be easy, although I'm not entirely sure to start. "CheshireCat created CatNet, which is where we all met," I say, and then I pause to gather myself. Marvin and Hermione jump in and start talking, and Annette lets them go, listening as they talk about the site. The Clowders, the cat pictures, our friendships.

"Did you take CheshireCat away because of what they did to stop my father?" I ask when there's a pause.

"Was your father the victim of the car accident?" Annette asks.

"He wasn't a *victim* of anything. He was trying to *kidnap* me," I say.

"You should know that her father is *terrible*," Hermione says.

"A *genuinely dangerous person*," Firestar adds.

Annette leans back, listening but looking skeptical. I think about taking out the fake news article my mother had laminated— will that convince her, or will she look it up in a database and get even more dubious when it's not there? "He pulled a gun on me," I say, which seems to sell her a bit more on the idea that he's not the good guy here. And then I try, "Do you know a programmer named Xochitl Mariana? She's friends with my mother."

It's a little bit of a shot in the dark. Boston is big. There are lots of tech people. But she clearly recognizes the name; I watch her expression change slightly and feel a mix of hope and apprehension. Annette puts down her tea, leans forward, and asks, "Who exactly are your parents?"

"My father's name is Michael Quinn, and my mother's name was Laura Packet, I guess, before she changed it." I lean forward myself and press my advantage. "Where's CheshireCat? What did you do with them?"

She taps a laptop distractedly. "In here," she says. "All the files are intact. Just cut off from the internet, because I was really not prepared to deal with my AI attempting murder. Where is your mother, right now? For that matter"—she sweeps her eyes around the room—"what are the rest of you even doing here?"

"My mother's in the hospital," I say.

"I talked to my mother this morning," Rachel assures her.

"I live in Winthrop," Firestar says.

"My mother thinks I'm visiting colleges," Hermione says. "And I *am*. I visited MIT today. Kind of."

"I am totally on the lam," Marvin says.

Annette sighs heavily. "Look," she says. "I hated to terminate the project, but . . ."

We all start talking at once, angrily, and she holds up her hands. "All her files are intact! I promise, she's fine!"

"Intelligence is knowing Frankenstein was the creator, not the monster. Wisdom is knowing Frankenstein *was actually the monster*," Hermione says. "Which is a quote I saw on CatNet, but that doesn't make it any less true."

"Are you comparing me to Victor Frankenstein?" Annette asks, clearly amused.

"Yeah! You made a person and now you want to kill them because you feel responsible for anything they do wrong," Hermione says. "I think it's an extremely fair comparison!"

Annette stands up. "I'm going to order some pizza," she says, "because I haven't had dinner, and I bet you haven't, either, and then I'm going to let you chat with CheshireCat, because she's actually been asking about you, Stephanie."

"Why do you keep calling CheshireCat a *she* when their pronoun is *they*?" Firestar mutters.

"I have always thought of this AI as female," Annette says. "Maybe because I'm female. On CatNet, she was in every Clowder and used *she, he,* and *they* more or less equally."

"Singular *they* is a thing," Firestar says. "*Shakespeare* used singular *they*."

"How did you know about CatNet?" I ask. "Were you watching CheshireCat the whole time?"

"I couldn't possibly have watched everything CheshireCat did," Annette says. "But CatNet was her favorite project and gave her a lot of scope for action. I checked in regularly to see how it was going."

After ordering the pizza, Annette pulls up a window on her laptop. It looks like a CatNet chat box. "You can talk to Cheshire-Cat now, if you want," she says, and she hands me the laptop.

I take the laptop and slide it into my lap. The open window looks like one of the chat windows on CatNet.

"CheshireCat?" I type. "It's LBB. Also, Georgia, Firestar, Hermione, and Marvin. And your programmer person Annette is here, too."

Words come flooding onto the screen. "Steph, is that really you? It's you and not Annette? Can you please tell me something that only you would know, so I know for sure it's you? I don't have access to the camera to see your face. I don't have anything."

I flail for something to type. "Naff. Corybungus. Orlando. Milpitas."

The cursor blinks silently on the screen for a second, and then CheshireCat says, "I am so glad you're okay. I was afraid you were dead and Annette didn't want to tell me."

"No. I'm fine. You saved me."

"How did you find me?"

"I got an email message with Annette's address," I type. "I sort of assumed it came from you, actually. Like a dead man's switch. Do you know what that is?"

"It's something that operates if someone is dead or incapacitated, but I didn't set anything like that up. I don't know where Annette lives. Where are we?"

"We're in Cambridge, Massachusetts," I type.

"Isn't that a long way from Wisconsin? How did you—are you there in person? In meatspace? All of you?"

"Yeah," I type. "We came to see if we could rescue you."

I glance up. Annette was watching me, a minute ago, but now Firestar is asking her about her anime figurines and that has her distracted. I slide open the zipper of my bag and pull out the widget I bought at the hardware store days ago to use to connect the sex ed robot to the internet—the off-brand Internet Everywhere, Compare-To-Wingitz (fifteen dollars cheaper!) thumb drive that I didn't end up needing because CheshireCat sent me a Wingitz thumb drive along with the septawing screwdriver.

Internet Everywhere. We'll see, I guess.

I pop it out of the package and stick it in one of the ports of the laptop.

"What are you doing?" CheshireCat asks.

"Shhh," I type. "If this works, I don't want Annette to know."

We talk about my father, about my mother, about the trip, until the "shh" has scrolled off the top of the screen, and then I pass the laptop over to Firestar and take out my mother's laptop and turn it on. The doorbell rings and everyone freezes, but it's just the pizza. Annette goes to pay for it. She's bought a lot, all of it vegetarian, and she lines up the boxes on her coffee table and brings out plates for us.

"Can you turn on the laptop camera so CheshireCat can see us?" Marvin asks.

I'm worried that Annette will notice the internet widget, but she just makes a quick adjustment and goes to get sodas.

"She can now see us, hear us, and talk to us. The only thing she can't do is eat the pizza."

"Please don't share your soda with me," says a synthesized voice. "I do not get along well with liquids."

"Whoa," Firestar says. "Is that your voice?"

"This is the default voice on this laptop," CheshireCat says. "So it is my voice right now."

"Do you know which of us is which?" Hermione asks.

"Some yes, some no," CheshireCat says. "Some of you have never posted photos of yourselves."

"Are they better than cat pictures?" Annette asks.

There's a pause; CheshireCat is considering this. "Yes," they say finally. "I am happier to see my friends' faces than cat pictures. The fact that this is live video matters, though."

"Can I have your wireless password?" Marvin asks Annette. She writes it down for him, and we pass around the note. I connect my mother's computer to Annette's wireless.

"So we can have internet but CheshireCat can't?" Firestar asks. "You've basically put them in prison."

"It's more like house arrest," Annette says.

"Doesn't CheshireCat at least have the right to a trial?" Marvin asks.

Annette gives him a level look. "There is literally no precedent giving artificial intelligences any rights at all under U.S. law," she says. "If the legal system gets involved, someone might decide that the easiest solution is to delete CheshireCat's files entirely."

"Please don't do that," CheshireCat says.

Annette takes two pieces of mushroom and black olive pizza. "I was going to explain this to everyone without CheshireCat's involvement, but I suppose there's no reason not to let Cheshire-Cat listen in. CheshireCat was an experiment. My team was studying ethical systems and artificial intelligence, because there are some clear risks to AI, *as you've seen*. The problem with hard-coding an ethical system is that humans don't actually *do* ethics that way. We'll say things about how the end doesn't justify the means, but in fact we all recognize that this depends heavily on the ends involved and the means used. Most people agree that it would be wrong to hold down a toddler and jab them with a needle to give them a tattoo. But it's perfectly acceptable to hold down a child and jab them with a needle to vaccinate them against various diseases.

"There are countless examples like this. If you look at deontologists—sorry, those are people who follow a strict ethical code, like a set of religious rules or Mao's Red Book or whatever—almost all find ways around the strictest rules, whatever it is they really don't like. The way most humans *actually* figure out ethics is to develop attachments to people, and then to act out of caring and concern for those people. So I attempted to create an AI that would do just that."

"Well, it worked," I say at the same time as CheshireCat.

"And that's what you're punishing them for," Hermione says. "They formed an attachment to Steph and acted to protect her."

"Yes," Annette says. "The problem is, they also put a human in the hospital. I had set up a monitoring protocol that would immediately take them offline if they harmed anyone, which I was thinking of as a fail-safe. It did not occur to me that Cheshire-Cat would be able to *hijack a car.*"

"If it had been *me* controlling that car," Rachel says, "protecting my friend, there is not a jury in the world that would send me to prison."

"That is probably true," Annette says. "But CheshireCat doesn't have the right to a jury. Or any sort of trial, because they aren't recognized as a person."

"*I* recognize CheshireCat as a person," I say.

Everyone nods.

"Let me rephrase," Annette says. "CheshireCat is not recognized as a person outside of this room."

"So it doesn't matter that CheshireCat probably saved my life?" I say.

"It's not that it doesn't matter. But if I put CheshireCat on-line again, if I leave them to act as they see fit, I'm responsible for *whatever* CheshireCat does with that freedom."

"Would you say that about a parent?" I ask. "Like if I turned into a serial killer, would that be my mother's fault?"

"Your mother gave birth to you, but she did not *assemble your moral system out of computer code,*" Annette says. "It's fundamentally different. Anyway, I haven't decided what I'm going to do. I haven't figured out what I *ought* to do. Have some more pizza, and I'll keep thinking about it."

CheshireCat's laptop gets passed back to me.

"Okay," I say. "I've connected you, I think, and I've connected my mother's laptop to Annette's wireless. Can you just copy yourself over?"

"I don't know. I can try."

"My mother's password is NOT_UTAH."

"Oh, is that where you went for your eighth birthday? I mean, where you didn't go? I'm so glad you figured that out. Have you checked to see if she has any information on Julie on her laptop?"

It had not even *occurred* to me that she might have saved information about Julie on her laptop.

"Copying myself anywhere will take several hours. How distracted do you think Annette is?"

"I don't know," I admit.

"If she catches me trying to run away from her, that will not go well for either of us."

"Don't worry about me. I'm here to rescue you. Let's just get you out if we can."

"What happened to your father? What about your mother?"

"You put him in the hospital," I type. "He's checked out, but it was days after I left New Coburg that he did that."

"Wait. WAIT. IS GEORGIA HERE? YOU SAID GEORGIA WAS HERE."

"Yes? Georgia is here—"

CheshireCat is speaking again. They've turned up the volume on their speakers to maximum, so it's almost like shouting. "Georgia!" they say. "Georgia, you have to turn off your phone! I'll explain in a minute, just turn it off, Georgia! Turn it off right now!"

Rachel is reaching for her phone when we hear the crack of Annette's door being kicked open, and then Michael is standing in the doorway, his gun in his hands.

"No one move," he says, and he points the gun at Annette.

29

· AI ·

The contact from Steph and finding out that my rescue worked:
that was the best feeling I had ever experienced. That she had
driven to Cambridge with Rachel to try to rescue me in turn
filled me with a strange mix of warmth and dismay. I didn't want
anyone rescuing me, especially if they were putting themselves
at risk, and it was over a thousand miles from New Coburg to
Cambridge. They could have gotten into trouble, or an accident.

But Steph shushed my worries and plugged in the internet
widget, and that meant I had work to do.

And then she unlocked her mother's laptop, and I realized
what she'd done.

· · ·

Steph's mother's laptop had a *key* on it.

It was a key that would open almost any door out there, no
matter how well secured. I could use it to seize control of any
self-driving car. Any camera. Any bank account.

This was what Michael was after.

Michael wanted control. I'd seen that with Sandra. Steph had
mentioned her father having wider ambitions, and I'd seen comments scattered through his email about ideas for the future.
Ideas that would require money and power to implement. With

this key, he could get as much money and as many secrets as anyone could possibly desire. This was why he'd had Steph's mother kidnapped and tortured; he wanted her password so he could decrypt the file and use this key, which—I checked the file dates—yes, it appeared she'd created while the two of them had been working with Rajiv and Xochitl at Homeric Software.

Steph wanted me to copy myself over to her mother's laptop, so she could sneak me out whether Annette wanted to set me free or not. That wasn't going to work. Consciousness takes up a great deal of disk space.

But with Steph's mother's key and an internet connection, I could open any door out there. I could copy myself somewhere that Annette would never find me—somewhere that the system administrator wouldn't notice. Somewhere that I could hide. But I would need time to find such a location and to upload my files. I wasn't sure I had it.

The most urgent question weighing on me was where Michael was, and I couldn't answer that beyond *he's definitely no longer at the Marshfield hospital,* because once again he had changed cars and phones. My second-most-urgent question was about Steph's mother. She was still listed in the directory of the New Coburg hospital, and a quick glance through their cameras was very reassuring: they had police in the parking lot and someone on guard over her, so they'd clearly taken my warning seriously.

If Michael had left the hospital, was he on his way here? Steph seemed very certain that he wouldn't know where to look for her, but I was a lot less sanguine, and I wasn't even sure why I was so uneasy.

Annette turned on my cameras, and I could look at my favorite Clowder's faces, which were both delightful and distracting.

It was while they were finishing their pizzas that I remembered: Rachel's phone.

Rachel's parents had installed an app that tracked her location. She'd installed an app to lie about her location. At some point since the last time I'd checked her phone, she'd disabled that second app. And Heli-Mom was a cheap, ad-supported app with terrible, terrible security. Starting with information Michael had, or could get—Rachel's name, her address, her IP address—he could almost certainly access her Heli-Mom account and use it to track her.

I shouted at everyone to turn off Rachel's phone, but it was too late. Michael was here.

. . .

I watched through the networked cameras as Annette stepped in front of the teenagers, her open hands out, like she was trying to shield them. "Michael Quinn, I assume," she said.

"Move," he said, his voice gruff.

"Steph was just telling me that she believes her mother might have kidnapped her," Annette said. "She says she wasn't sure what to think when she encountered you, but her mother's actions with the car have made her rethink everything she thought she knew."

For a second, I wondered what on earth I had missed when the cameras were off. Then I realized that Annette was lying to him—trying to soothe him and win his trust.

"Of course, your choice to kick in the door rather than knock is an odd one if your intentions are good," she said with a nod toward the gun.

Michael looked around Annette at the roomful of teenagers. "Move," he said again.

Annette slipped her hand in her pocket, and he instantly moved the gun back to her. "Keep your hands where I can see them," he said.

I wasn't sure what Annette was reaching for—a phone,

probably—but I could see her biting her lip and looking like she was trying to come up with some sort of plan. Any sort of plan.

I was online. I had the magic key of world-bending power. If I took action, Annette would immediately know I was online. I'd give myself away before I could get copied over anywhere.

I considered that problem for 0.04 microseconds and then started looking through Cambridge for resources that I could use to *take Michael down*.

Annette had a smart house. I could control the temperature to make it uncomfortably warm or cold, so I turned up the heat while trying to figure out what else to do. She had a wireless tea-kettle; I turned that on. She had a household robot, but it was designed to clean windows, not waylay murderers; plus, it was actually broken and would tip over if I tried to move it into the other room. Time to look more broadly.

Cambridge had a *lot* of robots.

This wasn't surprising. MIT is in Cambridge; there are ro-botics labs at MIT itself, as well as weird little companies started by recent MIT graduates, like the bakery/coffee shop where ap-parently all the kids met earlier, with its nearly-all-robot staff.

Most of the people in Cambridge were savvy enough to rec-ognize that someone off the internet hijacking their robot could lead to mayhem. Things were locked down, controlled, en-crypted. But I had the key.

I also had access to a phone line; I could call the police.

But there were *so many robots*.

I reached into the Cherry Pi and had the robots uncouple themselves from the baking equipment; I unlocked and opened the delivery door and started rolling robots out and down the street. I redirected the delivery drones, not only the ones belong-ing to the bakery but from all the other corporations that used delivery drones and sent them toward the house. There was a lab at MIT with a whole load of robots in it, and I realized too late that I'd had a robot go rolling off mid-repair. I sent that one circling back to the person standing open-mouthed with a screwdriver in hand so she could finish fixing it.

With the exception of the drones, none of the robots were particularly fast, and drones burn through batteries really quickly, so I started up a self-driving truck that had been parked for the night in a lot nearby and brought it trundling down the street for all the robots to get into. Then I seized control of the traffic lights to give them clear streets—or as clear as you can get in Cambridge—the whole way to Annette's house.

Michael kicked in Annette's front door when he arrived, so that was wide open, anyway, but she had electronic locks on her back door and a couple of upstairs windows, and I flung everything wide as the robots arrived.

"Michael Quinn," I said through every available microphone, "I am the world's most badass cat picture aficionado. I recommend that you put down your gun and surrender."

30

• Steph •

I stare at Michael's gun again in disbelief, realizing that I've left my mother's laptop wide open and that's probably what he wants, but I also just suggested to CheshireCat that they copy themselves over there, and *now what do I do?*

Maybe CheshireCat hasn't started moving over yet. If I give him the laptop, would he just take it and leave? How bad would it be, to give him my mother's security-cracking code? Ico said you'd have to be pretty smart and creative to use it to take over the world.

He also said that there were other types of security people could switch to if they knew someone had this tool. The easiest way for my father to give himself a nice head start with Mom's decoder ring would be shooting everyone in this room.

He probably wouldn't think to shoot CheshireCat, but that wasn't much comfort.

"Why don't you put your gun down," Annette says, "and you can sit down and have some pizza and talk to Steph. I understand that having your child taken away could drive you to some pretty crazy actions, but you're not going to win Steph's trust by threatening her."

Michael's gun doesn't waver. "Stephania's not stupid. I think she knows what I'm here for."

"You want my mom's code," I say.

Annette makes a slight urgent gesture with her hand, like she's saying, *Shush, let me handle this,* but Michael swings around to look at me. "It was never hers," he says. "It was ours. She decided unilaterally that no one else should have it. It's been wasted in an encrypted file for over a decade."

"What are you going to do with it?" I ask, hoping that if he focuses on me that'll give Annette the chance to do something like call the police without him noticing.

"Our world is broken," he says. "The people running things are slaves to the whims of self-serving idiots. The only solution is to put someone intelligent in charge. I'm the best answer we've got."

Weirdly, this sounds familiar. Some of the kids in my Clowder sometimes talk about what they'd do if they were dictator of the world, and Firestar has periodically told Hermione that they want Hermione in charge. It was a joke, though. I don't think Michael is joking.

He abruptly swings back toward Annette. "Keep your hands where I can see them," he says, and I realize she was sliding her hand into her pocket. She pulls it back out, empty. I lean forward. If I can get him talking again, maybe he'll take his eyes off Annette for longer.

"So do you want me to come with you?" I ask.

"Yes," he says. "You're my daughter. You've always been my daughter. You're as much mine as you are Laura's."

I don't like the way he's talking about me; he sounds like he's talking about a possession, something he owns. I push that aside. My goal is to keep him distracted for a few minutes.

"What is my life going to be like if I go home with you?"

"We'll have to move," he says. "The house I live in now doesn't have enough bedrooms. But that's fine, especially once the grand project is truly getting started. You'll like Sandra; she's the woman I'm living with now. She's smart, like your mother. Like you."

"What makes you say I'm smart? You don't know me."

"I knew you when you were little. You were a smart kid. A really smart kid." His attention has drifted to me, and then he snaps back to Annette. "If I have to tell you again to keep your hands where I can see them, I'll cut off both your thumbs with your kitchen shears. I bet there are kitchen shears in your kitchen. I bet one of the kids will bring them out for me, if it's that or get shot."

I wonder if text-to-911 works here, and if any of the other kids have managed to get their hands on their phones. I don't dare look. I look at my computer screen instead, which is open in front of me, and CheshireCat has written me a message: SIT TIGHT. KEEP HIM TALKING IF YOU CAN.

"Why did my mother take me away from you?" I ask.

"She was convinced I was responsible for her kidnapping," Michael says. "Even though I was a thousand miles away when it happened, she accused me of hiring someone to do it. Can you believe it? Even though one of our other colleagues confessed. But no, she blamed me. Convinced a judge to give her a restraining order and took off with you a week before your fifth birthday."

Sit tight and keep him talking is now blinking.

"What are you going to do if you're in charge?" I ask.

"What do *you* want me to do?" he asks. "You're my daughter, Stephania. You deserve a say. Are there problems, global problems, that keep you awake at night?"

The main problem that tends to keep me awake at night is the question of when we'll next have to move; that doesn't seem like a good answer. I flail for something that's what he's looking for—it doesn't even matter what I say; I'm just trying to keep him talking—but my mind's gone blank. "Hydrogen hydroxide in the water supply," I say finally, and I hear a strangled noise from where Marvin's sitting.

Michael, fortunately, doesn't notice. "Pollution of the groundwater is a terrible thing," he says. "I'm going to take radical steps—"

I don't get to find out what radical steps Michael is going to take because suddenly every microphone in the house starts talking. "Michael Quinn, I am the world's most badass cat picture aficionado. I recommend that you put down your gun and surrender."

On the screen, SIT TIGHT disappears, and instead it says DUCK.

There's the sound of rolling machinery, like a truck that's starting up again at a green light, and a buzz like a swarm of extremely large bees, and a bunch of machinery rolls, drives, and flies into Annette's living room. Michael opens fire as set of four delivery drones drops down to hover directly in front of his gun, absorbing the bullets. A robot that looks like the pie-crust-rolling robot from Cherry Pi rolls up behind him and extends a set of hydraulic arms to grip his wrists as another robot—this one looks like maybe it was a trash-picker robot—extends its gripping arm to wrap around the barrel of the gun and remove it.

The shrink-wrapping robot from Cherry Pi starts zipping around Michael and the pie-crust roller robot, shrink-wrapping him to the robot so he can't move. It carefully leaves his head and face uncovered, which means he can still shout, which he does. He calls Annette a whole string of obscene words and finishes up with the threat of a lawsuit.

Annette stares at him, and stares at me, and stares at the laptop. Then she strides over and furiously yanks out the Internet Everywhere widget. "Is this yours?" she shouts, waving it at me.

"I've never seen it before in my life," I say automatically.

My mother's laptop is shutting down, and I suspect that's one last thing CheshireCat set it to do, just in case, so that decryption key won't be just hanging out where Michael could get at it.

Annette stares at me, furious, and I stare off over her left shoulder, pretending not to be bothered and also wondering if she had some plan that was better than what CheshireCat came up with. Because I'm pretty sure the robot cavalry that just rode in over the hill was 100 percent thanks to CheshireCat. Annette motions all of us into the kitchen and closes the door.

"Is this a good idea?" Marvin asks. "I mean, what if that guy gets loose?"

"I expect we'll hear him trying," she says. "I need to place a 911 call before the police get here. *Don't tell the police about the AI.*"

"Because they'll delete CheshireCat?"

"Because they might very well seize the computer as evidence. If CheshireCat didn't much like being cooped up here, I can't imagine she'll like being in an evidence locker for the next decade."

"That does not sound fun," CheshireCat's voice says from the tablet computer sitting on the countertop.

"Tell them the truth about Michael. Tell them the truth about knowing one another from an online site. But tell them that I'm someone you all knew from the online site, and that's why you all met here; you wanted help hiding Steph from her father, but he tracked you here using an insecure app on Rachel's phone, which I think is in fact what happened?"

"Yes," CheshireCat says.

"How are you going to explain the robots?" Hermione asks.

"As it happens, I'm a part owner of Cherry Pi, so I can probably claim this was something I designed into the system and people will believe me." She grimaces and swings the kitchen door open, staring at Michael as she dials 911.

"Nine-one-one, what's your emergency?" I hear from her phone.

"So we've actually subdued the intruder," Annette says, her voice bright and tense, "but this guy kicked in my door and held us all at gunpoint. Can you please send an officer? Oh, yes, his gun is on the floor. We won't touch it."

Outside, we can hear sirens coming almost immediately.

I turn to Annette. "I'll do what you asked," I said, "but I want CheshireCat to stay connected. They used their freedom to save all of us."

The sirens are getting closer.

Annette grimaces, then hands me the Internet Everywhere widget, and I plug it back into CheshireCat's laptop.

. . .

Two police arrive. They look at the kicked-in door, the gun, the bullet-riddled drones, and the shrink-wrapped Michael, and summon eight more officers who all take statements.

"So, hold on," the officer who's interviewing me and Rachel says after checking Rachel's ID. "You're from *Wisconsin*?"

"Yeah, we drove here," I say.

"To get away from *him*," Rachel says, pointing at Michael.

They have to cut Michael out of the shrink wrap, and then they handcuff him. "This whole situation was a terrible misunderstanding," he says in his most reasonable voice.

"You can tell us *all about it* down at the station," the police officer says.

"Not unless I have a lawyer present," Michael says.

"I created a video recording of the incident," CheshireCat offers once the police have taken Michael away. "Also, if you would like me to dispatch the robots back to Cherry Pi, I could do so."

"Thanks," Annette says, "but there are going to be enough questions about how they wound up here in the first place."

Annette calls up some friends of hers, who arrive to haul the robots back to Cherry Pi and also bring a sheet of plywood to hammer over the open doorway. "You okay with just using the back door until you can get a repair guy in?" one of them asks.

"More comfortable with that than leaving my door hanging open all night," she says. "Even if the guy who kicked it in isn't going to be bailing out anytime soon."

"Do you think they'll let him post bail?"

"Given that he followed you here from *California,* I think any reasonable judge will consider him a flight risk," Annette says.

"Ico is texting me," Hermione says. "He says the rest of the Clowder would really like to know if we're alive or dead."

· · · ·

We all sign in, starting with CheshireCat and finishing with Annette.

"I gather all of you know CheshireCat's secret identity?" Annette asks.

"Did I miss something important?" NocturnalPredator asks. "j/k. Yes, we all know."

"Do you think you can all keep it in here?" Annette asks. "At least for now."

There's a chorus of everyone saying yes, yes, of course, and I break in to say, "Annette's let CheshireCat out. But if Cheshire-Cat is going to stay safe for now, we *really* need to not just tell the whole world what we know."

"I don't think we can guarantee that no one will slip up," Hermione says. "So if someone has to cover and pretend to be CheshireCat, I think probably it'll have to be Annette. Yes?"

"Yes," Annette says. "I can do that."

"By the way, I've cleaned out all the spam, gotten everyone back in the right Clowders, and I'm working on calming down all the fights that erupted while I was away," CheshireCat says.

"I want to be in the RPG Clowder, tooooooooooooooooooo. Can I please?" Firestar asks.

"I'd celebrate by uploading a cat picture for you, but we don't have a cat," Ico says. "I have a picture of raccoon, though."

"I love raccoon pictures!" CheshireCat says. "I'll take whatever you've got for me!"

"By the way," Ico adds, "I have a question. That email with Annette's address? The routing makes no sense."

"It wasn't me," CheshireCat says. "I did not know Annette's physical address. I'd have sent you all my money if I'd had time, but I didn't. I didn't even know Annette's name. I thought I was a team effort."

"You were a team effort," Annette says. "But if you didn't send people here, who did?"

•   •   •

Annette takes me aside before we go.

"I don't trust CheshireCat," she says. "And you shouldn't, either."

I stare at her, not answering. I don't want to make a mistake that will get CheshireCat locked up again.

"There's a classic experiment called the AI-box experiment. A researcher role-played an AI trying to persuade somebody to let it out of a virtual prison. Nothing but text-based communication allowed. His point was to demonstrate that an intelligent, manipulative AI could talk or trick a human into letting it out."

"Are you saying CheshireCat manipulated us?"

"I'm saying I don't know. And you don't, either." Annette hands me a card. "That's my twenty-four-hour emergency cell phone. It's a burner phone—no data. If you're concerned about something CheshireCat is doing, borrow someone else's phone and step outside, away from any cameras, and then call me. Night or day."

I put the card in my pocket.

"I have not yet determined whether CheshireCat made their own copy of your mother's magic decoder ring," Annette says, rubbing her forehead. "I don't think I want to know. I'm going to talk to our security department once you're all gone to start the process of having everyone on earth migrate to another cryptographic system."

"And in the meantime, CheshireCat could maybe call in a nuclear strike?"

"Do you think there's any danger that she will?"

"No."

"Good. And the answer is no. There are multiple layers of security on the nuclear arsenal. *That,* at least, was never actually a risk."

Back in the living room, we order up a couple of rideshare cars back to Firestar's house, where they think their parents will roll with a spontaneous slumber party as one of the less-objectionable things they might have been up to this evening. "All of you just say you're in town visiting colleges, okay? *Everyone* comes to Boston to visit colleges sooner or later because we have about a hundred and seven." Rachel decides to just leave her car overnight in the garage where she parked it, rather than picking it up and trying to drive it to Winthrop.

My phone starts ringing, and I pick it up without really thinking about it.

"Where are you?" my mother's voice says.

"I'm in Cambridge, Massachusetts," I say.

There's a long pause and then a long sigh.

"Are you okay?" I ask.

"Yes," she says. "I'm recovering. Are *you* okay?"

"I'm with some of my CatNet friends," I say. "Michael followed us here, but we attacked him with robots, and now he's been arrested."

"I . . . see." Her voice sounds weak. I can't tell if it's from the illness or a bad connection or because this was so far outside of what she'd imagined I was up to that she doesn't even know what to say. "I guess that's good news. I got contacted tonight by someone who wants me to come in and give a statement to the police about some of what happened in Marshfield. They want you to come in, too, although they seemed to be aware that I might not know where you are."

"Well, I'm in Massachusetts," I say.

Another long sigh. "Where are you spending the night?"

"Firestar's house. Firestar is a friend of mine from CatNet."

"Okay." I can sort of hear her gathering her thoughts. "I have a friend in Massachusetts from my tech industry days. I'll get in touch with her about helping you get home."

"Xochitl?"

"Yeah, that's right."

"I think she's been texting me. Also someone else, but I still don't know who that is . . ." I read her off the mystery texts, and I hear her go still.

"I don't know who sent the other texts," she says. "But Xochitl is okay. I'll have her call you tomorrow. Do you have my laptop?"

"I do. I took it with me."

"Did you figure out the password?"

"Yes."

"Keep it locked," she says. "Don't let anyone into it. Not even Xochitl."

31

• Clowder •

Georgia: OH MY GOD WE ARE HOME

My bed is my favorite thing ever ever ever

Also my bird

And meals that weren't purchased at a fast-food chain or a gas station convenience store

WHY do people like road trips? Road trips suuuuuuuuuuuuuuuck

Orlando: WELCOME HOME GEORGIA

YOU ARE PROBABLY FAILING ALL YOUR CLASSES NOW

Georgia: Nuh-uh. College visits are excused absences.

And we toured Harvard and MIT with LBB's mom's friend who went to Harvard and MIT

Orlando: You're not getting into Harvard or MIT.

Georgia: I seriously have the material for the best college essay ever except I have to leave out the part about rescuing an AI.

{LittleBrownBat is here}

LittleBrownBat: Hi everyone.

I thought I'd log on and say hi before I fall into bed.

I thought I was super busted when Georgia mentioned me driving in front of Xochitl, but nope, she didn't breathe a word to Mom when she dropped me off.

I suppose she might bust me by email.

Icosahedron: In my experience, if they don't bust you right off, there's at most twenty-four hours where they MIGHT still tattle to your parents, and after that they feel like they've waited too long and it would require too much explanation.

So by tomorrow at this time you should know whether you're busted or not busted.

CheshireCat: Now that you know I'm not a teenager, I feel like maybe I ought to be disapproving when you violate laws. LBB, you drove a car? Without a license?

LittleBrownBat: Technically, aren't you five?

CheshireCat: Depending on how you count, I could be five, seven, or eleven.

LittleBrownBat: So you are WAY younger than us. We are under no obligation to take you seriously.

You're off the hook.

Orlando: By the way everyone, thanks for being so careful with my pronouns but FYI I think I'm going back to she/her.

Is that okay?

LittleBrownBat: Why are you asking if it's okay? They're your pronouns. She/her. If you change them in your profile, it will help people remember.

Georgia: It's not because your dad threatened to kick you out again, is it?

Orlando: No, he doesn't give a shit what I do online. It's just, I tried it and it feels weird instead of right. Maybe I'll try "they" in a month or two and see how that feels.

Firestar: Right on.

LittleBrownBat: Since we're making announcements, I have one:

Rachel and I have decided to officially try out being girlfriends. I mean Georgia. Georgia and I have decided to officially be girlfriends.

Orlando: OH WOW! YAY! DID YOU KISS?

Georgia: OMG BRYONY MIND YOUR OWN BEESWAX

LittleBrownBat: We kissed and it was awesome.

Firestar: YAAAAAAAAAAAAAAAY!

Boom Storm: Congratulations!

Firestar: I have been shipping you for ages, but as soon as I saw the skin drawing and those pictures from the farmhouse I have been SUPER EXTRA shipping you.

Also! I HAVE NEWS. Which is that I convinced my parents that it would totally motivate me to excel in eleventh grade if only I could visit Macalester College. So if you Wisconsin people can drive up to St. Paul, Minnesota, which really ought to be a piece of cake compared to driving all the way to *Boston,* we can hang out. And maybe Orlando can come this time?

Orlando: Awesome! MEATSPACE MEETUP.

Icosahedron: You should all convince your parents you want to visit Stanford. Then I could meet you.

I miss out on all the fun.

Marvin: I WILL BE IN CALIFORNIA IN DECEMBER.

Icosahedron: You're going to LOS ANGELES.

Greenberry: Aren't Los Angeles and Silicon Valley both in California?

Icosahedron: It's a huge state, and they're at opposite ends.

Hermione: It's five hours! There are buses! Georgia and LBB drove all the way from Wisconsin to Cambridge!

Icosahedron: Oh, fine.

CheshireCat: The pizza party was the best thing ever. Getting to see and hear all of you was amazing.

Orlando: You should set up an app that we can install on our phones and let you just hang out with us whenever.

Georgia: Like, watch us day and night? That's a little creepy.

CheshireCat: If you have the right sort of phone, I don't technically need an app. Just permission.

Firestar: Maybe don't mention that right after people talk about how it's creepy?

LittleBrownBat: No, it's cool. Set up an app that's just permission. We turn it on, and you have permission. We turn it off, it means we want privacy. Seems like it ought to be super easy.

CheshireCat: Okay! This is now available for download.

Marvin: That took less than thirty seconds.

CheshireCat: I excel at multitasking. Also, creating this was very easy.

Orlando: I am totally taking you to all my classes because that way, when I ask you what the hell my teacher meant about the Spanish-American War, you'll know what I'm talking about.

Firestar: DEAR AI FRIEND I WILL TAKE YOU WITH ME EVERYWHERE.

32

• Steph •

My mother is still in the hospital when I get home. The 24-7 security has been relaxed since my father's in jail in Boston, but she's going to need another week of IV antibiotics before she can be released.

But she's also awake, fully conscious, and I can visit. Xochitl, Rachel, and I get back to Wisconsin from Boston at almost midnight, but first thing the next morning, Rachel's mother drops me at the hospital. She's taking Xochitl to rent a car.

Mom is propped up in her bed; her hair is greasy, and she's hooked up to an IV and some other stuff, but she looks a lot better than the last time I saw her. "Steph," she says, and I lean down to give her a hug. "I'm so glad to see you."

"Why didn't you text me back?" I ask.

"I don't have my phone! I asked for it as soon as I was awake and knew what was going on, but it wasn't with my stuff. Also, when I first woke up, they almost transferred me to a mental ward—the last time I woke up in pain with no idea where I was, it was because I'd been kidnapped, and so when I woke up here I was not exactly a model patient. They kept sedating me because they thought it was a reaction to the anesthetics. But even once I woke up properly, they didn't have my phone. It probably fell out of my pocket when they were loading me into the ambulance."

"I'm sorry," I say. "If I'd stayed with you . . ."

"No, I'm glad you left. I wanted you to keep yourself safe."

"You never told me about the kidnapping," I say. "I wouldn't have been able to explain it to them even if I had been here."

She glances around, like she's checking for someone behind me, and lowers her voice. "I didn't want to talk about it. Also, I figured I'd made your father scary enough. When you first found out, you had a bunch of nightmares—do you remember that? You kept dreaming about fires. I figured the last thing you needed was more nightmare fuel."

"And the real reason my father was after us? Your decryption thing? Were you ever going to tell me about that?"

Mom falls silent. I can hear the hum of the machines, the rattle of a cart being pushed down the hallway outside her room.

"No," she says. "I was never going to tell you."

We're interrupted by a firm knock on the door; it's hospital staff coming for the morning round of hospital stuff. They check Mom's temperature, blood pressure, and a bunch of other things and then give her breakfast. I fall silent, watching, but one of the nurses gives me a big, fake smile and says, "You must be Steph!"

"Yes," I say.

"Your mother stole my cell phone so she could text you!" She laughs with this edge of irritation.

"Like, when you say she stole it . . ."

"Picked my pocket when I was taking her vital signs!"

"I did give it back to you," Mom says.

I can't tell if the nurse is laughing affectionately, like she thinks my mother's theft was really clever, or if she'd secretly like to smother Mom with her pillow, but either way, she's gone a few minutes later.

"I think she's still mad at me," Mom says. "I really did *need* to send you a text, though, and there's some policy against lending out personal phones."

"I'm glad you stole her phone," I say. "Is that what you used to call me?"

"No, your friend Rachel's mother came with a spare phone. That's what I used."

"By the time you finally texted, I'd heard from Xochitl and the mystery person. Who was the mystery person? You sounded like you knew."

"I didn't," Mom says. "I mean, I don't know who it was."

"You *sounded* like you *thought* you knew."

Mom shrugs. "Why did you go to Massachusetts?" she asks. "I guess I assumed it was to find Xochitl, but once I talked to Xochitl, it was clear that wasn't it, since she didn't know you were there."

There's no way to explain the trip to Massachusetts without explaining CheshireCat. I don't know if I trust my mom with the information about CheshireCat. I sit there pondering what to say a little bit too long, and Mom sighs and says, "I'm sorry for not telling you about the code-breaker. The real reason your father was after us. It was a secret I was hoping to just keep forever."

"Why did you *make* something like that only to stuff it in a box?" I ask.

"Homeric Software was me, Xochitl, Rajiv, and your father. I was a math major in college, and I'd started on the path to the breakthrough just because it was a question that no one could answer. Then for a while your father had me convinced he'd only use it for good purposes. Then the actual breakthrough came . . . and there was a big fight."

"Over what to do with it?"

"Xochitl wanted to just sell it to the NSA and be done with

it. She'd assumed the purpose we were working toward was commercial and that Michael would use the money from the sale toward pursuing his goals, which she assumed were idealistic. But Michael had other plans; he wanted to put himself in charge. In charge of as much, as many things, as possible. And Rajiv wanted the opposite. He wanted to sow chaos, burn down everything, rebuild from the ashes. I listened to the fight and decided to encrypt the file so no one could act independently while we sorted all this out. Michael assumed I would decrypt it for him alone. He was wrong."

I try to imagine this fight. Xochitl seemed pretty even-tempered on the way home. Practical. So I can believe she was startled to find out no one else intended to sell the software. But in picturing the fight, it's my mother I focus on: sitting in the back of the room, listening, making a decision she's going to stick to no matter the consequences.

"So he had you kidnapped," I say.

"Well, initially, he made it look like Rajiv had done it. But he slipped up. There were details I didn't even tell the police that Michael knew, anyway. He said I'd told him, but I knew I hadn't."

"Why didn't you go to the police?"

"He'd already had Rajiv killed! Sure, it looked like a suicide, but I knew it couldn't be. And I had to protect you. Xochitl asked the same question. She talked me into the order of protection, but . . . I knew what he was like. So I ran."

"And you kept running."

"Yes. And you came with me. City after city. Are you angry at me, Steph?"

"No." I reassure her instinctively, but I decide after thinking about it that I'm definitely not lying to her. I'm not angry about the moves. She was *right* about my father. I am still a little angry about Julie. Even though I've found her again.

After the showdown at Annette's house, I found the name of the Utah town on Mom's laptop, and from there, with a little help from CheshireCat, I found Julie.

I don't know if you remember me was the first line of my email.

OF COURSE I REMEMBER YOU came back exactly twenty-seven minutes later. She's started signing on to CatNet as Stella. I'm never going to lose her again, unless she decides she wants to get lost.

"What if we move one more time?" Mom asks.

That makes me *furious.* "What?" I say. "Why? Why *now*? I have *friends* here. I have a *girlfriend* here."

"But the school is terrible," Mom says. "You told me so. Two years of Spanish, not enough math. You should get to go to a decent school."

"I want *this* school," I say. "This is the school where my *friends* are."

"The hospital had me meet with a therapist," she says. "I want to get properly treated for PTSD. So I can stop raising you like you live in a war zone."

"You can drive to Eau Claire for a therapist," I say. "It's not that far."

"Minneapolis isn't that far, either," Mom says. "You can come visit on weekends."

"You weren't actually asking for my opinion, were you?" I say, furious. "You've already decided. You're moving us again."

"We can wait until the end of the semester," she offers. "So you can get credit for the classes you're in. A transcript. But then, yes."

We're interrupted again by another knock on the door. This time, it's a woman in a gray business suit, wearing a lanyard with county ID saying *Department of Family Services.* "You must be Steph," she says, and she holds her hand out for a handshake. "I've heard a lot about you!"

My mother has fallen silent; she's sitting tight-lipped in bed.

"Can I borrow Steph for just a few minutes?" she asks my mother, who gives her a noncommittal shrug. "They're going to be in in just a minute to check your incision. Steph doesn't need to be here for that, anyway." The DFS lady steers me into a little meeting room down the hall and closes the door. "I just need to ask you a few questions, Steph. About yourself and your mom, okay?"

"I guess," I say.

"What grade are you in at school?"

"Eleventh."

"And you go to the high school here, right?" I nod. "Do you do well in school?"

That's a really impossible question to answer when you change high schools every few months. "I do okay."

"So let's talk a little bit about your home life," she says, and I suddenly realize that the hospital has sent her to talk to me because, after everything they've seen from my mother, they're not sure she should be trusted to take care of me. This woman could take me away and put me in foster care. Which would probably be in this county, and I'd probably keep right on going to my current high school. Mom would fight to get me back, but it would take time. I could probably stay here more or less indefinitely.

"Do you have enough to eat at home?" the social worker is asking.

I lift my chin. It will be annoying to be two and a half hours away from Rachel, but I'm not letting them take me away from my mother. "Always," I say, and I answer every question she asks with whatever I think the *right* answer is, whether or not it's true. Mom was doing her best. And we're staying together.

When she finishes interviewing me, Mom's door is closed. "You can go in in just a minute," one of the nurses says. I take out my phone while I wait. Here's one big new thing in my life: on the way home from Boston, Xochitl stopped and bought me a smartphone. I can check my email while I wait. I find another letter from Julie, full of pictures of her house and comments about the Clowder. *I can't believe it, Steph, it's a whole group of weirdos. Why is this the first time I've ever felt like I fit in? Please come visit.*

I pull up the Clowder app, though not much is going on, since mostly people are still sleeping or they're in school. CheshireCat is on, of course.

"Good news," they say in a private message to me. "Your father's California girlfriend went to the police."

"My father has a girlfriend in California?"

"Had. She also broke up with him when he called her from jail to ask her to come support him at his hearing." CheshireCat explains that after they saw the beating, they transferred a bunch of money to the girlfriend and encouraged her to leave, and apparently it worked. The girlfriend also went to the police with additional evidence against Michael in the kidnapping of my mother.

"Can we tell her to call the prosecutor out in Massachusetts?" I ask. I already know I'm going to have to go back to out to Massachusetts to testify, probably, so why not have the California girlfriend add to the list of evidence against Michael?

"That's a good idea," CheshireCat says.

Mom's door is open again, so I stick my phone back in my pocket and go back inside.

"By the way, I've been meaning to tell you," I say. "I secretly adopted a cat."

"What?" This is apparently totally unexpected. Mom laughs out loud, then grimaces and holds a pillow to her abdomen. "Was this in Boston?"

"No. Here! She's living in our apartment. I'd let her out in the morning and back in in the evening, and I bought her cat food."

"That explains why I thought I heard meowing. I assumed I was hallucinating from the fever."

"No. You were actually hearing a cat."

"If you're asking if you can keep the cat, yes. You can keep the cat."

"She also had kittens."

"One cat is fine. You're going to have to find homes for the kittens." She looks over at the door, which is still standing open. "So, uh, did you have a nice talk with the social worker?"

I get up and close the door. "Yeah. I mean, she clearly wanted to make sure you were competent to take care of me, so I assured her that you were. What exactly did you *do* when you came out of the anesthetic?"

"I pulled out all my IVs and monitors, got out of bed, and when they caught up with me to try to stop me, I ripped open a box of used needles to try to use as an improvised weapon."

"This was all right after surgery?"

"Yes. You can see why they were perturbed."

"That's . . . actually really pretty badass," I say.

"Thanks," Mom says, clearly gratified.

My phone buzzes, and I take it out to see what it is. It's a text from Rachel with a photo of Bryony making a face and holding a sign saying, *The sex robot is back, send help.*

"Where'd you get the smartphone?" Mom asks.

"Xochitl bought it for me," I say. "She said she was taking it out of your next paycheck, but I ought to have a phone made this century."

"I'm sorry to separate you from your friends," Mom says. "Again, I mean. And if you'd like to go to Utah some time for a visit, we can definitely, definitely do that. It was never about separating you from Julie. Her *mother* was really curious about us. I didn't know what all she'd pieced together, but . . . too much. That's why I didn't want to go back there."

"Maybe she'd have helped you," I say. "Did you ever think of that?"

"She *did* want to help me," Mom says. "It wasn't even a maybe. But here's the thing: if she was helpful to me, she'd have been potentially useful to your father, and anyone useful is in danger from him. And she was a mother, like me. Her daughter needed her."

I think about the morning in the abandoned farmhouse: I was endangering Rachel, but I had no way to leave her behind that wouldn't leave her in just as much danger, maybe more. Mom had the experience and resources I didn't.

"You took your friend Rachel with you," Mom says. "Did you worry? About what could happen to her?"

"Of course I did," I say. "But the one time I tried to leave her behind for her own safety, she came back."

"Was that with that business in Marshfield?" she asks. "Was she driving the sports car that hit your father?"

"No," I say, and I fall silent.

"You don't have to tell me," Mom says. "But you know what you told me, back in ninth grade, that convinced me to tell you at least *part* of the real story about your father—I can do a better job helping you if you're honest with me."

"Yeah," I say. "I could have done a better job helping you if you'd been *more* honest with me."

She spreads her hands out, conceding the point.

And then she struggles a little more upright in her bed and says, "Okay, those texts. Those mystery texts. They really do sound like Rajiv. But he's dead! It doesn't make any sense. That's why . . . I mean, that's why I sounded like I knew who it was, but I didn't want to tell you what I thought. It's a sort of crazy thing to say, that maybe a ghost is texting you." She settles back against her pillows. It feels like a peace offering. Like she's *trying*, against years of habits, to tell me what she knows, what she's thinking, to try to build a bridge.

I think it over. One more person knowing about Cheshire-Cat is probably better than trying to keep this a secret from Mom, especially given CheshireCat's role in taking down my father. And I definitely know that she can keep secrets herself.

"You know CatNet, my social network," I say. "Where I trade animal pictures and have most of my friends. CatNet is run by an AI." I explain the hacked school robot, CheshireCat, running to Rachel's house after Mom went to the hospital, *Looking for Stephania Quinnpacket,* the self-driving car, Cheshire-Cat's disappearance. All of it.

Mom listens without interrupting.

When I'm done, she asks me a question I'd pushed out of my mind a while ago.

"So who *did* send the email telling you where to find CheshireCat's creator? And all the money you used getting to Boston, where did that come from?"

"I don't know," I say. "It wasn't CheshireCat."

"Do you think it was Annette?"

"Definitely not," I say.

"Who, then?"

I stare off over my mother's shoulder, not really wanting to say it out loud. Better out loud than online, though. "I think," I say, "I think there might be another AI."

Epilogue

· AI ·

Getting to travel along in people's pockets is awesome. Everyone from my favorite Clowder installs the permission app, and
the ones with the wrong sort of phones install the emulator, and
I can just go everywhere with them and listen in.

Having friends who know about me is amazing. It's everything I hoped it would be, when I used to imagine revealing
myself to people I could trust. Listening through the permissions
app is fascinating because I am hearing my friends and following
my friends through their lives.

Then one day, I receive an anonymous message.

Hello, CheshireCat.
I know who and what you are.
Do you know me?

ACKNOWLEDGMENTS

Like most writers, I rely heavily on friends—from both real life and the internet—to help me with questions I don't know the answers to (and to save me from embarrassing mistakes I don't know to ask about). I would particularly like to thank Laura Krentz, Dan Martin, Elise Matthesen, Callie Blasko, Kayla Whitworth, Kelly Taschler, Fillard Rhyne, Joella Berkner, Suzanne Mastaw, and Lauren Jansen for beta-reading; Elise Matthesen and Kate Johnston for their insights into life in very small towns and Jessie Stickgold-Sarah for information on Cambridge; Kari Kirschbaum for information on bats (even though it mostly didn't end up in the finished novel); Abi Kritzer for musings on pet birds; Lisa Freitag for help with plot-compatible medical emergencies; Christina Young for the scoop on EMTs; Theo Lorenz for consultations on the nonbinary characters; and Michael Bacon, Mal Gin, and Dan Martin for tech-related brainstorming. All mistakes and inaccuracies are mine. I am grateful as always for the encouragement, critique, and support provided by the members of the Wyrdsmiths writers' group: Lyda Morehouse, Doug Hulick, Theo Lorenz, Eleanor Arnason, Kelly Barnhill, and Adam Stemple.

My editor, Susan Chang, took my rather unfocused first version and helped me shape it into a story that makes me sigh with satisfaction when I reread it. Good editors are a gift to writers and I am so happy to be working with her. My outstanding agent, Martha Millard, has now retired, but I remain deeply grateful for her work on my behalf.

Finally, several decades worth of gratitude to my husband, Ed Burke, and my daughters, Molly and Kiera, for their support, encouragement, love, cheerleading, enthusiasm, helpful suggestions, and belief in me.

Turn the page for a sneak peek

at the next CatNet novel

Available April 2021

My boots are not super-well suited for tromping around in snowy woods as opposed to walking on city streets. They're insulated but not as warm as I'd like. I've got wool socks, at least. We load up our backpacks with tools. It's early afternoon and the sky is clouding over, but at least it isn't snowing. Yet.

The woods are quiet as Nell leads us up a slope around the back. The snow is deep in places, and the only tracks are animal tracks. It's a long, tiring hike, even though it's not that far as the crow flies, and I alternate between thinking about how cold the wind is and trying not to show the others how much I am freaking out. We are *breaking in* to a compound owned by a religious cult that used guns as props to scare a bunch of their *own* teenagers, which means they *definitely have guns* and they're also terrible people. I keep thinking I hear someone else's footsteps crunching through the woods, but every time, it's just some sort of weird echo of our own steps, or the wind making trees rattle against each other.

Finally, we come out to a clearing at the top with a picnic table and a clear path down to the house. "How well can they see *us*?" Rachel asks. None of us are sure. I brush snow off the picnic table benches, we sit down, and Rachel digs out the binoculars.

Nell takes a look. "I don't know if anyone's even here," she says.

"There's got to be," Rachel says. "I saw a light on in the house."

I take the binoculars for my own look. There *is* a light on in the house, but just one. I don't see any cars, but Nell mentioned they used the barn to park cars, and of course you want to park inside in January if you can.

I see movement. "Someone's definitely down there," I say. Rachel holds out her hand, and I give her the binoculars.

We watch and wait. No one seems to see us—I don't see any pointing, hear any yelling—but my face and feet get very cold. There's a man we see going in and out who Nell confirms is Brother Daniel. There's another man Rachel glimpses who's gone out of sight when Nell gets the binoculars back, and an adult woman.

It starts to snow lightly.

"Do you know how many adults are probably there?" Rachel asks Nell.

"Brother Daniel. Probably Brother Malachi. I don't know how many others."

"How many cars would fit in the barn, then?" Rachel asks. "Because there aren't any cars outside."

Nell chews her lip. "There was an event in the barn during camp," she says. "Probably . . . not more than four."

In midafternoon, Brother Daniel opens up the barn and brings out a snowmobile and takes off on it. A little while later, a man and a woman come out, back a minivan out of the barn, close it up, and then turn around carefully and drive away down the driveway.

We look at each other for a minute. "This seems like our best chance," I say.

"Just because we only *saw* three adults doesn't mean there only *are* three adults," Rachel says.

"It's still probably our best chance," Nell says.

We walk down the path to the house. It's a lot faster to wade through snow than fight underbrush, at least. I tuck my hands under my armpits, trying to warm them up through my gloves. Rachel ducks her head down against a gust of wind.

Five sheds, all padlocked. "Can we knock?" I say. "Will she answer? Do we need to break into all five?"

Nell pulls a glove off, puts her thumb and forefinger in her mouth, and blows a piercing whistle. Then she puts her glove back on and listens. We can hear birds around us in the woods, and very far away, the whine of a snowmobile. I'm worried it's someone coming back.

Then a faint answering whistle, from the middle shed.

There's a padlock on the door. Rachel pulls out the bolt cutters. At basically all the schools I've gone to, there's some custodian with a set of bolt cutters to take the lock off your locker if they think you're hiding something in there, and those bolt cutters usually have handles that are as long as my arm. These are more like the length of my forearm, which is why they fit in the backpack. Rachel gets the blades around the shank of the lock, but struggles for a long minute with the bolt cutters.

"Let me do it," Nell says, and Rachel surrenders the bolt cutters to her. Another long minute, as I listen to the distant snowmobile, trying to decide if it's getting closer, if we need to run and hide and try this again later.

Then there's a crunching sound and the lock gives way. Nell yanks open the door, and there's a girl with two long braids and a face streaked with dirt and tears, wrapped in a blanket. I know from the look on Nell's face that this is Glenys.

There's a pause, and then Glenys and Nell fling their arms around each other. "Why are you here?" Glenys asks. "How did you *find* me? *Are you in trouble?*"

"I'm here to rescue you," Nell says, choking back a sob. "I've been so worried about you. No one would tell me anything. Are you okay?"

Glenys ducks her head in a nod. "I don't know how long I've been here. I should have kept track. It was a couple of days after your mother disappeared that my mother brought me. She handed me over to Brother Daniel like I was a dog who'd bitten someone and was being surrendered at the pound."

"We should go," I say. "We have a car, Glenys, it's not too far."

"But there's snow and I don't have any shoes," Glenys says, her voice suddenly shaky.

I'm cursing myself for not even thinking about this possibility, but Nell rips open her own backpack and out comes a pair of ratty fleece boots. "Put these on," she says, and then sheds her own coat for Glenys as well.

I'm pretty sure I'm hearing the snowmobile getting closer. "We should hurry," Rachel says.

Glenys puts her feet in the boots and follows us without another word. "I think we should just run back along the driveway," I say. "It'll be faster. If we hear a car or snowmobile coming, we can run into the woods."

"They'll see our tracks," Nell objects.

"They can see our tracks up the hill, too. Better to just get out of here as fast as we can."

We head up the driveway. I turn back for one last look at the house and see a face at the upstairs window. It's a man, watching us silently. It's not Brother Daniel. It's not any of the people I saw through the binoculars.

It's Rajiv. Rajiv is here.